Sailing Solo

EMILY HARVALE

Emily Harvale lives in East Sussex, in the UK.
You can contact her via her website, Twitter, Facebook or
Pinterest

Author contacts :
  www.emilyharvale.com
  www.twitter.com/emilyharvale
  www.facebook.com/emilyharvalewriter
  www.facebook.com/emilyharvale
  www.emilyharvale.com/blog
  www.pinterest.com/emilyharvale

Also by this author:

Highland Fling

Lizzie Marshall's Wedding

The Golf Widows' Club

Acknowledgements

Thanks, as always, to my wonderful friends for their support and friendship.

Thank you so much, Karina of Miss Nyss www.missnyss.com for another gorgeous cover. Karina is so talented and I always get excited about her covers.

Grateful thanks, once again, to Christina Harkness for editing this novel and for never saying, 'How many times do I have to tell you this?' Her input is much appreciated.

Heaps of thanks to David of DC Creation, for all the clever things he does with my website (which we're currently re-designing) and everything else to do with my technological needs. He is always at the end of a phone or email and never gets annoyed when I say, 'David, what's this button for?' for the thousandth time or 'David, could you just ...?' I don't know what I'd do without him. www.dccreation.com

Thanks to my Twitter followers and friends, Facebook friends and fans of my Facebook author page. It's great to chat with you.

And to you, the reader, wherever you may be, for buying this book – Thank You.

Love,

Emily x

ISBN 978-1-909917-00-2

Published by Crescent Gate Publishing

Print edition published worldwide 2013
E-edition published worldwide 2013

Editor Christina Harkness

Cover design by Miss Nyss

This book is dedicated to The Ladies of Posara, the fabulous group of women I met on a writing holiday in Posara, Italy, four years ago. They are good friends, wonderfully supportive women, and talented writers. It's a real pleasure to know you, Debbie Flint, Maggi Fox, Isabelle Goddard, Mary Jane Hallowell and Carolyn Mahony.

CHAPTER ONE

'You have got to be kidding, Willa. Are you telling me *this* is Mark Thornton?'

Wilhelmina Daventry nodded without glancing up from the pile of papers on her desk. She hadn't taken her eyes from her work since her colleague and friend, Blossom Appleyard burst into her office minutes before, breathlessly asking if she had ever seen a picture of Mark Thornton.

Instead, Willa silently took the travel magazine, *Only The Best Will Do*, from one of the other piles on her desk and handed it to Blossom. Curiously enough, it was open at a double- page spread featuring an article entitled, 'Hero Mark, Saves Six Lovely Ladies from Certain Death'.

'This … this gorgeous hunk is the man you would rather *not* be spending a week with,' Blossom said, jabbing one long, blue-painted fingernail at a picture of a half-naked man in his mid-thirties. 'Are you mad? Or do you just need new glasses?'

Willa still didn't look up. 'Yes, Blossom, that's him apparently but as usual you're exaggerating. He's not bad looking I admit but I wouldn't call him a gorgeous hunk. And I'd rather not be spending any time at all with him but I don't have a choice. I still can't believe Dad has done this. He knows better than anyone that there are always teething problems during the first week of the holiday season.' At this point, she did look up. 'Did you manage to sort out the flights?'

Blossom cocked her head to one side and turned the magazine so that she could study Mark Thornton from all angles.

'What? Oh yeah. All sorted. I couldn't get him on the same flight as the rest of the holiday group but I managed to find one that arrives four hours later. It means either we'll all have to wait at Athens airport for him to arrive or

1

someone will have to go back and pick him up. Sorry. That's the best I could do. Phwoar! The man is bloody gorgeous. Can I volunteer to collect him, please? I mean just look at him!'

Willa grinned, grabbed the magazine and tossed it onto the mountain of papers in her out tray.

'I'd better do it. You'd probably take him on some detour of your own. Besides, it'll look better if it's me and we do need to make a good impression.'

'What, the hired help isn't good enough for such esteemed guests as Mark Thornton?'

'I didn't mean it like that.'

'Yeah, yeah. I was only teasing. Don't take things so seriously,' Blossom said, making a grumpy-looking face at Willa.

'I'm sorry. It's just I'm so nervous about all this and having *him* here during the first week is really not what I would have wanted. I just wish Dad had asked me before inviting him. I'd have suggested letting him stay at the end of the season, not the beginning. I'm not looking forward to it one bit.'

'So you keep saying.' Blossom frowned, picked up the magazine again and waved it in front of Willa's nose. 'Then you do need new glasses. Hellooo. Look at him, woman. Look at those eyes. Look at that body!'

'Look at that ego,' Willa replied.

Blossom grinned coquettishly. 'How can you see it? He's got his trousers on.'

Willa tutted and put down her pen. 'You know that's not what I meant. You've got a one- track mind, woman – and it's a dirt track.'

'It's a four-lane motorway,' Blossom said, fluttering her eyelashes in a comical fashion.

Willa took the magazine from her. 'You're the one who needs glasses,' she said, studying the photograph. 'His hair's a mess.'

'It's windswept. That's a good thing. It proves it's not

covered in lacquer or gel or something. I thought you liked the rugged, outdoor type. He obviously spends a lot of time outdoors. You can see his hair's got that sun-lightened look.'

'Hmm. He probably has it highlighted at some posh London salon.'

'Willa! There's no way a man like that has highlights,' Blossom exclaimed, letting out a long, swoony sigh.

Willa shot her a look. 'His mouth's uneven.'

'No it's not. That's a devilish grin.'

'Looks more like a self-satisfied sneer to me.'

'You can trash him as much as you like. I think he looks pretty damn hot.'

Willa's eyes scanned the page and she had to admit to herself that Blossom had a point. Most women would probably class Mark Thornton as handsome. His mouth wore a lopsided grin that made you want to smile back at him and his hair was just asking you to run your fingers through it. With his rather intense, blue eyes and – judging by his bare torso in the photograph – a pretty fit body, Willa could imagine that most women would succumb to his adventurous, action-man charms. But she wasn't 'most women' and she definitely wouldn't be succumbing. She placed the magazine back in the out tray, photograph-side down.

'I bet his tan's sprayed on,' she added.

She returned her attention to the papers she had been working on and dismissed Mark Thornton from her mind, pleased that she would be more than capable of resisting him. Next week would be difficult enough to get through as it was; the last thing she wanted was to get a foolish crush on the one man who could make or break her with just his fingers. Well, his fingers and his keyboard. A bad review of the holiday either in his regular, award-winning article, 'Thornton's Travel Truths' or on his blog, 'Tripping with Thornton' could ruin her.

Besides, she already had a bit of a crush on someone

else, and that was just as complicated and inconvenient. She thanked her lucky stars that she now had the ability to keep her personal and professional life separate, even though that could sometimes prove extremely difficult. She'd made a huge mistake once and she wouldn't do that again in a hurry.

'You really don't like him, do you?' Blossom said, dropping down onto a chair and leaning her elbows on Willa's desk.

'I don't know him. I have read some of his articles though, at least some of the recent ones, and he can be quite sarcastic. He's given less than glowing reports about several travel companies and places where he's stayed. He's built up quite a following so a good or bad word from him can make or break you if you're in the travel business.'

Blossom reached for the magazine again, turned it over and sighed. 'I'd follow him, given half the chance.'

Willa glanced up and grinned. 'Yes, Blossom, but you'd follow almost any man so that doesn't say much.'

'True. So ... it's really important that he has a good time then? Next week, I mean.'

Willa leant back in her chair and studied Blossom's deceptively angelic features. It never ceased to amaze her that her friend looked so innocent, facially, yet possessed the body of a sex goddess; had such a soft, mellifluous voice, yet with a slight huskiness, which made even a simple sentence sound like a sexual invitation. Even her name was a contradiction. 'Blossom' hinted at a fresh, spring morning and a gentle breeze – she was more of a whirlwind on a hot and steamy night.

'Not too much of a good time though,' Willa said, pushing back a lock of brown curly hair from her face. 'We want him to say that our singles sailing holidays are for beginners and experts alike and a place where everyone can come to make new friends, possibly find romance all in a relaxed, friendly and welcoming atmosphere. Not, that they're a hotbed of writhing bodies and hedonistic pursuits

4

fuelled by alcohol and lust.'

'Oh! Are you saying we've got to change our entire programme then?'

Willa giggled. 'Not all of it. And I'm sure the *outdoorsy* Mark Thornton, intrepid traveller, fearless adventurer, hero and tamer of all things wild, would like nothing better than to try out a few stretches, poses and strange positions in your break of dawn, Pilates class.'

'Well,' Blossom said, hugging the magazine to her chest so that the photograph of Mark was pressed against her ample bosom, 'I could think up a few new positions especially for him if that would help.'

'I'm sure you could. Let's just play it by ear, shall we? Personally I wouldn't be at all surprised if it turns out that he's gay or that the photograph has been touched up and he's old, overweight and ugly.'

Blossom tossed the magazine towards Willa and it landed on her desk with Mark's face and those intense, blue eyes, staring up at her.

'Gay! There is absolutely no way that man is gay. Haven't you read what he did to that woman? And he's thirty-five. It says so under his photograph.'

'I read it. And I'm pretty certain that article's a work of fantasy. According to that, he single-handedly saved a group of six female campers in Canada from a marauding bear, a pack of wild dogs ... and drowning – without even breaking into a sweat or wearing a shirt, it seems. And he still had the energy for a night of wild sex. The man's a superhero, obviously.'

'And you say *he's* sarcastic. He did save them. And it was a pack of wolves, not wild dogs. As for the sex part, all I can say is, wow! That's why I came and asked if you'd ever seen a picture of him. The story is all over the internet but the bloody thing kept crashing and the couple of pictures I did see aren't as clear, or as good, as the one in the magazine.'

'Of course they're not. As I said, this one has

undoubtedly been enhanced – like the story. The bear was probably still hibernating and they walked near its den. The wolves were probably husky sled dogs pulling at their reins and the river rapids were probably a gentle, babbling brook.'

Blossom tutted. 'Well, we can ask him in just a few days' time can't we? I can't wait to see what he looks like in the flesh. If he's even half as hot as he is in that photo I wouldn't be at all surprised if one of us ends up falling in love with the man by the end of the week. Or falling into bed with him at the very least.'

'Well, I can assure you, Blossom, it won't be me.' Willa shook her head, pushed the magazine to one side, picked up her pen and resumed what she was doing before Blossom's interruption.

Blossom smirked. 'Not even for a five-star review?'

'Not even for that. Besides, if going to bed with the man would get us a good review, I'd delegate that chore to you. We'd probably end up with ten stars!'

'And that's a chore I'd be more than willing to accept. I suppose you're saving your charms for a certain Greek, hotel owner you met just three weeks ago and are clearly half in love with already. Which reminds me, I'm meeting the divine Aristaios for lunch – and a few glasses of ouzo. Fancy joining us?'

Willa shot a look at Blossom. 'I'm not half in love with Aristaios, if that's what you're suggesting. I'm not even slightly in love with him. I merely said that I hadn't realised he was so good-looking and that I could now see why Dad had been so concerned. I knew his voice was like chocolate covered honeycomb but voices can be deceiving. Until I came out here, I had no idea what he looked like. Dad didn't say anything about him, of course, and Daniel only told me that Aristaios was about thirty-eight. When I asked you what he was like, your exact words were, "He's okay, I suppose." You never even hinted at the fact that the man has the looks and physique of a Greek god.'

'Yeah, well. Your dad worries about you every single season and I'm surprised your brother even told you how old Aristaios was. That's more information than you'd usually get out of him. And perhaps I didn't tell you because I didn't want the competition. If I'd told you how handsome Aristaios is, you'd have been on the first plane over here instead of letting me come out early to have a week's holiday before we started preparing for the season. Oh, and don't give me that aggrieved look. I was only joking. What is wrong with you today? You're not usually this serious. Anyway, you haven't answered the question. Do you fancy joining us for lunch?'

Willa sighed. 'I'd love to but I must get this report written for Dad. You know what he's like when he asks for something – he wants it immediately. He'll be chasing me if it's not with him soon. Thanks to all the problems with Mark Thornton's travel arrangements, it's already an hour overdue. Oh! I didn't thank you for sorting all that out, did I? Thank you. Although it sounds as if you spent more time searching the internet for pictures of the man than you did on the phone with the airline.'

Blossom winked. 'Well, I had to do something whilst they kept me on hold. You were right about that. Twenty minutes just to see if they had a seat available – and they didn't! I eventually managed to get one with British Airways. I've emailed you the details so that you can forward them on to him. Anyway, I'll love you and leave you. Join us later if you can. We'll be at Demeter's for a couple of hours at least. And yes, we will be talking business. Well, some of the time. See ya!'

Blossom waggled her fingers in a wave and positively bounced from the room across the white and grey marble tiled floor.

Willa sighed deeply. There was nothing she'd like more than to spend a few hours at the local taverna enjoying a glass or two of ouzo whilst ogling the undeniably gorgeous Aristaios Nikolades. A long lunch of bread and

7

taramasalata; houmous; tzatsiki; olives; feta cheese and salad, washed down with retsina, followed by black coffee, thick enough to coat the pothole strewn roads, appealed almost as much.

She'd been stuck at her desk all morning doing paperwork and the weather was much hotter than predicted for this time of year. To make matters worse, the air conditioning was having one of its 'off-days'. The sooner, Christos, the hotel handyman repaired that, the better but like everything else before the start of the main tourist season, the reply was, "Tomorrow, I'll fix it tomorrow." Tomorrow had lasted for two weeks and Willa's patience was wearing as thin as her flimsy, pale green cotton dress.

'Don't forget to ask Aristaios to speak to Christos about the air conditioning!' Willa yelled.

'I won't,' Blossom replied without a backward glance as she headed towards the bougainvillea-covered terrace.

Willa watched her through the open French windows of the room Aristaios was letting her use as her office. It was a small room next door to Aristaios' larger office, on the ground floor of the Argolis Bay Hotel but it was big enough for a desk and a few chairs. More importantly, in Willa's opinion, it had breathtaking views of the bay, the Gulf of Argolis, the hotel gardens and the village of Kritiopoli, which was about two kilometres away.

She saw Blossom skip down the steps leading to the lower terrace and the gardens and then turn and walk in the direction of the road until finally disappearing from sight. Willa let out another long sigh and glanced up towards the sun. Removing her glasses and screwing up hers eyes against the glare, she basked in the warmth of the rays streaming through the open French windows.

She loved Greece. She fell in love with it on her very first holiday here as a child and had returned at every opportunity. She had visited all of the islands and much of the mainland but this was her first time on the Peloponnese peninsula. She only arrived three weeks ago but the

Argolida district of the peninsula, where they were situated, was fast becoming her favourite place in the world and she longed to visit all of the historic sites in the area.

The ancient Greeks and Greek mythology fascinated her and as she relaxed, her mind drifting into a dream-like state, she could visualise Apollo driving his chariot across the palatinate blue sky. A soft smile formed on her lips as she realised that her Apollo, with his shoulder-length, black wavy hair, chiselled features, olive skin and large chocolate brown eyes, looked much like Aristaios Nikolades. He would now be sitting with Blossom in the shade of the olive trees on the terrace of Demeter's restaurant less than ten minutes' walk away.

She opened her eyes as a flock of birds, too far in the distance to identify, glided majestically in the thermal pockets above the hills, swooping down towards the waters of the gulf, no doubt to follow the fishing boats in the hope of scavenging some lunch.

Reluctantly looking away from the cloudless sky, her gaze lingered on the glistening, azure waters of the bay and she giggled at her own foolishness. She could almost hear the Sirens' song calling her; luring her away from her desk to swim in the cooling waters, whilst shoals of tiny fish darted around her and wound in and out of the craggy rocks at the foot of the cliffs nearby. Although, if she were honest, the lure of Aristaios' eyes washing over her was far more tempting than the water.

She shook her head and large curls of glossy brown hair fell about her lightly tanned, make-up free face. She had to stop daydreaming, she told herself and concentrate her thoughts on the report to her father. This was the first time their travel company had used the Argolis Bay Hotel and although her father had carried out the original negotiations last year, he had not been back since.

This morning he had sent Willa another rather lengthy email asking her to report back on a number of points. It had been one of many over the course of the three weeks and on top of the numerous phone calls, she knew that he was still checking up on her. The thought irritated her but it was always the same and she knew she should be accustomed to it by now.

She wiped her glasses with a tissue, put them back on and took a final look at the magazine, which was still on her desk. Mark Thornton's photo stared up at her. She didn't expect the first week of the season to be all 'plain sailing' but for some reason she had the distinct impression that Mark Thornton would turn out to be a very hard man to please. She could feel the butterflies in her tummy unpacking their bags and preparing for a long stay.

'Please don't be a pain in the arse,' she said to Mark's photograph. Cocking her head to one side, she drew a beard and moustache on his clean-shaven face, gave him a few spots, including a large one on the tip of his otherwise perfect nose, blacked out one of his exceptionally white teeth and added a bulbous, beer belly to his washboard stomach. Then she wrote a few lines of her own and changed the feature heading.

She studied her work and with a brief smile, she tossed the magazine towards her out tray. It landed on the pile but slipped off onto the floor with a resounding 'thwack'.

'Sod it!' she said, making a mental note to pick it up later; she must get on with the report to her father. She was determined to make a success of this season and prove to her dad, once and for all that she was as good at her job as Daniel was – and she'd already wasted far too much of her day on Mark Thornton.

CHAPTER TWO

Willa leant back in her chair and stretched her arms above her head. She had sent the report to her father, answered several emails, re-written some of the details about the day trips on offer and done a hundred and one other things. She deserved a break.

She wondered what the first week's guests would be like. She knew by the details on their booking forms that they ranged in age from about twenty-five to around fifty. She also knew there were a few more women than men, but this it seemed was usual on singles holidays. Out of twenty people booked for week one, there were twelve women and eight men so it wasn't a bad ratio. She was just praying they'd all get on.

The sailing holidays had been her idea and her father had taken a lot of convincing. If her brother Daniel hadn't supported her and helped persuade their father, she was sure he would never have given his go ahead.

She still felt a little peeved that she hadn't been involved in the original talks with the potential hoteliers though. It was her idea after all, and she'd been the one to draw up a list of suitable hotels, putting the Argolis Bay Hotel at the top.

Her father said that he needed to thrash out the first deal, to get the best price, as he had years of experience in such matters. Once the deal was agreed for the first season, he'd consider letting Willa handle things from then on. She knew it made sense but she was even more disappointed when he hadn't asked her to accompany him on the trip, taking her elder brother, Daniel, instead.

As a result, she wasn't quite sure what to expect when she arrived in Greece three weeks ago. She had seen photographs of the hotel; read reviews on Trip Advisor, on the internet and in the travel press; seen write-ups of it in a few brochures and discussed it with various people in the business, including her father and brother, but it wasn't the same as actually being there.

The moment she arrived though, she knew the hotel was perfect. It was also paradise in comparison to her noisy office back in England in a converted Georgian town house, metres from the bustling pedestrian precinct of Eastbourne's town centre.

The fact that Aristaios Nikolades, the thirty-eight-year-old owner and live-in manager was drop-dead gorgeous was an added bonus as far as she was concerned but it was that very fact, she knew, that would be giving her father nightmares.

She smiled, remembering her conversation with her brother, when he'd returned from the negotiating trip last year.

'What's the place like, Daniel?' she had said.

'Pretty much what we were expecting. You'll have a really easy summer season. The hotel's family-owned, four star going on five, although Dad had a few issues with the place. It's right on the bay and it's got forty en-suite bedrooms all of which have balconies and sea views and views of the nearby village, which seems to have been caught in a time warp if you ask me. The pool's a good size just a few metres from the beach and there's a pool bar. You'll love it.'

'It looks good in all the photos I've seen and I love the pictures of the terraces overlooking the bay. One has tables and chairs shaded by a pergola covered in bougainvillea and the lower one's open, with tables, chairs and sun loungers. Do they look like that in reality?'

'Exactly like that. Dad really liked the gardens. There're paved paths leading down to the pool and the beach and also in the opposite direction, leading to the road and the village. I can't remember the name of the place to be honest. There's not much there. Just a taverna or two, a few shops and some pretty little houses. That's about it.'

12

'Kritiopoli,' Willa said, grinning. 'It's a traditional fishing village according to the stuff I've read.'

'It smells like it,' Daniel replied, wrinkling his nose.

'What's the hotel restaurant like?'

Daniel shrugged. 'Pretty much like all the other hotel restaurants. It was spotless, I'll give them that and the food was very good. The pool bar serves snacks too and there's a varied menu, so food-wise, you shouldn't have any complaints. Mind you, the English abroad will always find something to complain about but the pool bar serves chips, so that should keep most of them happy.'

'Daniel! These are our clients – and there's nothing wrong with eating chips. Did you see the sailing centre?'

'Yeah. It looks pretty good. There's a wood-covered, concrete quay where the sailing dinghies are moored and there're windsurfers on the beach. The guy who runs it is an uncle or something of the hotel owner. He seemed pleasant enough and he knows what he's talking about, according to Dad, so that was a good sign. He's older too, so he's got years of experience – or so he told us. He also owns a pretty good restaurant which is fairly close to the hotel. It's called Demeter's and it looks like everyone's idea of a traditional Greek taverna. He also owns a disco called Persephone's. That's downstairs from the restaurant.'

'Oh, I like that. Demeter, the Goddess of the Harvest above and Persephone, her daughter, Queen of the Underworld below.'

'Yes. I knew that would appeal to you with your fascination of anything to do with Greek mythology.'

'And the hotel owner?' Willa asked. She was always nervous of meeting hoteliers for the first time, especially as it was so important for her to establish a good relationship with them to ensure the season went without a hitch.

'Well.' Daniel fidgeted and gave her a troubled look. 'Dad did have a few doubts about him but I told him not to worry.'

'What sort of doubts?' she said, hoping her suspicions

were wrong.

Daniel shrugged. 'The guy's about my age. Thirty-eight, I think, and Dad felt he was a bit young to be running a hotel. He lives in and manages it but he has a friendly and efficient staff so I don't think there'll be any problems.'

'Daniel? That wasn't really what concerned Dad, was it? The guy being too young to run a hotel, I mean. It was because of me wasn't it?'

He gave her a sympathetic look. 'Well, you know Dad.'

Willa tutted. Unfortunately she did. 'What did he say?'

Daniel shuffled his feet. 'That he had thought the chap would be older and that he hoped you'd be sensible and professional about it. Don't get mad. I told him that he had got to let it go. That you're a big girl now and you can handle anything if he'd just give you the chance. I also reminded him that you've run scores of seasons since, without a hitch and it was about time he started trusting you – and your judgement. You can, can't you? Handle it, I mean?'

'Of course, I can! Will you and Dad never let me forget it? It happened years ago. I was only eighteen and it was my first holiday season. It hasn't happened since has it? And I'm thirty-two now.'

'Okay! Don't bite my head off. You asked what Dad said. I told him you'd be fine. I ... I just wanted to be sure, that's all. This is the first time you'll be going out on your own. You know how Dad worries.'

'I won't be on my own. Blossom will be there. Oh, God. Dad's not thinking of making you come with me for the first week, is he? I was really hoping we'd got past that.'

Daniel shook his head. 'No, I told him these sailing holidays were your idea and he should trust you to get on with it. I still think you should have gone on the negotiating trip but Dad said you were "too emotional about it". Anyway, he was reluctant but I managed to convince him – so don't blow it.'

She saw her brother's mocking smile and relaxed. Her

dad may think she was still a silly, naive eighteen-year-old but at least her brother had some faith in her.

'So ... what's he like then? This hotelier, I mean,' Willa said, teasing him.

Daniel gave her a curious look. 'What do you mean, what's he like? He's a thirty-something Greek.'

That was clearly description enough as far as Daniel was concerned.

He was right about Willa loving the place though. He'd also been right about the hotel staff being friendly and efficient; they were, every one of them, even Christos, despite his answer to every question being "Tomorrow". Willa was certain the air conditioning would be fixed and everything would be working perfectly by the time the first guests of the season arrived next week, on the 18th of May.

She was also sure they'd have no complaints regarding the hotel in general. The white and slate grey marble interior was the epitome of the chic sophistication one would expect from such a hotel, and the spacious reception area was a welcoming haven from the heat of the sun; it was cool even when the air conditioning wasn't working.

The charcoal grey sofas and chairs near the French windows were comfortable and inviting and the low coffee tables offered leaflets and maps providing information about the bay, the Gulf of Argolis and the Peloponnese peninsula. There were many culturally important sites within a few hours' drive or ferries could be taken from the bay to visit the islands of Spetses and Hydra, just a short distance away.

To the right of the reception was a bar and more French windows opened onto the terrace from here. Beyond that was the restaurant to the front, leading out to more dining tables on the terrace, and large picture windows to the side.

Back in the reception area a large, sweeping staircase led up to the bedrooms or guests could take one of the two lifts if they preferred, transporting them to a peaceful night's sleep in comfy beds covered in crisp white cotton sheets.

That's what Willa had put in the holiday brochure anyway – and all of it was accurate.

She heard her email 'ping' and turned her attention back to her work. It was another email from her father. It said that he had received the report and was satisfied that everything was on schedule. It also said that he was glad that Mark Thornton's flights had been arranged although why one of the staff in the Eastbourne office couldn't have dealt with it, he had no idea.

Willa had no idea either. She'd assumed that as her father's secretary had forwarded Mark's confirmation email to her, her dad wanted her to book them. She cursed under her breath. She should have checked. It would have saved both her and Blossom a lot of time this morning.

Oh well, she thought. It's all done now, so all's well that ends well. Then she remembered that Blossom said she'd emailed her the details for her to forward to Mark – and she hadn't done that.

'Bugger!' she said out loud. 'Dad'll kill me if he finds out.'

She hastily knocked up an email, attached the e-tickets and sent it to Mark Thornton, marked urgent.

CHAPTER THREE

Mark Thornton read the email that pinged into his inbox, and he grinned. It was from Wilhelmina Daventry of Daventry Travel and he could see why she was in the singles holiday business. It read:

Dear Mr Thornton,

This is to let you know that we have arranged flights for you with British Airways departing from Heathrow at ten past twelve on Saturday the 18th of May, arriving at Athens at five forty-five p.m. I shall personally greet you at the airport and I'm looking forward to meeting you. Your e-tickets are attached.

We're all thrilled that you will be joining us for our inaugural week of Daventry Travel's Sailing Solo holidays. Our programme is action-packed but there's plenty of time for relaxing by the pool after a fun-filled day sailing or visiting one of the many ancient sites nearby, before joining your fellow holiday-makers and new friends for a refreshing pre-dinner drink.

The menu for the restaurant is as varied as our programme and you'll be eager to sample the delicious food, freshly prepared in the pristine kitchens of the Argolis Bay Hotel, using mainly local produce.

The district of Argolida remains largely unspoilt and this area of the Peloponnese offers spectacular sunsets followed by night skies blanketed with a million stars. When you finally retire to your spacious room and climb into your comfy bed, you'll fall asleep to the soothing sound of the balmy waters of the bay and find yourself dreaming of times long since past and of a land ruled by gods and won by heroes.

I'm positive you'll have no complaints but if I may assist you with anything, please be assured that I am available day or night, to ensure your stay with us is perfect in every way.

Myself, my colleague, Blossom Appleyard and everyone at Daventry Travel wishes you a splendid week's stay at the spectacular Argolis Bay Hotel, on a Sailing Solo holiday.

Yours,

Wilhelmina Daventry. (Willa)

Mark shook his head and sniggered, running his long fingers through a shock of light brown hair. Was the woman mad? Did she really think that kind of twaddle would impress him? The last time he'd dreamt of the heroes of ancient Greece was when he was about eight years old, and compared to some of the night skies he'd seen on his travels, those in Greece were really nothing special.

He wondered again why he'd let himself be talked into writing this review. He'd made no bones about the fact that he thought singles holidays were a joke. Surely, everyone had friends? And if not, what was wrong with going on a bog-standard holiday on your own or, better still, organising your own travel arrangements? Why would anyone want to pay extra just to be surrounded by other single people? He smiled to himself, realising he'd answered his own question.

Nevertheless, singles holidays were, to his way of thinking, no different from those dating sites that seemed to be sprouting up everywhere like triffids, eating away at people's wallets as well as their hearts. Why didn't people just go out and meet one another any more?

Still, at least he'd be flying B.A. That was some small consolation. And a week relaxing by a pool or sailing to some secluded inlet wouldn't be that bad, he supposed. Besides, there was one redeeming feature about a singles holiday as he'd just realised; there'd be a selection of single women to choose from, and that might be fun.

His last relationship ended more than two years ago. She wanted to move in with him and settle down; he wanted to go on an assignment to Argentina for six months – so they split up. In his line of work, he often spent months at a time out of the country and it took a very special woman to cope with that or to want to go with him. Not many women wanted to be sweating in a tent in somewhere like the Amazon rainforest or hiding their charms under layers of thermals in the frozen wastes of Siberia. His mother didn't even go to Norway with him and his father to film the Aurora Borealis, all those years ago, and they were staying in a hotel for that assignment – for two months.

Mark stopped that line of thought. This wasn't the time for unhappy memories. The week in Greece was going to be fun – he'd make sure of that. Since his break-up, he hadn't really had time for women. He'd enjoyed a few casual flings but he he'd been so busy that he couldn't actually remember the last time he'd spent more than one night with a woman. He racked his brain.

'Nope!' he said to himself. They'd all been just one night and the last one was a very pretty but very foolish, blonde he'd met a few weeks ago in Canada. What was her name?

The shrill ring of his telephone snapped him out of his thoughts.

'Hi, Dad. How are you?' he said.

'I'm good, thanks. Especially now I know my son is a real live hero.'

Mark wondered what his father meant. He was clearly being facetious but Mark couldn't think of anything he'd done since he'd last seen his dad five weeks ago and he'd spoken to him at least four times since then. One of those times was only yesterday, so all he said was, 'What?'

James Thornton chuckled. 'I take it you haven't read this month's issue of *Only The Best Will Do*, then?'

'I don't think I have ever read *any* month's issue of that crappy magazine and if you're reading it, I clearly need to start worrying about your sanity. How they can call it a travel mag. is beyond me. Where are you anyway? I thought you were flying up to the Arctic today.'

'I am. I'm at the airport for the first leg of the journey. You can imagine my surprise when I sat at a table for a relaxing cup of coffee and saw a picture of you half-naked spread before my eyes. A fellow traveller was reading it. A woman, obviously.'

'Obviously,' Mark said, trying to fathom how any picture of him could have got into that publication, let alone one of him half-naked, although photographs of half-naked men seemed to be the only ones in the rather trashy periodical from what he'd heard. Photographs of travel destinations were few and far between. 'Are you sure it was a picture of me?'

'Definitely. Your name and age are under the photo. Although I had to look twice. I didn't realise you like to smother yourself in ... oil.'

Mark sat bolt upright. 'I don't. What are you talking about, Dad?'

'I'm talking about the two-page spread about you in this month's edition. There's definitely a distinct sheen to your torso.'

'What? Hold on. I'm going to look it up on line.' He tapped a few keys and the colour drained from his deeply tanned face as he saw his image under the headline, 'Hero Mark, Saves Six Lovely Ladies from Certain Death'.

'At least they got your age right,' James said, making no attempt to hide his amusement. 'So, you saved them from a bear, a pack of wolves, *and* drowning. You *have* been a busy boy. I'm in awe, especially as you still had the stamina to sleep with one of the women.

'Fuck!' Mark said.

'Oh! Okay, if you want to put it that bluntly, you still had the stamina to–'

'No Dad, I meant ... fuck! How did this happen?'

'Oh! Well it seems the lovely lady you ... slept with, happens to be a feature writer for the magazine. Didn't you know?'

'How the hell was I supposed to know? They were

camping and I had to get them out of a couple of awkward situations. No one told me one of them worked for that crappy title.'

'Well it's not something you would brag about, is it? Those people couldn't even think up a good title for their magazine, let alone write good copy. You really need to check who you're spending the night with in future, son.'

'Yeah, thanks Dad. I'll ask what a woman does for a living before I jump into bed with her from now on, shall I? Shit! I'll be a laughing stock around here for a few days.'

James sniggered. 'At least a week I should think. Possibly longer. I've bought copies for all my crew. It'll give us all a good laugh stuck in our tents in the freezing wilderness of the Arctic waiting to capture footage of the local wildlife. If only we had you to protect us.'

'Yes, very funny, Dad. It's so good to know I've boosted the magazines sales figures for the month and provided amusing bedtime reading for you and your film crew. Mind you, I may get a bit worried thinking of eight men, in tents, hundreds of miles from a woman, staring at a picture of me.'

'Don't worry, son. There are women out there ... somewhere. There's still time to join us, you know.'

'I can't. I've got the assignment in Greece next week.'

'Oh yes. The ... singles holiday, isn't it? Now that's also the sort of article you'd find in the pages of *Only The Best Will Do*. Remind me again, why are you doing this one?'

Mark sighed. 'I told you. It's a favour for Mum's new husband. He's a friend of the owner of Daventry Travel.'

'Oh yes, I remember. Your mother phoned me and told me in no uncertain terms, not to try to talk you out of doing it. You really shouldn't call him her new husband though, Mark. Your mother wouldn't like that and they have been married for about fifteen years now.'

'Twenty, actually. It's their wedding anniversary next month and they're having a big do. Anyway, I said I'd do this Greece thing but I'm going to be completely honest in my review so the holiday had better be good or it may backfire and end up not being a favour at all.'

'Is it really twenty years? Oddly enough, I haven't been invited to the bash. Anyway, if you change your mind and decide you'd rather be in the Arctic, just ring me.'

'Hmm. I think I'd rather be in Greece than freezing my nuts off – especially as you'll all be reading, *Only The Best Will Do*. Besides, you're the hero and intrepid traveller in this family. The older I get, the more I prefer a few comforts with my travel writing, like a bed, a bar and a woman. Not necessarily in that order.'

'Yes, so Candice Cornwell says.'

'Who's Candice Cornwell?'

James tutted. 'Really, Mark. You may not ask what they do for a living but you could at least find out their names! She's the one who wrote this delightful story about you. I'm still reading it actually – the woman goes on and on – but apparently, you're as impressive *in* bed as you are out of it. Who knew?'

'Oh, fuck! She hasn't written about that as well, has she?'

'Don't worry. She hasn't gone into specifics. Just a line or two, and it's really rather flattering, albeit unintentionally amusing drivel. You should buy some copies at the airport on your way to Greece. Leave them spread around the hotel and I can guarantee you'll have every single woman for miles chasing after you. Just remember to ask what they do in their day job – and their names.'

'Thanks, Dad. Any more advice?' Mark said sarcastically.

'Not at present. Right, I must dash. Enjoy Greece. I'll be in the Arctic for five weeks – if you need a place to hide from screaming women or the gutter press. Oh, that should be howling women according to Candice. Apparently, you made her howl like a wolf. Now that's a trick you must teach me. See you soon.'

'Dear God! Go away, Dad. And don't get eaten by anything in the wilds.'

Mark hung up and taking a deep breath, he read the article Candice Cornwell had written. By the time he'd finished he was seriously considering cancelling the trip to Greece and going to the Arctic instead – frozen body parts or not.

CHAPTER FOUR

D-day finally arrived and Blossom escorted the guests booked on the inaugural week of Daventry Travel's Sailing Solo holidays into the spacious, white and grey marbled reception area of the hotel. Willa and Aristaios were there to welcome them. They were a mixed bunch, as Willa had expected, ranging in age from mid-twenties to early-fifties but they all had one thing in common: they were looking forward to a week of fun in the Greek sunshine.

'Hello and welcome,' Willa said to the group of twenty holidaymakers. 'I'm Willa Daventry of Daventry Travel and this is Aristaios Nikolades, the owner of the Argolis Bay Hotel. You've already met my colleague, Blossom Appleyard. Help yourselves to a glass of wine whilst we get you checked in. Your bags will be sent to your rooms where you'll find your welcome pack. Settle in and relax or explore the hotel and grounds. The pool and the pool bar are open if you fancy a dip and another refreshing drink. Blossom and Aristaios will see you all on the upper terrace at six-thirty p.m. for the welcome chat and to discuss the itinerary but for now, I'll let you enjoy your drink and I'll come and say hi to each of you.'

Willa worked her way through the crowd and less than half an hour later, the guests were all settling into their rooms and she was having a cup of coffee in her office with Blossom.

'They appear to be a friendly lot,' Blossom said. 'Did you meet Harry 'Banner' Bullen, the advertising executive? He's rather tasty.'

'He's been in the country for less than four hours. Give the guy a chance to settle in before you pounce on him.'

'Hey! Don't jump to conclusions. I was thinking about you. Didn't you say you'd love to have the money to do a big ad campaign? Well, play your cards right and you might

24

get one for free – or some ideas, at the very least. And the fact that he's 'fit' is an added bonus. Don't look at me like that! I'm thinking about your family's business.'

'You're thinking about sex, Blossom, as usual.'

'Yes, but I'm thinking about *you* having sex and that's *unusual.* I know you don't like mixing business with pleasure but I suspect that man would make it worth the risk – in more ways than one.'

'Actually, that's just plain weird,' Willa said, giggling. 'Not me having sex, of course, just you thinking about it. And no, I'm not sure it is worth the risk. I didn't realise he had a double-barrelled surname though. I thought it was just, Bullen, not Banner-Bullen.'

'It's not. Banner is his nickname or so he says. Apparently, because he makes 'banner headlines' with his ads.'

'Modest as well,' Willa said, grinning. 'Speaking of modest, what's the time? I've got to leave by three to go and pick up the delightful, Mark Thornton.'

'Then you should have left ten minutes ago,' Blossom said. 'Where's your watch?'

Willa was halfway out of the door before Blossom finished the sentence.

***

'*You're* Wilhelmina Daventry? I mean ... hi, I'm Mark Thornton.'

Willa eyed the tall, good-looking man standing in front of her in the arrivals hall at Athens airport and hoped she didn't look as surprised as he did. Because she was surprised. That photograph of him in *Only The Best Will Do* clearly hadn't been enhanced. If anything, it didn't do him justice and she prayed that when she opened her mouth to reply, her voice wouldn't sound as shocked as she felt.

She folded up the large piece of paper she was holding, with his name written on it, stuffed it in her handbag and took the hand he held out to her. She shook it firmly but briefly and coughed lightly before replying.

'Yes. But please call me, Willa. Everyone does. I hope you had a pleasant flight.'

She saw his eyes examine the length of her body and despite being a UK size twelve, she pulled her tummy in, lifted her shoulders up and stuck her chest out slightly. She hoped he didn't notice.

'Very pleasant, thanks but it's even more pleasant to be on the ground, standing here.'

Willa blushed although she wasn't sure if he was flirting with her or being sarcastic. There was something in his tone she couldn't quite place and his eyes – which were even more intense, and a much deeper blue than they were in the picture – held a look something akin to irritation.

'Well, let's not keep you standing here,' she said. 'The car is this way, if you'll follow me.'

'With pleasure,' he said, running a hand through his light brown, dishevelled hair and grinning lopsidedly before picking up his bag and falling into step beside her.

'Is this your first time in Greece?' she asked, keeping her eyes straight ahead.

'No, I've been here many times.'

'Oh. Have you been to the Agolida district?'

'Frequently. I often spend several weeks in Greece and I spent six months sailing around the islands some years ago. You may have read the book I wrote about it. It was called *On the Waves of Poseidon*.'

'Oh, no, I haven't.'

'Just as well really. It was a crappy title and the book wasn't much better. I think it sunk to the bottom of the ocean.'

Willa stole a look at him from beneath her long, dark lashes. Self-deprecating humour wasn't something she'd expected from him.

'Have you written many books?'

He stopped in his tracks and when she turned to face

him, his handsome features wore a despondent look.

'Are you telling me you haven't read any of them? I'm crestfallen.'

'Oh, I'm sorry. I–'

'I'm joking,' he said.

Willa watched his lips twitch into the lopsided grin and she felt herself smiling back. He resumed walking and she fell into step beside him.

'It must be wonderful to travel all over the world for free and then sit and write about it.'

He stopped again. 'You're determined to put me in my place, aren't you?' he said, grinning broadly. Then he marched forward again. 'Don't worry, I'm being facetious. It's a great way of life but it doesn't come without risks.'

'Yes. I read about some the other day. I believe you fought off a bear and a pack of wolves to rescue a group of female campers and then saved one of them from drowning in the swollen river. In Canada, I think it was. Oh! Have I said the wrong thing again?'

Mark sighed and shook his head. 'Don't tell me, you read that in *Only The Best Will Do*?'

'Yes. It's the only travel magazine written especially for women.'

'It certainly is,' he said.

She saw something flash across his eyes but it was gone in a second and the smile returned. She was going to say that she read it because she had placed an advert in this month's edition, along with adverts in a fitness and health magazine and a couple of men's magazines, and she wanted to check that it looked as she'd expected, but something about his expression stopped her. She seemed to be saying all the wrong things and she didn't want to slag off a travel magazine on top of everything else.

'But I didn't really mean those type of risks,' he continued. 'I meant financial insecurity. You never know when you'll get your next assignment or if your book will sell enough copies to allow you to write the next one.'

'Oh.'

'And you shouldn't believe everything you read, you know.'

'I don't. Are you saying it's not true then? Are you telling me you didn't face danger and save the women from almost certain death?' she said, wondering if he'd detect the sarcasm in her tone.

His lips twitched. 'I did get a nasty bite from a mosquito. Seriously though, I got them out of a couple of ... awkward situations, that's all. Nothing worth writing about.'

'Really? Well, Candice Cornwell seemed to have rather a lot to write about it.'

'So I keep hearing.'

Mark quickened his pace and Willa was almost jogging to keep up with his lengthy strides. They covered the remaining distance in an awkward silence – and in five minutes flat.

'This is me,' Willa said, gasping for breath when they finally reached her car. She opened the boot with the remote and waited whilst he threw his bag inside.

'Is this insured for anyone to drive?' he asked.

'Er ... yes it is. It's our company car and Blossom and I – Blossom Appleyard, my colleague and flatmate – share it. Why?'

'Would you allow me to drive to the hotel then? When I spoke to your father he told me this is your first time to this part of Greece and the motorway will be hectic at this time of day. I know the back roads and there's a particularly pleasant taverna right beside the Corinth Canal. A friend of mine owns it and it's a great place for a halfway stop and a drink – and I could use one, believe me.'

'You ... you spoke to my father ... about me?' Willa was horrified. This was the first time she'd heard mention of it.

'Not specifically about you, no,' Mark said, walking round to the driver's side and taking the keys from her hand. 'He called me to say how pleased he was that I was going to be spending the week here and doing the review.

He just mentioned that this was your first time running an entire season on your own and that you were a little nervous, but the sailing holidays were your idea so he'd let you take the helm. He also said that he hoped I'd be ... kind, I think. Anyway, that was all.'

'That was all!' Willa screeched, feeling her face go as red as the paintwork of the car. 'Mr Thornton, this may be my first time running a season without another member of my family hanging around at the start and dropping in unannounced to check up on me but there is absolutely no need for you to treat me any differently than you would anyone else! Is that clear? I neither want nor expect any special treatment from you.'

Mark's brows shot up in surprise as she grabbed the keys back from him and got into the driver's seat. 'You can give me directions to this ... taverna but I'll drive there. You can drive from there to the hotel if you like, because, Mr Thornton, you're not the only one who could use a drink, and I plan on having more than one!'

'Oh!' was all she heard him say before she slammed the car door and turned on the ignition.

CHAPTER FIVE

Mark made several attempts at small talk once they left the airport but he received one monosyllabic reply after another, so, other than giving her directions they passed the first half hour of the journey in comparative silence. He didn't mind but he wondered whether his comment about conversing with her father had upset her. When he asked her, her response was a very firm, "No."

He tried pointing out things he thought she might not have seen before and would find interesting but she said she knew about each of them and was hoping to visit them all, over the course of the summer.

Finally, he asked her about the Argolis Bay Hotel and Kritiopoli and was astonished to see that not just her large hazel eyes lit up but her entire face seemed to glow. She was clearly very taken with the place.

'It's beautiful,' she said. 'The hotel was built by the owner, Aristaios Nikolades' grandfather in 1960 and, as a tribute to his English wife, who was an artist, he designed it to sit at a very slight angle from the beach, to make the most of the spectacular sunsets. Have you seen the sunsets in this part of the country? They are truly stunning!'

Mark thought that was a bit of an exaggeration but decided not to say so. He merely nodded. He didn't want to upset her again by saying the wrong thing.

'I don't think I'll ever tire of seeing them,' she continued. 'They must have been so inspiring for an artist. Several paintings by Aristaios' grandmother are hanging in the hotel's public areas. He's clearly very proud of her talent and rightly so. She was a very gifted lady.'

'I take it by "was", that she's no longer around?' He saw the sad look she threw him.

'No. It was very tragic but somehow romantic. She died at the age of sixty-seven and just a few months later,

Aristaios' grandfather died too, they say from grief.'

Mark thought that was rather morbid, not romantic but he just nodded.

'To make things worse,' Willa said, 'Aristaios' parents along with his aunt, also died in a tragic accident, not many years after, when Aristaios was fifteen. His uncle brought him up.'

'Wow. They're a rather unlucky family, aren't they?' He realised that was a mistake almost immediately.

'Is it much further to the taverna?' Willa asked stiffly.

'No,' Mark said, feeling relieved that this was true. He *really* needed that drink. 'We've been driving for about fifty minutes so there's about another fifteen to go.'

His head shot back as Willa accelerated and neither of them spoke again until finally, a little over an hour after leaving Athens, they approached the Corinth Canal via the coast road and the small, ancient town of Isthmia.

'It's really not far now,' Mark said, glad that he'd soon have a cold beer in his hand. 'You can see the entrance to the canal over there.' He pointed ahead of him and slightly to the left but you couldn't really miss it.

'I didn't realise you could come this way,' Willa said. 'When I arrived last month we drove across one of the bridges at the top and stopped to look down into the canal. I didn't know you could get to it via the coast road. Do we have to get a ferry across from here or something?'

Perhaps the prospect of a drink has improved Willa's mood too, he thought.

'Most people use the high bridges,' he said, 'but no, there's a bridge here too. There're a couple actually, at this level.'

'Where?' Willa asked, 'And how do the ships get through them then? Do they open like Tower Bridge in London?'

'No. The one we'll be using submerges. It can take about half an hour or so because it descends to a depth of about eight metres but it's fascinating to sit in the taverna and watch. Often, when the bridge comes up again, there're fish flapping about on top of it and the bridge operator strolls out, picks them up and takes them home for his supper – if the stray cats don't get to them first, that is. There's Stavros' place. Turn left here and park.'

They got out of the car and Mark led the way to a very traditional looking taverna situated right by the canal.

'Mark! Welcome! Welcome.'

A red-faced, rather rotund Greek man in his late fifties barrelled towards Mark as they entered. He grabbed him by the shoulders, shook him and slapped him on the back several times before hugging him.

'Hello, Stavros,' Mark said when Stavros eventually released him. 'It's good to see you. May I introduce Willa Daventry?'

'Beautiful! Beautiful!' Stavros said, grasping Willa in a bear hug. 'You are a lucky man, my friend. You treat her well, you hear or you will have me to answer to. Come. Come. Sit, eat and drink. I will call Aglaia. She will be happy to see you.'

He dashed off into the kitchen calling his wife's name.

'I ... I think he's got the wrong end of the stick,' Willa said, looking a little distressed.

Mark shrugged. For some reason he found Willa's concern irritating. Was it really so bad for someone to think they were a couple for a few minutes?

'Yeah. I'll explain when he comes back. Sit down. Are you hungry? What would you like to drink?'

Willa seemed reluctant and looked from side to side as if planning her escape.

'It's okay,' Mark said, a little annoyed. 'There isn't some ancient tradition where you'll suddenly find yourself engaged to me just by sitting at the same table in an old friend's taverna.' He pulled out a chair and sat down.

Willa's eyebrows shot up and she tutted. 'I'm not stupid, you know! I realise that. I ... I was just wondering where the loo is, if you must know.'

'Oh, sorry. It's over there to your right.'

'Thank you. Are you going to drive from here to the hotel as originally agreed?'

Mark wanted to say, 'told, don't you mean?' but instead he nodded. 'Yes. Why?'

'Because if you are, I'm going to have a glass of ouzo, followed by a large glass of wine, washed down with a glass of Metaxa, if that's okay with you?'

Mark was surprised. 'That's absolutely fine with me,' he said. 'And Stavros will be your friend forever. He likes a woman who can take her drink.'

'And I expect you've introduced him to many before me,' Willa replied, marching off towards the loo.

Stavros returned with Aglaia, and Mark saw him look around for Willa.

'She's gone to the loo,' he said, rising from his seat to hug Aglaia. 'How are you, gorgeous? You're looking well.'

'I'm well, Mark. Very well. Stavros tells me you have a young lady now. She is beautiful, he says. You love her?'

'No! I ... I haven't known her long.' Why hadn't he said they'd only just met and that it was strictly business? He grinned. Why not have some fun, he thought. 'She's ... temperamental ... and she's very shy. I'm not really sure how we feel about one another, to be honest.' Well, that wasn't a lie.

Aglaia tapped his arm and nodded sagely. 'I understand this. I will speak to her. I will tell her not to let you go. The rest – it is with Aphrodite.' She raised her arms towards the heavens.

Mark kissed her on the cheek just as Willa returned. 'Speaking of Aphrodite, this is Willa.'

Aglaia held out her arms and swept Willa into them, hugging her as tightly as Stavros had.

'Welcome, Willa. I am so happy to meet you. Mark is very special to us. We love him like our son,' she said, leading Willa towards a bench seat and coaxing her to sit. 'You could look far and wide and never will you see a man like him. You understand? He's kind, handsome. Other men they come, they go. Pfft!' She clicked her fingers in the air. 'Like that! Mark, he's there when you need him.'

Mark saw Willa's perplexed expression. He could hear everything Aglaia was saying and he wondered how Willa would react.

'That's good to know,' Willa said, casting a pleading look in his direction.

It was time to intervene. He took Willa a glass of ouzo and kissed Aglaia on the cheek.

'Let's leave it to Aphrodite now, shall we?' he said.

'You hungry?' Aglaia asked. 'I will cook for you.' With that, she disappeared into the kitchen.

'What was all that about?' Willa said, taking the ouzo from him. 'I told you they'd got the wrong impression. I think they think we're dating or something. Why don't you tell them we've only just met and that this is strictly business?'

'That's exactly what I asked myself just a moment ago but they're Greek and Greeks think everyone's in love – or they should be.'

Willa screwed up her eyes, her brows knitting together. 'No they don't!'

He shrugged again. 'Aglaia and Stavros do. What can I tell you? Is it such a dreadful prospect?'

'What?'

'Having people think we're in love.'

Willa's mouth fell open. 'Yes! Because we're not so it's not true and people shouldn't play games when it comes to things like love. That's my opinion, anyway.'

'Duly noted,' Mark replied.

'Don't be sarcastic.'

'I wasn't.'

Willa glared at him and gulped down the ouzo. 'Did you order my wine?'

'It's on its way.'

'Good. I think I'm going to need it. Do you often pretend

to be in love with someone you've only just met? Is that how it was with Candice Cornwell after you saved her from the bear and wolves and drowning?'

He thought it was too good to be true. He thought he'd dodged that bullet at the airport but it seemed everyone had read the intimate details of his night with Candice Cornwell – everyone except Aglaia and Stavros, thankfully. Aglaia would have given him her usual lecture on finding a woman, settling down and having babies.

'Look. I know you read *Only The Best Will Do* and you believe it's a bona fide travel magazine written for women but I have to tell you, most of the articles in there are more fiction than fact – and as far as I know, they don't have much to do with travel either.'

Willa raised her eyebrows and removed her glasses. He noticed for the first time that her hazel eyes had little flecks of green in them. He studied her face. She wasn't beautiful in the strict sense of the word but she was stunning. He'd definitely been stunned when he'd seen her waiting for him at the airport. Long, dark lashes framed her eyes and even with her glasses on, they were amazing. Thick brown curls danced around her lightly tanned face and her lips were a Cupid's bow – although perhaps that should be Eros's bow as they were in Greece, he thought cynically – beneath a nose that Aphrodite herself, would have envied. He silently chastised himself: Now who was talking twaddle?

'Actually,' Willa said, putting her glasses back on, 'I don't read it, but I did read this month's edition. We'd placed an advert in there to attract women to our sailing holidays, just as we've placed some in men's magazines and I was checking that it was what I wanted. Then I saw your name and the story. I only read it because Dad told me that he'd arranged at the last minute for a travel writer to come and stay and do a review. When he said it was you and then I spotted your name just minutes later, well, naturally I wanted to find out a little bit about you.'

'From reading that article? Really? You couldn't have

Googled my name and read about the books I've written and the wildlife and nature films I've made with my dad or the lectures I've given on survival techniques?'

'I ... I didn't think about it. I just saw your name and I read the article. What's wrong with that?'

'*What's wrong with that*? Oh, nothing! After all, why would you want fact when fiction is *so* much more entertaining? Especially when it's written by some airhead who doesn't read the regulations and clearly hasn't got the brains to realise that you *don't* leave food lying out in the open in bear country and that wolves are *not* just big fluffy dogs, or that when a river is in flood, there are likely to be rapids and that an hour watching a DVD on river rafting does *not* qualify you to go out on a river in a kayak you've hired, especially *not* to escape from a bear and a wolf!'

He gulped back his beer and emptied the glass. He saw Willa jump as he thumped it down on the table.

'Sorry. I shouldn't have said that. I didn't mean to snap at you. Please forgive me. Ah, here's Stavros with your wine. Thank you, Stavros. May I have another beer please?'

'Of course. Of course.' Stavros beamed at them and dashed off to the kitchen again.

'Thank you!' Willa called after him. She leant forward and looked Mark directly in the eye. 'Tell me, Mark, did you say all that to ... Candice before or after you made her – and I quote: "howl like a wolf during a night of sex so wild that I bit and clawed his rock-hard body as he rode me hour after hour in a frenzy of passion as hot as the lava bursting forth from a volcano, taking my very soul back to a time when the earth was new and men and women were little more than beasts ravaging one another's bodies and plundering each other's hearts," ... or something like that?'

Mark swallowed a lump, which seemed to have stuck in his throat and his eyes held hers.

'As I said, more fiction than fact. And most of it, unadulterated tripe. Actually, that was almost word perfect. How many times did you read it?'

'Once was more than enough, believe me. I have a photographic memory. Which part is fact and which part fiction? And did you tell her that you thought she was an airhead before or after you made her *howl*?'

'Does it matter?'

'Actually ... yes. Yes it does. I'd like to know.'

'Okay.' He leant forward so that their faces were just inches apart and he could feel her breath on his cheeks. 'Yes, I did tell her that she was an airhead. And it was before we slept together. In fact, I told her she was a fucking, stupid airhead. I might have had to shoot a bear or a wolf just because she and her silly friends wanted some 'wildlife' photos.'

'Oh!'

'That's right. They thought these beautiful, majestic, wild animals would just eat the food the women had left near their camp, pose for some photos and then go back the way they came. They didn't have the sense to realise that these creatures would want more and that, if they had been starving or the bear had been older, things might have become serious.'

'It was a good thing that you were in the right place at the right time then.'

'I suppose it was. It was a rather rare situation in any event. You don't normally see a bear and a wolf at the same time like that, or quite so close and I'm not sure which of us was the more surprised – me or the animals. They hate loud noises so thankfully for all concerned, a couple of warning shots into the soft ground were enough to make them both decide to leave but it could have ended very differently. I have never had to shoot a wild animal in my life in self-defence and I've been in far worse situations than that but it did get a bit hairy for a moment. Even I thought I might have to shoot one of them and believe me that was something I really didn't want to do, but the women behaved like complete idiots and sent all the wrong signals.' He dragged his eyes away from hers and ran a

37

hand through his hair, remembering that moment.

'You should've shot Candice,' Willa said light-heartedly after several seconds of silence.

His eyes darted back to meet hers and he burst out laughing. 'You know what? I wish I had. Then she wouldn't have been able to write that bloody stupid story about me.'

'But ... it wasn't fiction then? It ... it happened almost exactly as she said it did.'

Mark sighed. Why did it matter what Willa thought? he asked himself.

'That part yes, I suppose it did, although she still added a considerable amount of drama. The bear didn't stand up on its hind legs and *growl*, I can assure you and it wasn't over ten feet tall. It was a youngster, probably about three years old and still a little unsure of itself otherwise it might not have gone so quietly. And the wolf was just your average wolf, not 'frothing at the mouth with five-inch fangs still covered in blood from a recent kill'. I have a photographic memory too. To be honest, I thought the wolf would be more trouble than the bear. There was just something about its stance but it can't have been that desperate for food – which was just as well. And bears and wolves rarely attack humans unless they're provoked, surprised or starving, despite what people think. There is far easier prey out there, believe me. Most injuries happen because of the stupid things humans do when they're in a situation like that.'

Willa glanced towards her wine glass and Mark watched her fingertips slide up and down the stem. It was somehow quite erotic and he could feel himself getting a little uncomfortable.

'And the other part?' she asked, meeting his eyes again.

'The sex, you mean?' He thought his voice sounded odd and hoped she didn't notice.

Her eyes met his and she nodded slowly as the air crackled between them. Mark could hear his breath coming in short, sharp gasps. What the hell was happening to him?

He swallowed hard before answering.

'Let's just say, like the bear and the wolf, when someone offers me something on a plate, my instinct is to take it.'

The moment was gone.

'God, Mark! So it's all true then. After everything you said about the magazine, she told the truth.'

'No! Well, partly. She made a pass at me, we had sex, that was it. Oh, she did howl but that was afterwards when we'd finished and that was only because it was a full moon and she said she'd always wanted to – it had nothing to do with the sex and as for it lasting all night, as much as I'd like to say that bit is fact, it's most definitely fiction.'

He saw her glance down at the table and he wondered what she was thinking.

'Wolves don't just howl when it's a full moon, you know,' she said. 'They howl because of a lot of things. They also bark and growl and ... oh, sorry, I suppose if you've written books or given lectures about survival in the wild, I'm teaching my grandmother to suck eggs aren't I?'

Mark smiled. 'Yes, but it's good to meet someone who actually *knows* that about wolves.'

'Did ... did you see her again?'

'Who? The wolf or the woman? Sorry. A little joke. No way! I mean, no.'

They stared at one another until, a few minutes later, Aglaia brought out several plates of food and she and Stavros joined them. They dined on olives and bread, tomatoes, salad and sea bass followed by fresh figs.

'Did he tell you how we met?' Stavros asked Willa.

Mark tutted and shook his head. 'No Stavros, Willa doesn't want to hear about that. Please, I beg you.'

'No, Mark. She should hear it,' Aglaia said.

'I'd like to,' Willa said.

'Well, he was backpacking if I remember, yes?'

Mark nodded. 'Yes.' Then to Willa, 'This will be more fiction.'

'Fiction. No!' Stavros exclaimed. 'All true. He stopped

here for some food and a cold beer and the bridge, it came back up after being lowered to allow a ship to pass. This was a long time ago when fish they were plentiful. Not so much now. If there are ten you are surprised but then, there were many and when the bridge came up, it was covered in fish. Nico, he was the bridge operator and he told the people standing around they could help themselves to the fish. But so did the cats and one person, a big man, not from this area but a Greek I am ashamed to say, he kicked one of the cats into the canal.'

'No!' Willa shrieked.

'But yes!' Stavros continued. 'So Mark, he got up and ran to the man and told him to jump into the canal and get the cat out. It was swimming so it was safe and the man, he says, "No," so Mark, he says, "Either you jump in or I throw you in and if I throw you in, you won't get out." The man, he looked at Mark and then he jumped into the canal with a net Nico had given him and he pulled the cat out and Mark, he told the man to pay for the cat to have supper at my taverna. And the man, he did!' Stavros and Aglaia held one another and laughed heartily.

Mark shook his head. 'I told you. More fiction. The best part of that story is that Aglaia and Stavros adopted the cat and it lived a very happy life here with a full stomach.'

'This is true and the cat, we named him Markos,' Stavros said, his laughter subsiding. 'He has now gone to the Elysian Fields, we like to think.'

'We'd better get going soon ourselves or we won't reach the hotel before midnight,' Mark said, changing the subject.

'Oh my God! What's the time?' Willa asked.

'Ten o' clock and it's about an hour and forty minutes to Kritiopoli from here – assuming the bridge is still up.'

'Oh no. I hadn't realised it was getting so late. When I phoned Blossom to say we'd stopped on the way, I said we'd be there by ten-thirty. I'd better call her and explain.'

Willa spoke to Blossom whilst Mark explained to Stavros and Aglaia that they had to get to Kritiopoli.

40

Having refused his friends' kind offer of a bed for the night, Mark and Willa thanked them profusely and finally headed back towards the car.

'Sorry. This was actually rather selfish of me, wasn't it? I forgot that you've got other guests you should be attending to. I hope I haven't caused any problems.'

'No, it's fine. We knew that I'd be coming to get you and that at the earliest I wouldn't be back until nine-ish. Blossom and Aristaios were handling the welcome evening, and most of the guests like an early night on the first night but we do need to get you checked in. Not that that matters because there is someone on reception all night but still ...'

'It's late and you've got a busy day tomorrow. I'm sorry.'

'So have you, Mark. Unless you want to lounge by the pool, of course.'

'I might just do that. I've been fairly busy for the last few months. I could do with a rest.'

'Well, it must be tiring rescuing women from bears and wolves and rapids, not to mention spending all night making them howl like a wolf!'

He saw the smile spread across Willa's mouth and he had an almost overwhelming urge to pull her into his arms and see if he could make her *howl*. 'You're not going to let me forget that, are you?'

'Probably not. Did you really threaten to throw that man into the canal?'

'What? Yes I did. I don't like seeing people ill-treat animals – big or small. They have as much right to be here as we do and we should show them some respect. Nothing makes me angrier, to be honest. I don't think he actually jumped in though. I think he got the cat out with the net – but it was a long time ago and I forget. I suppose I was a bit of a bully but I'd do it again tomorrow if I had to.'

'I'm glad,' Willa said. 'I feel the same way about animals.'

He held the passenger door open for her and their eyes

met for the briefest of moments as she got in the car. He walked around to the driver's side and got in. He turned to her and grinned.

'Perhaps we should take Aglaia and Stavros up on their offer of a bed for the night. You seem to be rather concerned about what is fact and what is fiction, so if you really want to know if I can make love all night long and make a woman howl like a wolf, I'm willing to give it a go if you are.'

Willa's head shot round and her mouth fell open.

'I take it that's a 'no',' he said as he started the car and headed off in the direction of the Argolis Bay Hotel.

CHAPTER SIX

'He did what?' Willa said, horrified at the very thought of it and nearly dropping the mug of coffee Blossom had passed to her.

'He carried you into the apartment and laid you down on the bed,' Blossom repeated. 'Hey, don't look at me like that. You're the one who stopped off for a drink and clearly ended up knocking back several. Mark said you only had a couple but I'm not sure I believe him. You know you always fall asleep when you've had too many, so it's your own fault – and believe me, you were out like a light.'

'Why didn't you wake me up?'

'I wanted to. I did try but you were sparko and he said it was no problem to carry you to bed ... so I let him. To be honest, I'm not sure I was making much sense. Apart from the fact that the guy is drop-dead gorgeous and I was swooning like a schoolgirl, it was nearly midnight when he drove up and I was so surprised to see him get out of the driver's side and see you snoring your head off that I–'

'Snoring! I was snoring? Oh my God. This is so embarrassing. Could it get any worse? Blossom ... why are you looking at me like that? It didn't get worse, did it? Oh no! What else did I do?'

'Well ... okay, I'm just going to say it because I think it's best that you know and I'm not totally sure that they heard it ... really.'

'What? Who?'

'Mark and Aristaios.'

'Oh God, I didn't fart or something, did I?'

'No! You ... well, Aristaios and I came out to meet you and when Mark said you were asleep and we tried to wake you and couldn't, he asked where we lived and offered to carry you in.'

'Yes, you've told me that. What did I *do*?'

43

'Well, he lifted you out of the car and starting walking towards the apartment and ... you put your arms around his neck and ... sort of snuggled up to him ...' Blossom's voice trailed off and she took a large gulp of coffee.

'That's not so bad, I suppose,' Willa said. 'Anyone would do that if they were sleepy.'

'And then you said, "I think I'm a little bit in love with you, Aristaios. Are you taking me to bed?" Only it didn't come out that clearly. I heard it because I was right beside you, so I suppose Mark must have heard it because you were in his arms. He did seem to stiffen a little – and not in a good way. The tense up sort. Anyway, I'm not sure Aristaios heard although he did give you an odd look but that may just have been because of the situation. I immediately asked Aristaios if he'd arrange for Mark's bag to be taken to his room. Then I started waffling about something to Mark and no one commented on your little confession. I think you may have got away with it.'

Willa hung her head in her hands. 'Kill me now!'

'Don't be silly. I want to hear everything that happened between you picking, 'Magnificent Mark' up at Athens and him carrying you up to bed. Well, everything before you fell asleep that is. Besides, you don't want to give your dad the satisfaction of being able to say that he knew you couldn't cope, do you?'

Willa's head shot up. 'That's right. Throw Dad at me, why don't you? Oh God. I hope Mark doesn't include last night in his review. In fact, I hope he doesn't include any of yesterday in it. We ... we had a bit of a ... heated debate at one point and if Dad hears about that, he'll drag me back home and have me answering the phones in five seconds flat.'

'Then you'd better be nice to Mark and ask him not to. What did you have a row about?'

'It wasn't a row, it was ... a difference of opinion ... sort of.'

'Yeah, I can imagine. You do have a very short fuse

when you're stressed, you know.'

'I know. It wasn't an argument or anything. It just ... well, he just irritated me, that's all and I was ... perhaps a little ... difficult.'

'Obnoxious, you mean?'

'No. Well, maybe a little. We were discussing that article about him. He tried to say it was all fiction.'

'So why did you row about that? I thought you said it was all fiction too, so you were right and he agreed with you.'

'I told you, we didn't row. But he said it was fiction and it turns out that most of it was fact. Highly embellished but fact nonetheless, and then he was really ... mean about the woman who wrote it.'

'The one he spent the night with and made her howl, you mean?'

'Yes. And he seemed annoyed that she wrote about it.'

'Well, that's reasonable. You'd be annoyed if you spent the night with someone and they wrote about it, although, as she goes on about how great he was, I would have expected him to be pleased.'

'Well, he wasn't.'

'Well, he seemed perfectly happy when he arrived here and when he carried you to bed – until you made the comment about Aristaios, that is. After that, he didn't say much. Just that he was tired and would head off to his room. Anyway, speaking of Mark, I must get going. He and several of the other guests are going to be on the terrace for my break of dawn Pilates class in less than ten minutes' time.'

'Seriously? He's joining your class. Oh, I suppose he has to try out everything on offer if he's going to write a full review of the holiday.'

Blossom grabbed a bottle of water from the fridge and beamed at Willa. 'And I'm going to be offering him a whole lot more than Pilates, let me tell you. By the time I've finished with him, he'll be the one howling like a wolf.

See you at breakfast.'

Willa watched Blossom bounce out of the apartment and she didn't doubt it for one minute.

***

'Good morning, Aristaios. How are you today?' Willa said, having spent the last half an hour plucking up the courage to face him.

He glanced up from the newspaper he was reading and his eyes seemed to dance with delight. Willa hoped that meant he was pleased to see her but after what Blossom had told her, it could mean something else entirely.

'Willa! Good morning to you too. I am very well, thank you. You slept well?'

'I'm so sorry about last night,' she said. 'May I?' She pointed towards the empty chair at his table in the restaurant.

'Of course. Please sit,' he said smiling broadly. 'And there is no need to apologise, Willa. You were very tired. It was a long day and you have been working so hard. And the heat. You are not used to it yet, I think.' He leant forward and brushed a tendril of brown curl from her eyes.

She could smell his aftershave and her head swam, more from the intoxication of being so close to him than from the heady scent. She smiled back and poured herself a cup of coffee from the pot on the table.

'It is exceptionally hot,' she replied. 'I hope they've all brought plenty of sunscreen.' She nodded towards the ten people she could see on the lower terrace in Blossom's Pilates class, currently performing the sun god pose with differing degrees of success.

'Ah yes. The English abroad,' Aristaios said, directing his eyes towards the terrace.

'Weren't both your mother and grandmother English?'

He grinned. 'They were, but they both married Greeks.'

They watched in silence for a few minutes. Willa wasn't

really surprised to see that Mark was performing each position with ease but she was surprised that he was wearing a T-shirt and a pair of baggy shorts. For some reason she'd assumed he'd want to show off his physique, especially now that she knew the photo of him in *Only The Best Will Do* definitely wasn't enhanced.

A couple of the other men in the group were only wearing shorts and one man was wearing skin-tight swim briefs – what Blossom and others referred to as 'budgie-smugglers'. Willa made a mental note to be very wary of that one. He had a great body though and with his sandy blond hair and muscular frame, she imagined the demigod, Heracles. From the way that he kept stumbling and bumping into Mark who appeared to be accepting it all good naturedly, it looked as if Blossom's Pilates class should have been added to the twelve labours.

As she watched him stumble again, she tried to recall his name from the check-in introductions yesterday. If Mark hadn't grabbed his arm, he would have ended up flat on his ruggedly handsome face. Harry! That was it. Harry Bullen – the advertising executive Blossom had spoken of. Hmm. She could see what Blossom had meant by him being tasty. But a man wearing budgie-smugglers; that was a definite no-no, as far as she was concerned although even from this distance it looked as if he had a lot more than a budgie stuffed down the front.

He wasn't the only one who kept bumping into Mark, Willa noticed. A petite woman in a tight-fitting purple leotard seemed to be throwing her arms around him far more than was necessary to regain her balance.

'Poor Mark,' Aristaios said as if reading Willa's mind. 'He seems to be in the wrong place at the wrong time, as my dear mother used to say.'

He and Willa exchanged glances and grinned, knowingly.

'Although,' he said, suddenly leaning forward, his dark eyes sweeping over her and lingering longer than was necessary on her cleavage, 'last night he was in the right place at the right time. A place I would very much like to have been in, myself. A place that perhaps one day, I may be, if the gods are kind.'

Willa could feel her mouth falling open. She quickly snapped it shut, hoping she didn't resemble a fish. Had he just said what she thought he had? She felt her temperature rising and it had nothing to do with the blazing sun, now climbing in the early morning, cloudless, blue sky.

'I ... I am so embarrassed about that,' she said, glancing towards the table as she felt her cheeks redden and her heart jump around in her chest. 'We stopped for a drink and ... I think I may have had one too many. Plus, as you said, it was a long day and ...'

He put his hand on hers and she stared at it as if it were a lethal weapon.

'Willa, there is no need for explanations between you and me,' he said.

He slowly retracted his hand so that his fingers stroked hers, making several nerve endings throughout her body suddenly stand to attention and pass messages of sexual expectations to her increasingly bemused brain.

'Oh!' was all her voice could manage.

She thought he might elaborate but some of the guests were coming into the restaurant for breakfast and it was time for both she and Aristaios to get on with their jobs.

***

Willa could feel Mark's eyes watching her from the moment after breakfast when she strolled out onto the upper terrace to address the group on their first morning's programme. She had hoped to get him alone before the briefing, to discuss yesterday evening but it seemed he was intent on avoiding her. Three times, she waved at him to attract his attention and each time he pretended not to see her.

It was possible, of course, that he really *hadn't* seen her, surrounded as he was by females of all shapes, sizes and ages from the moment he entered the restaurant for breakfast until the moment he left and took a seat on the terrace. She was fairly certain though that she caught him looking in her direction more than once before hurriedly looking away. The few times he was alone and Willa approached him, he suddenly appeared to be talking on his phone and she wondered whether she had said or done anything else on the way to the hotel from the Corinth Canal. Surely, it couldn't just be her comment about being a little bit in love with Aristaios... could it?

'Good morning everyone,' she began. 'I was very pleased to see that many of you took part in Blossom's Pilates class this morning and I'm sure you're all raring to go after that workout.'

Several of the group cheered, none more loudly or enthusiastically than Harry Bullen and she knew instinctively that he was going to be the one to get into trouble if anyone was, this week. There was just something about him that seemed to indicate he would jump first and ask questions later.

'You've all, no doubt, read the programme but let me say right off the bat that none of this is obligatory. You can participate in as much or as little as you like, or none at all if you'd rather just do your own thing. Blossom, Aristaios and I are happy to help if you want to hire a car or go on any sightseeing tours other than those we have planned for you, so do please ask. And feel free to ask us questions at any time. We're all here to make sure this holiday is one you won't forget in a hurry – for all the best possible reasons!'

Another loud cheer from Harry brought a smile to several faces and a few tut-tuts from others.

'Well, let's get started then,' Willa continued. 'For those of you wishing to sail or windsurf this morning, please come with me. For those wishing to lounge by the pool, I'm sure you've already found it but if not, come with me and I'll show you where it is – although as you can all see, it is visible from here. It's just a question of which path to take through these gorgeous gardens.'

'You just follow the yellow brick road,' Harry cajoled.

'Except it's white limestone and marble tiles,' someone else said cheerily.

'I just want to know which one leads to the bar,' another person joked.

'Well, whichever one you take,' Willa said, smiling, 'Aristaios is happy for you to try a fresh fig on your way, and believe me, there is nothing quite so delicious as a fig warmed by the sun and plucked straight from the tree. They have ripened a little early this year so we are very fortunate. Just make sure it's a fig tree and not a prickly pear. You really do *not* want to grab one of those without thinking. Don't worry, there aren't any near the paths, so you won't take one by accident and the prickly pear tree is actually a cactus, so you won't mistake it. If you do want to try a prickly pear though, just ask Aristaios or Loukas Diamantidis, the sailing centre owner you'll be meeting in a few minutes, and they'll peel one for you. It's a skill acquired over time. Take my word for it.'

'Wasn't that what Baloo ate in the Jungle book?' asked Suki Thane, the woman who had been wearing the purple leotard earlier.

'Yes, it was and he warned you about them in the song, so it's not just my word you should heed.' Willa laughed. 'Right. Let's go and meet Loukas down on the beach. It looks like it'll be a good day for a gentle sail.'

Willa hoped she would get a chance to speak to Mark during the walk to the sailing centre but once again, he was surrounded and Suki Thane seemed to have become attached to him by an invisible thread.

'I'm really looking forward to this week.'

Willa looked round and saw that Harry was speaking to her.

'Good. I think you'll have a great time, Harry.'

'They seem a really fun bunch of people,' he continued, falling into step beside her. 'Especially Mark. I think he'll turn out to be a good sport. For someone so famous, he doesn't have any airs or graces.'

Now Harry had her attention. 'Someone so famous? I know he's built up quite a following with his blog and his articles have won a few awards. He also told me yesterday that he'd written a couple of books and made some wildlife films or something but I didn't realise he was that well known.'

'Where have you been hiding? He and his dad, James Thornton are the new Richard Attenborough, Ray Mears and Bear Grylls rolled into one – or two I suppose, strictly speaking. Haven't you seen any of their wildlife or survival in the wild documentaries on TV? They've also written a ton of books and Mark's written several in his own right. All his books have shot into the charts within weeks of being published and his blog, 'Tripping with Thornton' gets more hits on a daily basis than any other travel blog out there. Oh, and his first book, *On the Waves of Poseidon* was number one in the Times bestsellers' list for weeks and it's still one of the best selling travel books on record.'

Willa was stunned. Was this the book Mark had described as 'a crappy title and the book wasn't much better'? He told her it had sunk to the bottom of the ocean. She'd assumed that meant it hadn't sold many copies. Perhaps he wasn't quite as arrogant as she'd thought.

'Are you sure?' she said, glancing towards Mark who was picking figs and handing them to Suki Thane and three of the other women vying for his attention.

'Yep! I've got a copy of the Poseidon book with me as it happens. It's a really great book. It's very funny as well as being the quintessential travel guide to the Greek Islands. And he's certainly got a way with the ladies, hasn't he?' Harry said, nodding his head in Mark's direction.

Willa watched Mark run a hand through his hair and for

the briefest of moments, their eyes met. Almost immediately, he turned his attention back to Suki and the other women and they continued on their way to the beach.

'She's old enough to be his mother,' Willa said under her breath.

'What was that?' Harry asked.

'Oh! Nothing. I don't suppose I could borrow *On the Waves of Poseidon* for a day or two could I?'

'Sure. I've read it about six times, anyway. I only brought it with me because it gives some really useful info on the nearby islands of Spetses and Hydra plus he writes about sailing in the area so it seemed apt. He's an expert yachtsman, you know.'

Willa shot a look at Harry's face before staring at Mark's back. She let out a long, loud sigh of resignation. 'Of course he is,' she said.

CHAPTER SEVEN

Loukas Diamantidis looked more like a film star than a sailing instructor. He was tall, fit and ruggedly handsome in addition to looking much younger than his fifty-five years. When he spoke, his voice was deep and firm, and forty-five year old divorcée, Suki Thane wasn't the only woman in the group to clearly be swept off her feet by the tidal wave of Loukas' charm.

'It looks like you've got some competition, Mark,' Harry said as they stood on the shore listening to Loukas' instructions.

Mark grinned. 'A little competition never hurts. It only makes things more interesting!'

'I couldn't agree more. Some of the women here are quite something, aren't they? I wasn't sure if it was the exercise this morning that made me short of breath or watching Blossom's boobs under that T-shirt she was wearing. Now there're a couple of fruits I'd really like to get my hands on.'

Mark stole a glance at Willa and Harry obviously spotted it.

'And Willa's pretty hot too, in that sort of will she, won't she way, isn't she? She's very friendly but there's something about her that gives you the impression she's off limits – and there is nothing more attractive to a guy than a woman he thinks he can't have, is there? You just want to remove those glasses of hers, grab a handful of that hair and kiss those lips into submission, don't you?'

'Do I?' Mark said, thinking that was exactly what he'd like to do. That and a lot, lot more besides.

'I was speaking hypothetically,' Harry said, grinning. 'I wonder if either of them is spoken for.'

Mark met Harry's eyes. 'I have no idea but I think Willa may be, just from something she said.'

'Really? Oh well. We're all on holiday and holidays are all about having fun, so we'll have to see about that, won't we?'

Mark felt himself rise to the bait. 'Yes, I suppose we will,' he said.

'And you are Mark Thornton?' Loukas said, standing just a few feet from Mark.

'What? Oh, yes. Pleased to meet you.'

'No, no. It is I who am pleased to meet you! I have read all of your books. *On the Waves of Poseidon* was my favourite. You have captured the essence of Greece and her people in those pages. Perhaps you would be kind enough to sign my copy over a glass of ouzo?'

'I'd be delighted,' Mark said. 'Your English is excellent. Have you spent time abroad?'

'Yes. My father sent me to school there. That is where I met Aristaios' father, Georgiou and we became friends. Then I married Georgiou's sister, and their mother of course, was English so we spoke both English and Greek throughout our lives.'

'Ah. Yes, he told me a little about that last night and that he'd also been educated in England. So you're his uncle then?'

'Yes. His parents, and my beloved wife, Ariadne, died many years ago in a tragic accident. I came here to help run the hotel until Aristaios was old enough to take over. Then I decided I would stay. I own this sailing centre, Demeter's restaurant and Persephone's disco. You must come and dine with me one evening, yes?'

'I'd love to, Loukas. Thanks.'

'Well, there is no need for me to give you tuition, is there? You take whichever boat you like. The winds in this bay are gentle as you know but you are welcome to take one out into the gulf, if you like. I know she will be safe in your experienced hands.'

Mark glanced towards Willa. 'Thanks, Loukas but I think I'll stay in calmer waters for now.'

'As you wish. I must return to the novices.' He nudged Mark gently in the side. 'One or two of the women here are very attractive, no? I think I may enjoy this week more than I had thought.'

'Harry here was just saying the same thing, weren't you Harry? Harry?'

Mark turned to see Harry was walking towards Willa and he clearly had more on his mind than just sailing. Without thinking, Mark followed in his footsteps.

'Thanks, Harry, that's really nice of you to offer ... but I've already agreed to go out with Mark,' Willa said as Mark came into earshot.

'You have?' Mark said. 'I mean, you have. Sorry, Harry. Maybe next time.' He gave Harry a friendly pat on the arm and a triumphant smile.

'Yeah, next time,' Harry said cheerily and wandered off to one of the other women, who was clearly struggling with the concept of getting into a dinghy. 'Let me help you, love.'

Mark returned his attention to Willa. 'By "go out with" me you meant ... what exactly?'

Willa's brows knit together and she gave him an odd look. 'Sailing, of course. I know you didn't ask me and I do apologise for dumping myself on you like this but I've been trying to get a chance to talk to you all morning.'

'Oh.'

'What did you think I meant?'

'Sailing. But I was just checking. And I don't mind in the least. You can dump yourself on me anytime you like.'

Again, Willa's brows knit together. 'Why do I get the feeling that that means far more than I think it does?'

'I have no idea. You've clearly got an overactive imagination.'

'Uh, huh. Candice Cornwell and I have something in common then, it seems.'

'Dear God! Will you never let me forget that woman, Willa?'

'I got the distinct impression you'd forgotten her a long time ago but I'll do a deal with you.'

'Really? That sounds intriguing. What kind of a deal?'

'Let's take a boat out and I'll tell you.'

'O–kay. I take it you've sailed before – as you're running sailing holidays – although that doesn't necessarily signify. Candice Cornwell is supposed to be a writer but–'

'Don't be mean. We all do the best with what we've been given, Mark. Not everyone is as talented as you, you know.'

'Ouch! What have I done to deserve that?'

'Candice Cornwell!'

'That's not what, that's who. Sorry, that was a facetious remark. Which boat do you want to take out?'

'The Hobie. We won't need trap harnesses if we're staying in the bay and going for a gentle sail. I'll skipper on the way out. You can skipper on the way back.'

Mark raised his eyebrows in surprise. 'This is getting to be a habit,' he mumbled.

***

No sooner had Willa and Mark left the quayside than the wind died. Mark immediately shifted his position to sit opposite Willa to prevent the Hobie from tipping over and they drifted on the glasslike waters of the bay, staring at one another.

Mark still wore a T-shirt and baggy shorts although he had clearly changed them since the Pilates class as these were khaki and the ones he wore earlier were grey. Willa realised that the blue baggy shorts and T-shirt she was wearing were very similar in style to his. She had a bikini underneath hers and she found herself wondering what Mark had under his.

'So, you wanted to do a deal,' he said.

'What? Oh, yes. I did.' She dragged her mind back from what had been surprisingly pleasant thoughts.

56

'I'm listening.'

'It's about last night. Well, about all of yesterday really ... and I suppose, even just now.' She waited for him to comment but he eyed her silently. 'Firstly, I should apologise for falling asleep like that. I'm really sorry.'

'It wasn't a problem. It was late, you were tired and I knew where I was going so it didn't matter.'

'Yes, but ... you are a guest here and I should have paid more attention to you, not fallen asleep and let you drive me back here.'

'Don't worry about it, Willa. It's really not an issue. It was oddly comforting to have you sleeping beside me.'

Her eyes opened wide at that, even though she knew he meant it quite innocently.

'You know what I mean,' he added.

She nodded. 'I hope I didn't snore ... too loudly.'

He grinned at her. 'I've heard worse. No. Don't worry, I was teasing. You hardly snored at all. You just made odd, rather sweet, oohing sounds. I think you were dreaming.'

She saw his grin disappear suddenly but his eyes remained firmly focused on her.

'Um. I should also apologise for asking you all those questions about that article and for ... possibly snapping at you. I ... I was a little stressed yesterday and I may have taken it out on you which is totally unprofessional and–'

'It wasn't a problem. I actually rather enjoyed yesterday, so there's no need to apologise for that.'

'Er ... thank you. Um, and anything I may have said last night was just the drink speaking, not me. Well, it was me obviously but you know what I mean. Please take anything I said with a pinch of salt.'

His intense blue eye studied her face as if he could read her very thoughts.

'You mean it's not true that you're a little bit in love with Aristaios then? I can see why you would be. He's a very handsome man – not that he's my type, you understand but I can see why women would want to go to

57

bed with him. Do you want to go to bed with him, Willa?'

Her mouth fell open and stayed there.

'Sorry, was that question too direct?'

'Yes! And it's none of your business.'

'True. But it was none of your business whether I made Candice howl or not, or what I said to her and when, but you asked me and I told you the truth. I thought you might do me the same courtesy.'

'Oh! That was different. That was in the public domain. She published it for all to read.'

'You said it out loud last night for all to hear. Is there really a difference?'

'Yes! No, I suppose not. Why do you want to know?'

'Why did you?'

She could feel the tension rising in her chest; her breath caught in her throat. Why had she wanted to know?

'I was ... curious, I suppose.'

'I'm ... curious too. You seem to be having difficulty answering the question. I take it that means you are in love with him and you do want to sleep with him.'

'No!' she shrieked. Oddly enough for the first time since she'd laid eyes on the divine Aristaios Nikolades, she wasn't sure she did.

'No to both?'

'I ... I think so.'

She met his eyes and saw something in them that almost made her forget the reason she wanted to talk to him in the first place. Almost, but not quite.

'I need to ask you a favour – and this is the deal. I won't mention Candice Cornwell again if you don't mention in your review that I fell asleep last night and that you had to carry me to my apartment and put me to bed.'

He looked a little annoyed. 'I had no intention of mentioning that. What do you think I am? Oh, don't answer that. I think I know. Anyway, you have my word I won't write anything about it.'

She sighed loudly and smiled at him. 'I'm sorry for

58

thinking you might. It's just ... well, Dad would have a fit if he read that, and I'd be on the first plane back to Eastbourne.'

'I don't think planes fly to Eastbourne. Sorry! Being facetious again. Er ... you didn't ask me not to mention your little confession though. Does that mean that I can? I can see the headline now, 'Beautiful holiday rep bedded by British hero cries out for Greek god'. Is that too much?'

'You ... you *are* joking ... aren't you?'

'Yes,' he said, a smile hovering around his mouth. 'But not about you being beautiful.'

Before she had a chance to respond, a breeze caught the sail and the Hobie strained beneath them. Mark nimbly moved across the trampoline and sat beside Willa as the boat's hull lifted. Willa steered competently as they trimmed the sail, gained speed and headed out to deeper water.

***

'I enjoyed that,' Mark said as they pulled the Hobie out of the water onto the beach an hour later. 'You're very good. Perhaps we could do it again sometime.'

'Thanks. You're not that bad yourself and I'd like that. Maybe later in the week.'

'It's a date.'

'Willa!' Blossom yelled from the bar beside the pool just a few metres away. 'Your dad was on the phone about an hour ago. He wants you to call him back.'

'Oh dear. Sorry Mark, I'd better dash. Planes may not fly to Eastbourne but if I don't get back to him pretty sharpish he'll find a way to get them to fly from there to here.'

Mark watched her run up the beach towards Blossom and he smiled. This morning had gone better than he'd expected. He'd been genuinely surprised by how good a sailor Willa was and he'd thoroughly enjoyed being on the water with her. After the wind picked up they hadn't talked about anything other than sailing but he'd found her easy to get along with and they handled the Hobie well as a team.

Even more importantly, last night he'd thought she was in love with another man and for some reason that had ruined his holiday before it had really started. Today, she said she wasn't and whilst that didn't mean anything in itself, at least it meant he had a chance. The thought suddenly troubled him. A chance for what? To get to know her? To spend some time with her? To take her to bed?

'How was your morning?'

It was Harry. He was striding towards Mark, dripping wet and wearing just his swim trunks.

'Good thanks and yours? Have you been for a swim?'

Harry chuckled. 'Yes and no. I've been helping Loukas teach some of the women how to right a capsized dinghy. It was ... entertaining to say the least. There's nothing quite as exhilarating for a woman as being saved from drowning by a man – but you'd know all about that wouldn't you?'

Mark sighed. 'It's something I'm trying very hard to forget. Couldn't any of them save themselves?'

Harry grinned. 'Now where's the fun in that? Fancy a beer? I'm gasping.'

'Saving women does that to you, or so I've heard. Is Loukas joining us?'

'He said he'll be here in ten minutes. There seems to be one woman – Suki, I think her name is – he felt needed a little ... extra tuition.'

Mark found himself wondering which one of those two would be giving the tuition. He followed Harry up the beach to the pool bar where they found Aristaios having a glass of ouzo with Blossom.

'Mind if we join you?' Harry asked.

'Please do,' Aristaios said.

'Actually, I must love you and leave you,' Blossom said, getting to her feet. 'I'd better see what Mr Daventry wanted in case there's anything Willa needs me to do. Enjoy yourselves in my absence.'

'How can we possibly do that?' Aristaios said, taking her hand in his and kissing her fingers.

'Very easily, I can imagine,' Blossom said, clearly not in the least impressed by the gesture.

Mark and Harry sat and the three men watched Blossom saunter up the path towards the terraces and the hotel.

'What is it about English women?' Aristaios said. 'My father fell in love with one and married her as did my grandfather before him and I can't decide who is the most delicious,–Willa or Blossom.'

Mark's head shot round and his eyes met Aristaios' in what he felt was probably a challenge.

'Ah, I see you are interested in one of them, too. Let me guess. It is Willa, yes?'

Mark shrugged.

'Don't be coy, Mark,' Harry said. 'We're all men together and what's said here stays here, right?'

Aristaios nodded in agreement but Mark remained silent.

'Well,' Harry said, 'I wouldn't mind either of them but I think Willa would be more of a challenge. I don't know what it is about her but something tells me she would hold back.'

'I agree,' Aristaios said. 'I think she does not like mixing business and pleasure but Blossom … I think she thinks everything is pleasure and she will mix both if she wants to. Willa would take longer to … encourage, I think.'

'What do you think, Mark?' Harry asked.

'I think I need to go for a swim before lunch,' Mark said. 'I'll catch up with you later.'

For some reason, he didn't want to talk about Willa and whether or not she'd be a challenge to get into bed.

CHAPTER EIGHT

'Everything okay?' Blossom asked as she strolled into Willa's office. 'What did your dad want? Checking to see that we haven't eaten the delicious Mark Thornton yet?'

Willa smirked. 'You're not far off. He wanted to make sure that he has everything he wants and that we're giving him the V I P treatment.'

'I'd like to give him the V I P treatment – the Very Intensely Personal treatment, that is.'

'Yes, you and several other women it seems.'

'Well, what can I say? The man's a dreamboat. I wish he'd take his T-shirt off though. I want to check that his abs are as good as they looked in that picture we saw. All the other men are baring their bodies – and some of them *really shouldn't* be – but Magnificent Mark seems rather reluctant.'

'Perhaps he knows he doesn't need to. Even in his baggy shorts and loose fitting T-shirt, you can see he's got a perfect body.'

'Well, well, well. You've changed your tune. What happened out there on the Hobie? Last week he was the Devil incarnate, now he's the best thing since sliced bread.'

'Nothing happened out there or anywhere else before you ask, and aren't you mixing your metaphors?'

'Ooooh! You sounded just like your dad then. You're right, I am and as it's lunchtime, I'd rather be mixing my drinks. Are you coming?'

Willa got up, linked arms with Blossom and headed towards the door.

'I could use a drink, especially if I'm beginning to sound like Dad. He told me about five times just how important it is to get a good review from Mark – as if I didn't know that. One thing he did say though which I didn't know until now was that Mark is doing this review as a favour for his mum!

Apparently, Dad knows her husband – and that was also odd. He didn't call him Mark's father so perhaps Mark's parents are divorced and his mum's remarried. Anyway, Dad mentioned the holiday to the husband, Francis, I think he called him and Francis told him that he may be able to pull a few strings. That's why this was all so last minute. Mark only agreed to do it a day or so before Dad asked me to book the flight. Sorry, before *you* booked the flight, I should have said.'

'And it now seems that you're very glad I did. Am I going to have competition?' Blossom asked, grinning mischievously as they ambled through the gardens towards the pool bar.

'For Mark? Not from me you're not although I can't say the same about every other female here. He's good to look at, I'll now admit that and he's surprisingly good company but I get the distinct impression that he's a bit of a womaniser and I've got absolutely no intention of being one of his one-night stands.'

'Nor have I,' Blossom said. 'I'm banking on at least two and I plan to be lying down for some of the time.'

Willa giggled and waved at Aristaios who was still sitting near the pool with Harry. There was no sign of Mark and she wondered where he'd gone. She soon had her answer and it made both she and Blossom stop in their tracks.

Like one of those TV adverts for men's cologne, Mark suddenly rose up from beneath the water of the pool and shook his light brown hair, tossing droplets of water in all directions. He placed his hands flat on the tile surround and lifted himself out in one smooth, fluid movement. He landed on one foot and stood up straight as rivulets of water streamed down his tanned, rippling body, threatening to take his loose swim shorts with them.

'Fuck me!' Willa and Blossom gasped simultaneously, their mouths falling open as they feasted their eyes on the vision before them.

Willa was sure her eyes leapt from their sockets on stalks as they did in cartoons. When she was finally able to look away from Mark's body to Blossom's face, she could see Blossom was feeling exactly the same as she was.

'I've changed my mind,' she said when she could find her voice, her gaze sweeping over Mark once again. 'Can I have him when you've finished with him?'

'Over my dead body,' Blossom squeaked.

They weren't the only ones making the most of the view. It was as if time had stopped and every female within a ten-metre radius had her eyes firmly fixed in the direction of this Adonis.

Not that Mark seemed to notice. He grabbed his towel, rubbed his hair and his torso with it, tightened the knot on the cord in his trunks and flopped onto the chair he'd vacated earlier. He ran his hands through his wet hair and took several large swigs of the beer that Harry pushed in front of him.

'Willa! Blossom! Join us,' Aristaios called out to them, beckoning with his hand.

Mark twisted round in his seat and his eyes lit up, Willa was sure of it. Was he pleased to see her or Blossom? Perhaps it was both of them. Did it really matter? She was surprised to find that it did. This has to stop right now she told herself silently. Apart from anything else, Blossom clearly liked him a lot and there was no way she would get in the way of that.

'Did you have a good swim?' Blossom asked Mark, sitting on the empty seat beside him.

'Yes, thanks,' he said. 'The water's the perfect temperature. In fact, I'd say everything about this holiday has been perfect so far.'

Willa cast him a sideways glance as she walked around him to take a chair from another table but he jumped up, pushed his chair back and grabbed one for her, placing it to the other side of him so that she would be sitting between him and Aristaios.

'Thanks,' she said 'but I don't like facing the sun. I'll sit round the other side if you don't mind.'

She thought she saw a shadow flick across his eyes but it was gone in a second.

'Sure,' he said, picking up the chair and carrying it around the table to put it in the space between Aristaios and Harry. 'No problem.'

She definitely saw Harry wink and grin at Mark. That much she didn't imagine and she had an odd feeling that there was something going on that she wasn't aware of. She sat down and told herself over and over not to ogle Mark's body.

'What are you planning to do this afternoon? Blossom asked Mark when he returned to his seat.

He shook his head. 'I might just chill here or I may take a stroll down to the village. I haven't decided yet. The itinerary says 'free afternoon' so I guess I can do whatever I want. Well, not quite *whatever* I want but I'm hopeful.' His gaze settled on Willa and his mouth curved into his lopsided grin.

Willa felt her lips forming into a smile and made a determined effort to stop them. Mark was clearly flirting with her and she couldn't let that continue or be seen to encourage it.

'There's not much in the village,' Blossom said, 'although it is very pretty. I'm taking a few of the guests out on a bike ride later, once it's cooled down a bit. We're going into the hills to look at some of the flora and fauna. You're welcome to join us. You too, Harry. We'll be leaving around four and will be back by six-thirty in time for a shower and a few drinks before dinner.'

'You should go,' Willa said a little too quickly and firmly. 'I mean ... if you like cycling, that is. Aristaios, Blossom and I have been several times and it's well worth it. There's a surprising diversity of ... oh, sorry, I've just remembered, you know this area far better than I. You've probably seen everything it has to offer.'

'I thought I had,' Mark said, 'but it seems I was wrong.' Then he cast a glance in Harry's direction. 'You up for that? I'm going to go into the village first I think, but a bike ride sounds good to me.'

Harry nodded. 'Yep. I'm going to have a bit of a siesta after lunch but you can put me down for the bike ride. Will you personally come and wake me half an hour or so before, Blossom?' he joked.

His grin was as broad as the Corinth Canal, Willa thought.

'I'll do better than that,' Blossom said, leaning forward provocatively. 'I'll have afternoon tea sent to your room at three-fifteen. How's that for service?'

Everyone smiled, but Willa noticed that for one brief moment, Aristaios had fidgeted in his seat and looked rather annoyed. She couldn't fathom why though. Afternoon tea was a part of the package and several of the guests would ask for it to be sent to their rooms.

'I'm starving,' Mark said. 'What's on the menu for lunch?'

***

Willa heard Mark's voice in the reception area and she glanced up to see him strolling towards her office. She considered jumping up and shutting the door but he'd see her do that, so she thought better of it. She decided instead to pretend that she was on her way out but in her haste, she stumbled into one of the low armchairs to the left of her desk. She cursed loudly as a stabbing pain shot through her big toe.

'Ouch!' Mark said, reaching the open doorway. 'I bet that hurt. Are you okay?'

'I'm fine,' she said. 'I always scream and jump about like this when I'm enjoying myself.'

She saw Mark's dark brows knit together and knew she shouldn't have snapped at him. She wasn't sure why she had. Perhaps it was because she'd seen him come back from his walk to the village with Suki Thane, her arm tucked in his. Or maybe because Blossom had returned from the bike ride eager to tell Willa what fun they'd had and how Mark had done this and Mark had done that. Or possibly it was because she thought he was flirting with every single woman in the hotel, including her and that was reprehensible behaviour.

'I guess it beats howling,' he said.

Willa let go of her bruised toe and stood upright. 'I thought you didn't want to mention that topic again.'

'No, I don't want to mention the story or ... whatshername again. Howling, I'm fine with.'

'Candice! Her name is Candice Cornwell.'

A huge grin spread across his face. 'Now you're in breach of our agreement. You promised you wouldn't say her name again. That means you'll have to pay a penalty.'

He stepped towards her and instinctively, she backed away.

'You brought it up, not me. And I can't believe you keep forgetting her name. That's so ... so ...'

He raised his brows and took another step towards her. 'So ... what, exactly?'

'Cold,' she said, standing her ground and raising her chin.

The grin faded. 'I was teasing you, Willa. I do remember her name. I'll admit I had forgotten it until I heard about the article so I'll accept any criticism you want to level at me for that but to be honest, I'm not sure she ever told me her surname and only briefly mentioned her first name. In my defence, I did have other things on my mind at the time.'

'I'm sure you did!'

'No, not sex, so don't look at me like that. Things like making them move their campsite in case the bear or wolf returned in the night, and making sure they didn't leave any rubbish behind them which they were going to do, unbelievably. Some people clearly don't pay attention to the regulations. Anyway, I was fairly shattered by the time I'd set up another camp for them so we didn't talk much after that.'

'You spent the night with her. Didn't you talk then?'

Mark sighed. 'No, not really. Then, I admit, I was only thinking about sex and I was hardly going to say, 'Oh, what's your name by the way,' when she was unzipping my jeans, was I?' He took another step towards Willa and his lips twitched. 'And I generally don't make small talk when I'm having sex. I do ask certain questions, as I'm sure you can imagine but on the whole, I prefer action to words … don't you? '

Willa stepped back. 'I ... I ... this isn't about me.'

'It could be.'

Willa gasped. 'No, it could not! And please will you *stop* flirting with me.'

'Am I flirting with you? I thought I was just being honest. You do want me to be honest, don't you?'

His voice was dripping honey and Willa had to swallow several times and avert her gaze. There was something in his eyes that was making her feel completely tongue-tied.

'I ... I bet you didn't even take her number, did you? In the morning, I bet you just left without knowing her name or asking for her phone number.'

Mark's expression changed and he shook his head. 'Why would I take her number? I didn't want to see her again. Oh, okay, I suppose that confirms everything you appear to think about me. Fine, but at least I was honest. I didn't pretend I'd call her, knowing full well I wouldn't and she didn't seem upset about it in the story she wrote so I'm not sure why you're so cross about it. And let's not forget, she was the one who made the first move, not me.'

'No, I remember, 'like the bear and the wolf, when something's offered to you on a plate, your instinct is to take it'. And I'm not cross.' Willa turned away from him abruptly. 'I just want you to ...' At that moment, she stubbed her other big toe on the second chair. 'Fuck ... me!'

she shrieked as she lost her balance.

She put her hands out to steady herself and managed to grab the edge of her desk but her hand slipped, sending a pile of papers onto the floor.

He was by her side in an instant and caught her in his arms. 'I'm sorry,' he said, holding her close. 'Are you all right? Let me look at it.'

'I'm fine,' she squeaked, regaining her balance despite the pain, attempting to wriggle free from his arms.

'Sit down. I think it's bleeding. Do you have a first-aid kit in here or is it in reception?'

She looked down and saw a tiny pool of blood beneath her toe. 'There's a small kit in the drawer of my desk. It just needs a plaster.'

He sat her down, got the first aid kit and knelt in front of her taking her foot in his hands. 'By the way, was that an offer?' he quipped, dabbing at her toe with cotton wool and the Savlon wound wash he'd found in the kit.

'What?' she said, utterly confused by the strange sensations shooting through her, which had nothing to do with the pain in her toes.

He applied a plaster to the wound then lifted his head and looked her directly in the eye. 'You said you just wanted me to ... and then you said, "Fuck me." I was just wondering because if it was I ...' He trailed one finger slowly up her tibia towards her knee.

'No! It definitely *was not*,' she said, pulling her leg away. 'I was going to say that I just want you to remember her name.'

He grinned and shrugged. 'Oh well. You're going to have two very painful big toes tomorrow, you know.'

'Thank you, doctor,' she snapped.

His eyes held hers. 'Willa, have I done something to upset you? I thought we were getting on really well this morning but since then ...'

He seemed genuinely concerned and she realised she was behaving like a complete idiot. He was teasing her and flirting with her and she was taking it all so seriously. And he was right about Candice Cornwell. Far from being annoyed about the one night they had spent together, she had seemed deliriously happy about it.

'No. I'm sorry. It's just ... oh, I don't know. I ... I'm not very good at flirting and playing games, that's all.'

'And ... you think I'm flirting with you and playing games then?'

'Yes. Well … aren't you?'

His eyes seemed to search her face. 'I'll admit I've been teasing you and yes, I suppose I've been flirting but I don't think I'm playing games, exactly.'

She tutted. 'Of course you are! What is flirting and teasing if it isn't playing games? And I'd really rather you didn't. It may all be a bit of fun to you, Mark but I don't play those sort of games and ... and I need to keep things between us on a professional level. You ... you've been making ... suggestive remarks and ... and saying things since the moment we met at the airport.'

For a moment, he didn't respond and then he said, 'I'm sorry if I've upset you. That wasn't my intention.'

'Oh, you haven't really upset me, it's just ... well, like this morning, when you said I was beautiful – I know I'm not so–'

'You are beautiful! he interrupted. At least I think you are. That wasn't me flirting. That was me being honest. Okay, I may have been a little flirtatious at other times I'll admit but I said that because it's true. Did you think that I said it to try to get you into bed? Because I didn't. Not that I'm saying I wouldn't like to get you into bed because again, if I'm being honest, I rather think I would but I'd like to get to know you, spend some time with you ... then maybe ...'

Their eyes locked and he leant towards her. She thought she was moving away from him but was astonished to realise she was leaning in to meet him. Their lips met in a tentative kiss and her taste buds savoured every delicious moment. Tiny bursts of delight shot through her and the pain in her toes was completely forgotten.

His arms wrapped around her. He eased her towards him and her legs parted, allowing his body to slide between her thighs as the kiss deepened; his tongue exploring her mouth, licking her tongue and encircling it, tasting every inch it could reach and making her want more. Much, much more.

'I left it in Willa's office. I ... Oh!'

Willa pulled back as soon as she heard Blossom's voice, suddenly realising what she was doing, but it was too late.

Blossom stood in the open doorway, a look of horror on her face. Then she turned and marched away without a word.

Willa instinctively jumped up, knocking Mark backwards and he fell onto his rear with a stupefied expression on his face. She glanced at him and then at the empty doorway. Once again, she forgot her injured toes and ran after Blossom as fast as her damaged digits would allow.

CHAPTER NINE

Mark sat where he was for several seconds, wondering what on earth had just happened. He'd kissed Willa though he hadn't intended to and now she'd run off because Blossom had seen them. Feeling slightly bewildered, he began to pick up the papers that had fallen when Willa had grabbed at her desk and he realised exactly why he'd kissed her. From the moment he'd seen her at Athens airport, he'd been captivated by her.

He couldn't remember the last time he'd felt like this about a woman. Perhaps he never had and he wasn't sure whether he should be pleased or concerned. His way of life wasn't conducive to lasting relationships and it was clear that Willa wouldn't be interested in a quick fling. She'd basically said as much.

She'd also said she wanted to keep things on a professional level. Did she mean it or was she just scared? She did seem to be dwelling rather a lot on his one-night stand with Candice Cornwell. Was she really as appalled by it as she was making out or was she, in some strange way, intrigued by it? She hadn't backed away from him when he'd kissed her. In fact, she kissed him back. Surely, that meant something? So where did he go from here?

Perhaps it was best if he backed away before anyone got hurt. This sort of feeling could lead to serious stuff, and settling down, marriage, kids and all that baggage wasn't on his agenda – at least not for now.

And would it ever be? He vividly remembered the pain and heartache he'd suffered when his parents' marriage fell apart. He swore he would never put a kid through that. He also remembered how devastated his father had been when his mum had left them. His dad had no idea she was unhappy and in spite of the long absences, Mark knew his dad had been completely faithful to her throughout the thirteen years of their marriage.

Mark was almost twelve when his mum left, moved to Spain, and later married her new husband, but he remembered the heartache, the bitterness and the years of missing her as if it were only yesterday. Some things were just too painful to forget.

Spotting a few more papers, which had slid under the chair, he moved it to retrieve them. He saw the magazine *Only The Best Will Do* right at the back against the wall and he smirked. How ironic. Absentmindedly, he flicked through the pages, coming to an abrupt halt when he reached the article Candice Cornwell had written.

Someone had drawn a beard and moustache on his clean-shaven face, given him a few spots, including a large one on the tip of his nose, blacked out one of his teeth and added a bulbous, beer-belly to his stomach. And it got worse. The article was now headed, 'Arrogant Pain in the Arse Mark Meets His Match'.

He couldn't understand what he was reading but as he continued, any feelings he thought he may have had for Willa, disappeared in a puff of smoke. Underneath the new heading it read:

Having slathered fake tan and baby oil over his expensively re-sculptured body, Mark Thornton heads off to Greece, expecting a week of fun in the sun whilst thinking up new levels of criticisms and sarcastic barbs to hurl at the overworked and underappreciated Wilhelmina Daventry. But Mark is in for a surprise. Willa and her colleague, Blossom Appleyard have met his type before and know exactly how to handle him. A five-star review is theirs for the taking as this once arrogant man is left whimpering at their feet.

And that, he thought bitterly, was fact. Although he'd only been at the hotel for one day he had already decided that, unless something truly terrible happened – like everyone got food poisoning or the dinghies all sank – he would probably be giving Daventry Travel's Sailing Solo

Holidays a five-star review. What's more, he had just been kneeling at Willa's feet. Now, he definitely felt like whimpering. He stared at the magazine and screwed up his eyes as if he were in physical pain.

The feeling of dejection didn't last long and Mark got to his feet determined to ask Willa for an explanation. He had no idea when she'd written this but written it she had. That much was obvious and that meant she wasn't the person he'd thought she was. He couldn't understand what he'd done to deserve it though. Was her obvious dislike and contempt based merely upon Candice Cornwell's article and if so, why?

He needed answers but first he needed a drink and he made his way towards the bar as if his life depended on it.

'There you are,' Harry called out to him. 'We were looking for you. Loukas has invited us to have dinner at his restaurant this evening.'

'Us?' Mark said, half expecting him to say that Willa and Blossom were invited although he didn't know why.

'You, me and Aristaios. He's gone down to the pool to look for you. We'll meet him on his way back. You didn't have any plans this evening, did you?'

Mark felt the magazine scrunch up in his clenched fist and he forced himself to take a few deep breaths. 'Nothing that can't wait. But I warn you, Harry, I'm in the mood to get drunk. Very, very drunk.'

'What are we standing around here talking for then?' Harry said, throwing his arm around Mark's shoulder and leading him towards Demeter's.

***

'Blossom! Please let me explain,' Willa said, standing outside Blossom's bedroom door and feeling more than a little faint. Her toes were throbbing, swelling up and beginning to turn a rather vivid shade of blue but the pain in her feet was nothing compared to the pain in her heart that

74

she felt for hurting her friend.

'I can't believe you!' Blossom shouted through the bolted door. 'After everything you said about him. All that, "well it won't be me who falls in love with him or in bed with him" or whatever. All that, and what happens? On the first night you end up in his arms and on the second, you end up kissing him and you're virtually having sex with him on a chair!'

'I wasn't! Having sex, I mean. We were kissing I admit and I swear I really don't know how it happened. That's the truth. What can I say? I was cross with him and we were having a bit of a ... disagreement to be honest and then I stubbed my toe and then my other toe and it started bleeding and he put a plaster on it and the next thing I know we're kissing. It ... it was just one of those stupid, spur of the moment things. It didn't mean anything to me and it certainly didn't mean anything to him. If I could turn the clock back I would. I would never do anything to hurt you, you know that. Please open the door, Blossom.'

Willa heard the bolt slide back and Blossom stood in the doorway.

'Did ... did you say your toe is bleeding?'

Willa nodded. 'Yes, and it hurts like hell. They both do but I deserve it for being such a shitty friend. I'm so, so sorry Blossom. I promise you it won't happen again.'

'You'd better sit down,' Blossom said, sighing deeply. 'I'll open a bottle of wine and we can talk about it. Are the guests okay tonight? Do we need to be there?'

'No, well, not unless any of them needs to ask us something but hotel reception will call us if they do. Anyway, right now, you're more important than the guests.'

'Don't let your dad hear you say that. You'll be back in Eastbourne before you can say 'complaint form'. Where ... where's Mark?'

'Oh! I have no idea. The last time I saw him he was sitting on his backside in my office because I'd shoved him out of the way to come after you.'

'He'll be pleased,' Blossom said, grinning.

'I don't care about him. I care about you.'

'You care about your five-star review, or you will do this time next week or whenever your dad gets the report.'

Willa sighed. 'If Mark gives me a bad review because of this then he's not the man I suspect he is. I don't think he's the type to get his own back or anything. I don't think he'd give someone a bad review just because they've upset him. I think he tells it like it is – good or bad. I ... I definitely think he's a bit of a lad as far as women are concerned but I get the impression that he's a basically honest person. Some men will do anything to get a woman into bed with them but I think ... I think he'd be truthful about it – although he knows exactly how to turn on the charm, make no mistake about that! Oh, what do I know? I've only known the guy for just over twenty-four hours. He could be a complete and utter shit.'

Blossom opened the wine and eyed Willa whilst she poured out two glasses. 'You really like him now, don't you?'

'No! And if I did, it wouldn't matter. You like him and that's what's important to me. There is no way I'd ever try to get between you and a man you like.'

'And there's no way I'd ever get between you and a man you like – and you do like him. I can see it in your eyes when you talk about him. What's more, he seems to like you so I think we'd better be sensible about this. I'll back off and you can have him.'

'No! You said you liked him long before me. I'll back off and you can have him.'

Blossom sighed loudly. 'We sound as if we're back in school, not thirty-two-year-old women. Look Willa, I like him, I'll admit that but I just like his body. You like *him* and that's more important. Men with good bodies are ten a penny. There's Harry and Loukas and some of the other holidaymakers are rather hot. Besides, this is only the first week of the season so I'll have plenty of choice. It's not like I'm desperate after all. Well ... not *that* desperate.'

Willa giggled. 'Yeah, right! And you're forgetting someone. There's also Aristaios. He's gorgeous!'

'But not as gorgeous as Mark it now seems, in your eyes. Yeah, Aristaios is gorgeous but there's something about him. I'm not sure what it is, but he's just not my type.' Blossom handed a glass of wine to Willa and they clinked their glasses together. 'Here's to love and sex and always having plenty of choice,' Blossom said.

'Here, here. Does this mean I'm forgiven?'

'Yeah. Now let me look at your toes.' Blossom knelt down and her eyes shot open. 'Shit, Willa. I'll be amazed if you can walk tomorrow, let alone sail. Perhaps we should get you to the doctor.'

'I'll be fine,' Willa said, praying that she would be. 'I'll have a bath and an early night and everything will be as right as rain in the morning.'

'Okay,' Blossom said, not sounding totally convinced. 'Do you think you should phone through to reception and ask them to check that Mark isn't still in your office waiting for you?'

'Um, I suppose I should. Chuck me my phone would you? I'll do that now.'

Willa dialled the number and spoke to the receptionist.

'Apparently, he, Harry and Aristaios have gone to dinner at Demeter's so Aristaios told reception anyway,' Willa said, repeating what the receptionist had told her.

'That's good then,' Blossom said. 'At least you know he's in safe hands ... even if you'd rather he were in your hands.'

Willa blushed. 'Do you know something? I'm not really sure that I do ... want him in my hands, I mean. I ... I think I could easily end up getting hurt. I was once. You know that and I don't ever want to go there again, believe me. Besides, I've never been good at these one- night stand things and this season is really important to me. I don't want to screw it up although I may have done that already. I

... I did tell him I don't mix business with pleasure but I'm not sure he believed me. I think I need to make it clear. I think–'

'I think you think too much. Are you mad, woman? You had the most gorgeous man either of us has seen in years kneeling at your feet and kissing you and you're worried about getting hurt. That was almost fourteen years ago. You've had a couple of flings since then and you've been okay. Live a little, Willa. Have some fun. Mix business with pleasure for a change and get something in return. Why shouldn't you have some fun and get a five-star review in the process?'

'I'm not sure it's that easy.'

'I think you'll find it is. Now go and have your bath and get your feet up or you won't be in any fit state to do anything and that would be a real pity.' Blossom took a large gulp of wine and smiled. 'On second thoughts, you'll still be able to lie on your back with your feet in the air, so it isn't all doom and gloom!'

***

'Read it!' Mark said several hours and empty beer bottles later as he shoved *Only The Best Will Do* under Aristaios' nose. It was still open at the page with the rewritten article. 'You've known her for a month or so now. Is this the type of woman she is?' Having moved on to the brandy, he poured himself another Metaxa and knocked it back in one gulp just as he had the five before.

Aristaios shrugged and tried to focus. 'I didn't think so. Blossom perhaps. I think she knows exactly how to manipulate a man but ... Willa' He shrugged again. 'Who knows with women? They let us see only what they want us to until it is too late and they have us like this.' He grabbed himself by the throat and then moved his hand to his groin. 'Or this. And we ... we are the ones made out to be the villains, the bastards, the users, but it is them! They have

78

what they want and they throw us aside like that.' He tossed his arm up and his glass flew out of his hand, smashing on the terrace and only just missing Loukas who was bringing another bottle of Metaxa to the table. 'And now you see, I nearly kill my uncle because of them.'

'We need to show them,' Harry said.

Mark nodded vigorously. 'I agree! Er ... show them what, exactly?'

'That they're not the only ones who can play games. We can too. And we're better at it because we're men and men are better at games than women are. Take football. When do you hear of a female footballer with a transfer fee of hundreds of thousands of pounds? Never. That's when. Or cricket? Who gives a toss about women's cricket?'

'Women cricketers?' Mark suggested.

'Hmm. Apart from them? Anyway, what I think is we should show them how to really play.'

'Women cricketers or women footballers?' Aristaios asked.

'What? No, Willsom and Blossa. I mean, Blosso and Wilma. I mean … Oh fuck it! You know who I mean.'

'How?' Mark said. 'And play what, exactly? I was never very good at football but I can play cricket rather well if that helps although I haven't played for years.'

'Why are you going on about football and cricket? I'm not talking about that type of game,' Harry said.

'Oh! Well, you brought them up, not me. What are you talking about then? Do you know what he's talking about, Aristaios?'

Aristaios shook his head.

Loukas sat down and refilled their glasses with brandy. 'I think what Harry is suggesting is playing a game of love.'

'Fuck that!' Mark said. 'Count me out. I'm not falling in love with anyone – ever!' He knocked back his glass of brandy and screwed up his face as the liquid hit the back of his throat.

'He's not suggesting you do, Mark. I think Harry's plan is just the opposite. He wants you to get the women to fall in love with you.'

'Not necessarararily. I mean not necess...appily. I mean. No. Not in love – just in bed. I think we should show them that we can get them into bed just like that.' Harry's thumb rubbed against his fingers several times but he couldn't get his fingers to make the clicking sound he hoped they would.

Mark snapped his fingers in the air. 'Like that, you mean?'

'Exactly like that,' Harry said. 'How d'you do that? I can't do that.' To prove his point, he showed he couldn't – several times.

'Mark is clearly better at certain things than you, Harry,' Aristaios said as he tried to click his fingers but could only make a quiet snap.

'Mark is better than everyone,' Harry said.

'No, I'm not!'

'Don't you like to win?' Loukas asked.

'Everyone likes to win,' Mark replied.

'Well, then let's make this even more of a game,' Harry said. 'Let's put money on it.'

'On what?' Mark said, having lost the thread of the conversation completely.

'On whether we can get the women into bed.'

'Which women?' Aristaios asked.

Harry tutted. 'Wilsure and Bloshop!'

'He means Willa and Blossom,' Loukas clarified.

'I don't want to get Bloshop ... Blossom into bed,' Mark said.

'Okay. You get Willa. I'll get Blossom. Hey! I got it right!'

'Who do I get?' Aristaios asked. 'What about Loukas?'

'Oh! Well if you want to get Loukas into bed that's entirely up to you, but he's your uncle and I think there may be a law against that. Although as we're in Greece ...'

'Shit, Harry! I did not mean that! I meant who do

Loukas and I try to get into bed?'

'Oh, anyone you like.'

'I like both Willa and Blossom.'

'I think I shall stay out of this,' Loukas said. 'And I am not sure you should be doing it either. You will all regret it when you are sober but a bet is a bet and once it is made, you cannot go back. I have an alternative. Your problem, it is with Willa, Mark? She is the one you are most angry with, no?'

Mark nodded. 'Livid!'

'Well then, let us do this. You will all make a bet of 100 euros to see who will be the first to get Willa to go out with them on a date.'

'A date! That's nothing,' Harry exclaimed. 'What will that show her?'

'It will show her that she is not the only one able to play such games – if indeed she is,' Loukas said. 'It may also show her what she cannot have and sometimes knowing that you cannot have something and wanting it is the worst punishment of all.'

'What's the fun in that?' Harry asked. 'I want to have sex.'

'You can have sex on a date,' Aristaios said.

'Oh, okay then. I'm in.'

'Wait a minute,' Mark said. 'What are we doing? I'm lost.'

'We're making a bet of 100 euros each to see who will be the first to get Willa to go on a date with them. And the winner gets the money and goes to bed with Willa,' Aristaios said.

'Only if they want to and Willa wants to,' Loukas said. 'It is not compulsory. The first man to go on the date wins. Sex is optional.'

'Not for me, it's not,' Harry said. 'A date's not a real date unless you have sex at the end of it ... but only if she wants to, obviously and she will want to, I'll make sure of that.'

'Okay,' Aristaios said. 'I am in.'

'Mark?' Loukas said.

'Er ... I'm not sure we should be doing this. Not that I'm really sure what it is we *are* doing. Something seems wrong but I have no idea what it is.'

'Okay then, it's just between me and Aristaios. I bet I can get Willa to go on a real date with me before you can and that means getting her into bed as far as I'm concerned,' Harry said. He reached for his wallet and counted out several notes.

'We will see about that,' Aristaios said. 'Loukas, I have no money with me. I need to borrow 100 euros from you.'

Loukas placed 100 euros on the table and gave Harry back five 20 euro notes. 'It was only 100 euros, Harry, not 200.'

'Why not?' Harry asked. 'Let's make it 200. It's more interesting.'

'Let us make it 500,' Aristaios said. 'Unless you do not think you can win.'

'500 euros it is!' Harry handed his wallet to Loukas. 'Count out 500 euros for me would you? I can't seem to see the numbers properly.'

'Are you sure about this?' Loukas said. '500 euros is a lot of money.'

'It's nothing. Perhaps we should make it 1000?'

'Done!' Aristaios said. 'Loukas, I need to borrow 1000 euros.'

'This is very serious now,' Loukas said. 'Mark? They have bet 1000 euros to see who can get a date with Willa. Are you in or are you out?'

'Okay, I'm in!' Mark said, realising that this bet would go ahead whether he agreed to it or not and suddenly feeling that at all costs, he had to win. He counted out 1000 euros and handed it to Loukas.

'Then you must all shake hands – it is binding,' Loukas declared. 'I will keep the stake money in this bottle and I will be the judge of who wins. The date must start here at this restaurant and then I will arrange for the couple to go to Aphrodite's Bed. If Willa goes and does not ask to return within two hours then the bet, it shall be won.' He pushed the 3000 euros into the recently emptied Metaxa bottle.

'Hold on,' Harry said. 'Why do we have to use this Aphrodite's Bed? Why can't I just take her back to my room and use mine?'

'Aphrodite's Bed is not a bed,' Loukas said. 'It is a secluded, privately owned island just outside of the bay, in the gulf. It is named this because it is shaped like a scallop shell. You know the legend of Aphrodite, yes?'

Harry nodded. 'But ... I don't want to spend the night on a beach!'

'You do not have to, my friend. The bet, it is won if Willa stays for two hours. There is not much to do in this place at night but there is a small villa set above the beach. It is popular with newly-weds, if you understand me. You do not have to stay the night ... unless you both wish to but if Willa goes with one of you to this place, and she does not ask to return within two hours, then ...' Loukas shrugged and held out his hands.

'And if she does ask to return?' Mark queried.

'Ah, then the bet, it still exists.'

'But won't she realise there's something up if each of us tries to take her to the same place?' Harry asked.

'That, my friends, is a problem for you,' Loukas said. 'You agree to the terms?'

Harry and Aristaios nodded and held out their hands.

'I think I may regret this in the morning,' Mark said but he shook hands with them nonetheless.

CHAPTER TEN

Mark hadn't had a hangover like this since his eighteenth birthday and he couldn't decide whether his head was currently spinning like a top, swaying like a branch or banging like a drum. It was probably a combination of all three, he thought and he wondered just how much he'd had to drink last night.

He also wondered exactly what had happened. This morning he'd woken up not only with the hangover from Hell but also with a feeling that, like Damocles, he had a sword hanging over his head – he just couldn't figure out why.

Having finished the pot of coffee, which Aristaios had kindly sent up to his room, he stumbled into the restaurant in search of more, only to see Harry sitting there. At least the man looked as bad as he felt, Mark thought.

'Morning,' Mark said in a hushed tone although even that seemed to reverberate around his brain like a ricocheting bullet.

Harry opened one eye but quickly closed it, lifting his right hand a few centimetres off the table instead in an attempt at a wave. He made a grunting sound and nodded once.

'That bad, huh?' Mark said, joining him at the table. He swallowed two headache pills and one large glassful of orange juice. 'I hope these are as fast acting as it says on the packet.'

'They're not,' Harry said. 'I took some five minutes ago and I still feel as if my head's trapped inside the Hadron Collider. What the fuck did we have to drink last night?'

'I think it was more a question of how much we had to drink, not what, although I do remember several beers, ouzos and glasses of brandy – and that's not a good combination. Have you seen Aristaios or Loukas yet?'

Harry shook his head and clearly regretted it. 'Aristaios sent coffee up to my room with a note saying he'd see me at breakfast but I've only been here a few minutes and ... ah, speak of the devil, here they are.'

'Good morning, Mark, Harry. How are you both feeling?' Aristaios asked, looking and sounding as if he didn't have a care in the world let alone a hangover.

'How come you're so bloody cheery?' Harry remarked. 'And you, Loukas. You look as fresh as a daisy.'

Aristaios and Loukas grinned and joined Mark and Harry at the table.

'We are Greek,' Loukas said as if that answered the question. 'Do you remember last night?'

'Not much of it,' Mark said, reaching out for the pot of coffee one of the waiters had deposited on the table. 'What?' he said, seeing the odd look pass between Aristaios and his uncle.

'So ... you do not remember the bet?' Loukas asked.

'What bet?' Harry said, grabbing the cup of coffee Mark had poured for him.

'The bet about Willa and the date,' Aristaios said.

And there it was. Mark could almost feel the falling sword as it pierced what he thought was probably his last surviving brain cell.

Why on earth had he agreed to it? Why had he let Aristaios and Harry agree to it? It wasn't that he was against betting or against going on a date with Willa. He didn't mind a bit of rivalry or competition but actually entering into a wager over a woman was not something he'd normally stoop to. And he could just imagine what Willa would do if she found out. There was nothing else for it, he'd have to call it off.

Then he remembered what Loukas had said. That once a bet was made, it could not be called off and he knew that was true. Every Greek male he'd ever met had a strong sense of 'honour' and however dishonourable this bet may be, the thought of backing out of it would be a far greater

85

dishonour. The bet would have to stand, he realised that. He also realised that at all costs, Willa must not find out about it and equally importantly, he must win.

'I missed you two at this morning's Pilates class,' Blossom said to Mark and Harry as she strolled towards the table where the four men sat. 'I hear you had a bit of a session with these two.' She stood behind Aristaios and Loukas, resting her hands on their shoulders and grinning.

'They should come with a health warning,' Mark said, trying to smile but finding it was far too difficult. 'I really can't remember ever feeling quite as bad as this and I've been drunk on beer, ouzo and Metaxa more often than I care to admit.'

'The Tsipouro may have been the ... straw that broke the camel's back,' Loukas said, shrugging.

Mark let out a sigh of comprehension.

'Does that mean you won't be sailing today?' Blossom asked.

'I'm having trouble just sitting here,' Harry said.

Mark nodded slowly in agreement. 'I may be able to attempt walking again later but sailing ... I think that's a no-no.'

'It seems a few people are the worse for wear today,' Blossom said. 'One person's in bed with a nasty case of sunburn, you two and three others are hungover and let's not forget Willa and her toes.'

'Her toes?' Aristaios asked. 'What is wrong with Willa's toes?'

Blossom glanced towards Mark who shook his head as if in silent answer.

'Oh, Willa banged both her big toes on the chairs in her office yesterday evening. They're not broken, thankfully – her toes or the chairs – and she'll be fine but they are rather bruised so she won't be going out sailing today. I've also told her to limit walking to essential journeys only.'

'Is she at home?' Aristaios asked.

Blossom grinned. 'You've known her for over a month

now, do you honestly think she'd be at home? She's at her desk as usual.'

'Well. I must go and see how she is,' Aristaios said, grinning at Mark and Harry. 'I shall give her your best wishes.' He rose from his seat.

'We'll go with you,' Mark said, completely forgetting about his hangover and that the last time he'd seen her was when he'd kissed her. He also forgot about finding the rewritten article. The only thing he remembered was the bet, and the fact that he just had to win, no matter what.

'Will we?' Harry asked, frowning. 'Oh yes, we will.' And he too forgot his hangover.

'Competition is a powerful medicine,' Loukas said as the three men got to their feet.

'Competition?' Blossom queried. 'You don't mean that all three of them have a thing for Willa, do you?'

'A thing? Yes. I suppose you could call it that.'

Mark decided it was best not to comment.

***

'Yes, Dad. Everything is fine with Mark Thornton,' Willa said to her father, who was calling her for the third time in two days. 'I told you that yesterday. It's just that ... well, this isn't the sort of holiday he's used to and I think you ought not to expect a five-star review. I mean he ...' Her voice trailed off as she saw, Mark, Aristaios and Harry heading towards her open door.

'He what, Wilhelmina?' Donald Daventry asked.

'Sorry, Dad. I've got to go. Mark's actually heading towards my office now so I'd better not keep him waiting. I'll talk to you tomorrow. Bye.'

'Wilhelmina!'

Willa hung up the phone and wondered briefly for the umpteenth time why her father would never call her Willa.

'Good morning, Willa,' Aristaios said. 'We have all come to see how you are. Blossom told us of your injuries and we ... wanted to see if we could be of assistance to you.'

Willa shot a look in Mark's direction but he seemed to be studying the wall behind her.

'Thank you, gentlemen. That is so sweet of you but I'm fine. Really I am. They hardly hurt at all this morning and once the bruising goes down, I'll be as right as rain.'

'Well, if you need anything, don't hesitate to call me,' Aristaios said.

'Or me,' Harry added.

'Oh, um. Or me,' Mark said, his gaze going in every direction except Willa's.

'Er ... I don't know what to say. That is so kind. But honestly, I'm fine. Are you two sailing today? I'm afraid that I shan't be this morning, but hopefully by tomorrow I'll be able to.'

She studied Mark's face and then Harry's for a few seconds and decided that they looked far worse than she felt.

'Er ... we're giving it a miss today,' Harry said. 'We were going to just hang around the pool, I think but if there's anything I can do for you then please feel free to ask.'

'Same here,' Mark said.

'Really? And you, Aristaios?' She realised that something very odd was going on but she had no idea what and she couldn't help smiling at the evident discomfort they all seemed to be under. 'Haven't you got anything to do around the hotel?'

'I ... I will be in my office ... next door ... all day,' he said.

Willa noticed the look he gave to Mark and Harry and the glares they gave him in return.

'Okay,' she said. 'What's going on?'

Three pairs of eyes peered at her.

'Going on?' Aristaios said. 'Nothing is going on. We ... we were just concerned about you, that is all.'

She watched them glance at one another and fidget and she felt as if she were a headmistress about to reprimand three delinquent schoolboys. She also noticed that Mark seemed to have very little to say and wondered whether he was embarrassed about yesterday and the kiss. Had he thought better of it and regretted it this morning?

'Well, that's lovely. Thank you,' she said, 'but now I really must get on with some work.' She bent her head over her papers and hoped they would realise they had been dismissed.

She heard them shuffle their feet and glanced up under her lashes to see all three of them turn towards the doorway.

'Mark,' she said, her head still bent down, 'may I have a quick word with you, please?'

'Of course,' Mark said after a moment's hesitation.

Willa heard the triumphal tone and wondered again what was going on. She looked up and saw the slightly resentful expressions on the faces of Harry and Aristaios as they left the room. There was a huge grin on Mark's.

'Would you mind shutting the door, please?' She waited until he had before continuing. 'Okay. What's going on? And don't tell me you're just all so concerned. I'm not a complete idiot.'

'Don't look at me like that,' he said. 'We are all concerned. What's wrong with that?'

'Nothing. It just seems rather odd to me. I get the distinct impression that there is something going on. What are you three up to?'

'Up to? We ... we're not up to anything. You make us sound like naughty children.'

'You all looked like it just now when you were all offering to ... assist me. It was as if ... well, as if you were in competition or something.'

'Competition! What ... what makes you say that? Most women would like three men offering to run around after her all day.'

'Well, I'm not most women.'

'Don't I know it!'

'What's that supposed to mean?' Willa could feel her hackles rise.

'It doesn't matter.'

Mark had a slightly angry expression on his face and Willa glowered at him, wondering what on earth he had to be angry about. Unless it was about that kiss.

She leant back in her chair and looked him full in the face. 'Does this have something to do with last night?'

'Last night? Why ... what happened last night?'

He was avoiding her eyes and she could feel herself getting crosser by the minute. Was he now trying to pretend that he didn't remember kissing her?

'Are you saying you don't remember?'

'Well, we had rather a lot to drink so ...' He shrugged as his voice trailed off.

'So you're telling me that you don't remember kissing me.'

For the briefest of moments his eyes met hers. Then he looked away and shrugged again.

That was too much for her to take. 'This *is* because of last night, isn't it? You do remember, don't you? And your pride's hurt because, unlike most women you've met, I pushed you away and ran after Blossom instead of falling into your arms and into your bed!'

Mark's eyebrows shot up in evident surprise and his blue eyes darkened with anger.

'From what I remember, you were in my arms and if I'd been trying to get you into my bed, you'd have been there, believe me. But no, this has nothing to do with last night – well, not the kiss anyway.'

Willa's temper got the better of her. 'Of all the arrogant ...! My God! So all that self-deprecating humour was just an act after all? All that, I'm being totally honest – crap. What is it with men like you? Just because you're every woman's idea of the perfect man, you think you can just take us and leave us when you please. Well, believe me, *Mr Thornton*, there is absolutely no way on this planet that you will get me into your bed – ever! Do I make myself clear?'

'Abundantly! But you're hardly one to talk about putting on an act. Playing the innocent virgin who doesn't think love is a game and doesn't want people to think she's someone's lover when she's not.'

'It wasn't an act! And I never said I was a virgin. I've had hundreds of men.'

She saw Mark's nostrils flare and his lips form a tight hard line.

'Why doesn't *that* surprise me?' he sneered.

'How dare you! How fucking dare you! You're the one who sleeps with people without even knowing their names. I know the name of every man I've ever had sex with. And you're the one who thinks women are here for your pleasure and that we're all rather stupid.'

'At no time did I think you were stupid.'

'Oh, sure. Candice was "a fucking stupid airhead" and you told my dad that you'd be "kind" to me as if I'm some little lost puppy or something. You even said you'd drive to the hotel because I couldn't possibly follow the roads sign could I? And ... and at Stavros' when I was looking for the loo, you actually thought I was so stupid that I was scared of being alone with you. As if I would ever be scared of being alone with you. I'm alone with you now and the only thing that scares me about it is whether there is really enough room for the three of us. You, me and your gigantic-sized ego!'

'Candice was a fucking stupid airhead and I didn't tell your dad that I'd be kind to you. He asked me to be. If anyone thinks you're a little lost puppy, it's him, not me. And I didn't say I'd drive to the hotel because I didn't think you could. I offered because I needed something to occupy my mind so that I would stop worrying about what you thought of me and concentrate on the road instead. Though why I should have bothered about your opinion of me is beyond me, especially as you'd clearly made up your mind about that before we even met – which *is* stupid, come to think of it. And at Stavros', I was just plain annoyed that you seemed so worried about people thinking we were a couple. There are several women who would like to be part of a couple with me. There are worse things, you know. Like using your charms and kissing someone to get a five-star review!'

Willa gasped. 'I did *not* use my charms to get a five-star review – or anything else for that matter, if that's what you're suggesting. And that wasn't why I kissed you. I have no idea why I kissed you. In fact, I have no idea why I'm sitting here, arguing with you. Why don't you just go and annoy someone else because you're wasting your time with me!'

He stepped towards her and she felt herself grip the arms of her chair. His eyes flickered over her and he smirked. 'I hope you don't regret that request,' he said. He turned and headed towards the door.

'Oh, I suppose that means you'll give me a bad review now. Well, you know what, *Mr Thornton,* you can take your review and you can shove it!'

He turned back to face her, his eyes taking in every inch of her body before coming to rest on her face.

'Oh no, Willa. Your holiday will get the review it deserves, but you – you deserve ten stars at the very least. I can't ever recall being taken in so thoroughly by a woman, and several have tried, believe me.'

He yanked open the door and stormed from the room before she had a chance to respond.

Willa gasped for breath and tried to calm her shattered nerves, wondering what on earth had just happened. All she had really wanted to do was apologise for last night and ask him if they could keep their relationship on a friendly but professional footing. How had it turned into a slanging match so quickly and so thoroughly? Her head dropped into her hands and she wondered whether she was angry at him or at herself. She also wondered how they were going to get through the week.

She was stunned when he returned shortly after, marched up to her desk and tossed a copy of the magazine, *Only The Best Will Do* in front of her.

'And that, I believe … belongs to you. You and Candice Cornwell have the same talent for the written word it seems.'

He almost spat the words at her and it wasn't until he'd left the room again and she cast her eyes over the magazine that she remembered what she'd written in her copy. She flicked through the pages praying that she was wrong and that this wasn't her copy but there it was in black and white – well, in blue ink if she was going to be precise – the rewritten headline, 'Arrogant Pain in the Arse Mark Meets His Match'.

And beneath that, the words she'd written:

Having slathered fake tan and baby oil over his expensively re-sculptured body, Mark Thornton heads off to Greece, expecting a week of fun in the sun whilst thinking up new levels of criticisms and sarcastic barbs to hurl at the overworked and underappreciated Wilhelmina Daventry. But Mark is in for a surprise. Willa and her colleague, Blossom Appleyard have met his type before and know exactly how to handle him. A five-star review is theirs for the taking as this once arrogant man is left whimpering at their feet.

Dear God, she thought, no wonder he'd been so cross and lost his temper with her. But she'd lost her temper first – hadn't she? She couldn't actually remember who had started it but she could clearly remember who had finished it and she could still picture the look of contempt and disgust in those intense blue eyes.

A thought suddenly occurred to her. How had he got hold of her copy of the magazine? She racked her brain and remembered last week when she'd tossed it onto the pile in her out tray and it had slid to the floor. Then she

93

remembered last night when she had stumbled and knocked a pile of papers onto the floor – a pile that she had noticed was on one of the chairs this morning when she had come into her office. Then it dawned on her. The magazine must have somehow gone under one of the chairs. She'd forgotten all about it and yesterday, Mark must have picked up the papers and found the magazine when she'd run after Blossom.

Surely, the cleaners would have moved the chairs before yesterday and picked it up? Obviously not, she realised and she made a mental note to speak to Aristaios about the cleaning staff; they were clearly *not* doing a very thorough job.

CHAPTER ELEVEN

Mark was furious when he stormed out of Willa's office. How dare she have a go at him and berate him for putting on an act when she was clearly the one doing just that.

He'd really been taken in by it and since setting eyes on her at the airport he had thought of little else but her. Shit, he thought, he'd even felt slightly jealous when she'd been in his arms that first night and said that she was a little in love with Aristaios.

Was that all part of her plan he wondered – to make him think she wasn't interested in him in the hope that he'd want her all the more? Well, it had worked, hadn't it? He did want her. He wanted her so much that he'd entered into a stupid bet to try to stop Aristaios and Harry from going on a date with her – and possibly getting her into bed.

He stopped in his tracks. 'Fuck,' he said to himself, 'you've really blown that, haven't you?'

He shook his head and wondered how things had got so crazy in just a couple of days. When he'd got on the plane on Saturday, the only thing he was worried about was that the holiday would be dreadful and he'd have to tell his mum and her new husband that he couldn't give it a five-star review. There was no way he'd lie, not even for his mum.

Here he was, at ten o'clock on Monday morning, worrying about how he'd just blown his chances with the first woman he'd felt anything for in ages; worrying about the fact that she had clearly led him on and deceived him; worrying about the fact that he'd entered into a rather nefarious, drunken wager over her. This only proved that he was just as bad as she seemed to think he was, and just as bad as she was, but most importantly, he was worried about what he was going to do now.

He plodded towards the pool bar. It may only be ten o'

clock but he could use a drink. It might help him think this through. The hair of the dog and all that. Let's face it, it certainly couldn't make things any worse.

'Shit!' Harry said as Mark approached the pool area. 'You look like you've just had a thrashing – and not in a good way.'

Mark smirked. 'I feel as if I have. Why is it that no matter how badly they've behaved or whatever they've done wrong, women can always make us men feel that it's all our fault?'

'It's one of the talents they're born with,' Harry said. 'Did you ask her about her comments on the article then and why she'd written it?'

Mark shook his head. 'She didn't give me a chance. She was too busy confirming that that was her opinion of me. She seems to think I'm a bit of an arrogant, womanising, little shit with, possibly, misogynistic leanings – or something very similar.'

Harry's brows knit together and he burst out laughing. 'Sorry, Mark,' he said, slapping him playfully on his back as Mark sat down. 'It seems your chances of winning our little wager are rather slim then, aren't they? Although what you've done to deserve that opinion is beyond me. Did something happen between you two that Aristaios and I don't know about?'

Mark shrugged his shoulders and glared at him. There was no way he was going to tell Harry or Aristaios that he'd already kissed Willa. 'Not that I'm aware. I think it has quite a lot to do with Candice Cornwell, for some reason. I don't think Willa approves of one-night stands. Oh! Perhaps that means you and Aristaios might not find the bet so easy to win either.' That was a thought that cheered him, even if only for a moment.

Harry shrugged too. 'Oh well. We'll have to see how things go. Are you having coffee or hair of the dog, like I am?'

'Dog!' Mark said. 'And make it a St Bernard-sized one,

please.'

'Ah, there you are,' Aristaios called out. He was heading towards them, a huge grin spread across his mouth. 'I had to come and ask what all that shouting was about in Willa's office. I hope nothing ... unpleasant ... has happened between you two. I would hate for you to lose the bet before it has really begun.'

Mark sighed and waited until Aristaios had joined him and Harry at the table before replying.

'Yes. I can see how dreadfully upset you are about it by the size of that grin.'

'Can I get you a drink?' Harry asked Aristaios as he handed Mark a beer and a large glass of Metaxa.

'Not for me, thank you,' he said, still grinning. 'I'm going to ask Willa to lunch and I don't want her to smell alcohol on my breath at ten o'clock in the morning. What would she think of me?' He chuckled loudly.

'Knock yourself out,' Mark said. 'You may find I'll have the last laugh yet.'

'You think so?' Aristaios said, his eyebrows arching in amused surprise.

'Mark doesn't give up easily,' Harry said. 'And let's not forget, this is the man who fought off a bear and a pack of wolves, saved a woman from drowning and still had the energy for a night of wild sex, so getting a date with a woman who seems to despise him should be as easy as a stroll in the park.'

Harry and Aristaios both chuckled and Mark nodded his head from side to side.

'Yeah, yeah. Laugh all you want but let's see if you're still laughing when you're both standing at Demeter's, watching me sail off into the sunset taking Willa to Aphrodite's Bed.'

He had absolutely no idea how he was going to do it but he was now even more determined to win the bet, no matter what the cost.

'What's up?' Blossom asked, dashing into Willa's office and closing the door behind her. 'I came as soon as I could get away. Most of the guests are sailing and the rest are lounging by the pool so I should be fine for a while. What did you mean in your text by "something awful has happened"? Don't tell me your dad's coming over already.'

Willa snorted. 'If only! That would seem nothing in comparison now. No. It's Mark.' She held out the magazine *Only The Best Will Do*, open at the article she'd rewritten.

Blossom took it and read it. She gave Willa a look of utter astonishment. 'Did you write this?'

Willa nodded.

'When? And more importantly I guess, has Mark seen it? Is that what you meant by something awful has happened?'

Willa nodded again. 'I wrote it last week. That day you booked the flights and came and asked about a picture of him. I ... added to the image and wrote that stuff when you went for lunch with Aristaios. Don't give me that 'you're insane' look. I don't know why I did it but I did, and I threw it onto my out tray but it slid off and somehow, it's been hiding somewhere, waiting for Mark to find it.'

'Well, you are insane and nothing's going to change that. When did he find it then? Today? Just now?'

Willa shook her head and sighed. 'Nope. He must have found it last night after I pushed past him. When I stubbed my toes yesterday, I knocked a pile of papers onto the floor and this morning they were in a heap on the chair. I think Mark picked them up and found the magazine. That's the only explanation. Reception would have locked the office last night when I said I wouldn't be back. It was locked when I came in this morning, so the only time he could have found it was then. The only other people who could get access would be the cleaning staff – and they obviously haven't been in here for ages!'

'So ... what happened? The last time I saw him was at breakfast and he looked fine – well, he looked awful to be honest but that was because he's clearly got a hangover – but he seemed okay and he came to see you with the others, didn't he? Did he have the magazine with him then? Did he confront you with it?'

'No. It was weird because they came in and were all falling over themselves to be of assistance to me – even Mark. Then I asked if I could speak to him – I was going to apologise for last night and ask if we could keep things professional – I know. Don't say it. I'm crazy. Anyway, I asked him what was going on because there is clearly something, for all of them to do that, and he got rather ... defensive and I thought he was just annoyed with me because I'd run off last night, so I said that and then things went berserk. I said things and he said things and then he stormed off and came back with the magazine and threw it at me.'

'He threw it at you? Did he say anything?'

'Several things, none of which were pleasant, although to tell you the truth, I can't really remember exactly what he did say – or what I said, come to that.'

'Did ... did he say anything about the review?'

Willa sighed. 'Yes – and that was weird too. He said that he'd give the holiday whatever it deserved – as if this wouldn't affect his opinion one bit. But he then said that I deserved ten stars for my act! I have no idea what he meant by that.'

'I'm guessing he meant that you've been pretending to like him just to get a good review. I suppose that would be rather annoying. And that's basically what this rewritten article says – that you and I know exactly how to get what we want. Oh, and thanks for including me in that by the way. That really was *sooooo* kind!'

Willa let her head flop down towards her chest. 'I'm sorry about that and you're right, of course. He said as much now that I think about it. Oh God. What am I going to do?'

Blossom dropped down onto one of the chairs and tossed

the magazine into the waste bin beside her.

'Firstly, we get rid of *that* rubbish,' she said, 'and secondly, we think of a way for you to apologise to Mark without making him think you're only doing it to get a good review.'

CHAPTER TWELVE

'Come in,' Willa said an hour later on hearing the knock on her office door. For an instant, she was annoyed at herself for wondering whether it might be Mark.

Aristaios popped his head around the door and beamed at her, his chocolate brown eyes glinting in the sunlight streaming through the open French windows diagonally opposite him.

'I have come to take you to lunch,' he said, striding towards her.

'Oh! I ... I was just going to have something at my desk.'

'Nonsense. It is a glorious day and you have been here since early this morning. You need to take a break from all this paperwork. There is nothing here that cannot wait – of this I am certain.'

He came round to her side of the desk and gently took her hands in his, easing her up from her chair.

'Oh! I ... er. Okay,' she said, feeling that resistance was probably futile and besides, he was right. She could use a break from reports and figures and booking enquiries.

Aristaios was also right about it being a glorious day but she hadn't seen much of it. She'd spent the morning with her head bent over her desk apart from during the 'row' with Mark and the half an hour or so she and Blossom had tried – and failed – to come up with a solution to what they had decided to call, the Meltemi problem. Just like this whole 'business' with Mark, the strong, dry winds experienced annually around the Aegean and known as the Meltemi, sprang up from a clear, untroubled sky often causing serious problems for sailors and severe delays for the ferries from Athens and the islands. Mark may not be affecting seafarers but he was definitely causing problems to spring up from nowhere.

Holding her hand, Aristaios led her out onto the terrace

and to a table laden with wine, bread and meze.

'Wow!' she said. 'You clearly had this planned. What would you have done if I'd said no?'

He smiled and raised her hand to his lips, brushing her fingers with the softest of kisses.

'I would have been heartbroken,' he said, his eyes meeting hers and holding her gaze.

She averted hers after a minute or two and quickly took a seat. She wasn't sure what was happening but she had the distinct impression that Aristaios Nikolades was attempting to seduce her. At the very least, he was flirting with her and although he had done so on many occasions since her arrival here one month ago now, this was the first time he'd done anything like this.

Usually, they just met for lunch by chance and Blossom and Loukas were there more often than not. Aristaios had never actually come to her office and asked her, unless they needed to talk business, in which case it was always pre-arranged but never like this. This, she thought with some apprehension, felt almost like ... a date.

He poured two glasses of wine and raised his in a toast. 'To the most beautiful woman to set foot on these shores since Aphrodite,' he said.

Willa felt she needed a drink and had already taken a large gulp of wine before she almost spat it out across the table. She had to put her hand to her mouth and swallow quickly to prevent that from happening. If Aristaios hadn't been Greek and a native of the area, she'd have sworn he was suffering from sunstroke. The most beautiful woman since Aphrodite, she thought. Huh, he was clearly suffering from something and she was more convinced than ever that there was something very strange going on between Aristaios, Harry and Mark.

She smiled benignly. 'Aw. Thank you,' she said. 'That's really sweet of you. Actually, I hadn't realised but I really am very hungry. Do you mind if I just dig in?'

She could see he tried valiantly to hide his startled

expression and possibly even a touch of hurt pride but she wasn't sure she cared.

'No! Please. Help yourself.'

And help herself she did. She wasn't lying when she said she was hungry. She was ravenous and she thought she could very probably have eaten the Trojan horse if it had been all that was on offer. Thankfully for her – although not so much for the Trojans – it was not. As soon as one large plate was emptied, the waiters brought another and then another until she realised that Aristaios was looking more than a little surprised by her capacity to eat. Every time he reached out to take her hand, she reached out to take some food and even to her, it felt like one of those weird scientific experiments, only in reverse. Finally, she decided to put her hands in her lap.

'Have you had enough to eat?' he asked.

She wasn't sure whether he was being attentive or sarcastic but she smiled her sweetest smile.

'Yes, thank you. That was delicious. I couldn't eat another bite.' She flopped back against her chair and held her stomach, puffing out her cheeks as she did so.

'I have enjoyed this very much, Willa,' he said, leaning towards her, his dark eyes twinkling and his generous mouth curving into a full smile. 'I know you do not mix business with pleasure as a general rule but I cannot hold back. I like you, Willa. I like you very much indeed and I would be honoured if you would agree to go out with me, this evening perhaps or tomorrow if you do not feel up to it tonight.'

Willa stared at him in astonishment. 'Are you asking me out on a date?'

He leaned in closer and made a move towards her hands but she pulled back and sat bolt upright.

'Yes. Are you so surprised? Surely you must know that I have felt something for you since the moment you arrived. I have ... held back because I did not want you to think badly of me but now, I can do so no longer. You are a goddess,

Willa. Ah, perhaps it is pre-determined by the Moirai, the Fates as you call them, that the Nikolades men, they all fall in love with English women. I do not know but I cannot deny the attraction I feel for you or the jealousy I felt when I saw you on Saturday night in the arms of another man.'

Willa swallowed and wondered if the slight feeling of nausea she was experiencing was because she had had too much to eat or because of the syrupy chat-up lines Aristaios was now feeding her.

'Are ... are you saying you're in love with me?' she asked.

'In love?' He looked startled. 'I cannot put this feeling into words. Perhaps yes. I know that I can think of nothing but you, now. Can concentrate on nothing but you. Want nothing but you. Say you feel the same. And if not, say that you will at least give me the opportunity to show you how much you mean to me. Please, Willa. Please say you will go on a date with me. I have something very special in mind.'

He looked so sincere, she thought and it was true that he had been flirting with her on and off since she had arrived in Greece but she couldn't help feeling that this was all a bit ... sudden. She also couldn't help wondering whether he had in fact heard what she'd said whilst she was in Mark's arms that night, about her being a little bit in love with Aristaios and asking if he were taking her to bed. Perhaps he now thought he was onto a 'sure thing'. The oddest thing about it all though was the fact that she wasn't over the moon about it.

'May I think about it?' she said. 'This is the first week of the holiday season and I've got quite a lot on my mind at the moment as you know. And then there's Mark and the review. I really need to ensure that he gives us a glowing report and to be honest, Aristaios, he and I have had a bit of a ... misunderstanding and I really need to smooth the waters with him.'

'Yes, I have heard.'

'Oh! Did ...did he tell you about it?'

Aristaios' eyes searched her face and she waited for his reply with a touch of trepidation.

'Yes,' he said. 'He was ... laughing about it just now, down at the pool bar ... with Harry. I do not know exactly what he said before I arrived but ... I do not think it will affect his review of the holiday. He said he does not allow his personal feelings to influence his reviews – or some such thing and he appeared to find the whole thing rather ... amusing.'

Willa felt her face burning with anger. So Mark and Harry were having a good laugh about it, were they? Why had he pretended to be so cross about it then? She was really confused now.

'Did he say anything else?'

Aristaios shrugged. 'I do not think so. Some of the women attracted his attention and he ... changed the subject. I left just as he was taking one of them ... somewhere.'

Willa sucked in her breath, grabbed her empty wine glass and filled it to the brim with retsina from the second bottle the waiter had brought them. She drank the whole glassful in several large gulps.

'I'd love to go on a date with you, Aristaios,' she said as she deposited the glass back on the table and refilled it. 'You just say when and where and I'll be there.'

***

'What do you mean you're going on a date with Aristaios this evening?' Blossom asked, clearly surprised by Willa's news when she returned from lunch.

'Exactly that. He asked me out. I said yes. That's it.'

Blossom sank into one of the two low armchairs in Willa's office and fell back against the cushion. 'A real date, you mean?'

Willa leant back in her chair and sighed. 'Yes. A real date. Apparently, I'm the most beautiful woman since

Aphrodite, or some such crap and he can't hold back his feelings for me any longer.'

'Don't make fun of him!'

'Ooh! What are you getting so upset about? Anyone would think you were jealous. Oh God!' Willa sat bolt upright and studied Blossom's face. 'You're not, are you? You don't have a secret thing for him, do you and I've jumped right in the middle of that too? I thought you said he isn't your type.'

'No! He isn't my type. And what do you mean, "jumped in the middle of that too"? Oh, I know. You meant first Mark's all over you and now, Aristaios. Well, no, I'm not jealous and I wouldn't be at all surprised if you have Harry beating down your door next and I won't be jealous of that either. It's just that you're usually so adamant about not mixing business with pleasure and it doesn't sound as if you even want to go out with Aristaios and if that's the case, then why are you?'

Willa relaxed. The last thing she wanted to do was upset Blossom again.

'To be honest,' she said. 'I'm not sure I do want to really. And I am still concerned about mixing business with pleasure but ... I don't know. I'm much older now. I'm sure I can handle it. At least I hope I can. The strange thing is though, if he'd said this to me a week ago I'd have been dancing on the ceiling but now ...'

'But now you've found a bigger and better fish but you're having trouble reeling him in.'

Willa tutted and then grinned. 'Actually, you could be right. I don't know though,' she said, sighing. 'I'm just ... just so confused. I think I'm better off steering clear of all men, to be honest. I did fancy Aristaios but now, I'll admit, I do think Mark is bloody gorgeous but he's just so ... annoying and arrogant and ...'

'Popular,' Blossom said. 'I saw you glare at Suki Thane and those other two women – whose names I can't remember for the life of me – yes I can – Susan and Sonia.'

Blossom shook her head as if trying to get her brain around that. 'Anyway, I saw you, and if looks could kill.'

'When?' Willa glanced away and shuffled some papers on her desk.

'Don't pretend you don't know. When you were finishing lunch with Aristaios, and Mark appeared with Suki on one arm and Susan – or was it Sonia – on the other and either Sonia – or Susan – dancing about in front of him. I *saw* you!'

Willa exhaled and puffed out her cheeks. 'Okay, I'll admit I was a little ...'

'Jealous. And I'd say a lot, not a little.'

'Rubbish! I was slightly peeved that he seemed intent on ignoring me, that's all. And did he really have to laugh quite so loudly at Suki's jokes or ... or rush quite so quickly to help Sonia – or Susan – when her bikini top *conveniently* came undone, or give her his shirt. And did he *really* have to feed each one of them quite so many olives by hand!'

'I see what you mean,' Blossom said, getting to her feet. 'You're not even the slightest bit jealous and I now realise exactly why you agreed to the date with Aristaios – you're hoping to make Mark *not* feel jealous just like you!' She shook her head again, this time closing her eyes and tutting. 'Well, good luck with that.'

'Do you think I shouldn't do it then?' Willa asked. 'Go on the date, I mean.'

'No. I think you should go but just don't spend the whole night talking about Mark and don't do anything you might regret just because you think it might make him jealous. Remember, we may think Mark is basically a decent bloke but we both agree he clearly has a way with women and ... well, he may not actually *be* jealous so you might be wasting your time. And although I don't think Aristaios is the type of guy to ... take advantage of a situation, we don't really know him very well either, so just be careful, that's all I'm saying.'

'Wow! What's happened to your usual 'throw caution to

the wind and have the time of your life', attitude?'

'That only works when you don't have feelings for someone.' Blossom turned towards the open door. 'And here comes Harry!' she said, glancing back at Willa and smirking. 'How much would you like to bet that he's come to ask you out?'

'What?' Willa said. 'Why would Harry want to ask me out?'

'Because apparently Aristaios, Mark and Harry all have a bit of a 'thing' for you – or so Loukas said. I'll explain later,' Blossom replied as she sauntered passed Harry and headed out towards the terrace bar.

***

Mark finally managed to shake off Suki, Susan and Sonia although it took him almost an hour to do so. It was his own fault, he knew that but even so, could the women not take a hint? And why, he wondered, did they all have to have names beginning with the letter 'S'? It was just plain weird and more than a little confusing. They were all nice enough; that wasn't the problem and they were all good to look at. In fact, if he hadn't been so preoccupied with Willa and this stupid bet, he may well have been happy to spend more time with any one of them, or all three of them. But for now, all he could think about was Willa – and winning.

When he'd seen Willa and Aristaios having what appeared to be a rather intimate lunch, he'd been furious. The man was one step ahead already and Mark had no idea how he was going to get things back on a friendly footing with Willa after their row. He hadn't meant to go back to his room and get the magazine and confront her with it. He still wasn't sure why he had but it was too late to worry about that now. The damage was done. He just had to find a way to repair it.

He shouldn't really have flirted quite so much with Suki, Susan and Sonia either, he realised. That probably hadn't helped his cause, but there was no way he was going to let Aristaios see how concerned he was by finding him at lunch with Willa – or Willa for that matter. He may be wrong but he could have sworn that she looked a little ... jealous. Either that or she thought he was an even bigger shit now. He'd noticed she had definitely given him the evil eye a couple of times when he had stolen a look in her direction.

Anyway, there was only one thing for him to do. He'd have to go and talk to her. He wasn't sure what he was going to say but he'd think of something. There was no time like the present, he decided. Perhaps he'd just have one beer to settle his nerves. He spotted Blossom sitting on the terrace and strolled over to her.

'You look as if you're miles away,' he said. 'Thinking of something good – or someone?'

Blossom looked startled. 'Sorry, Mark, I *was* miles away. At least I was wishing I were. How are you? No entourage, I see.' She grinned at him and winked.

'No. I've left them in Loukas' capable hands. I said I needed to pop back for something. Call me a coward but I can't handle more than one woman at a time. May I join you for a drink?'

Blossom nodded. 'Of course, please do. I could use the company.'

Mark pulled out a chair and sat astride it leaning on the back. 'Really? I would have thought you'd welcome a bit of time to yourself. It must be hectic having to look after all these holidaymakers.'

'Oddly enough, it isn't. They sort of look after themselves most of the time and it's only the Pilates in the mornings and early evenings and the occasional bike ride or daytrip that I do. Loukas and his team – and Willa of course, handle all the sailing, so I get quite a bit of free time. Don't tell her dad that though and *please* don't mention it in your review. Mr Daventry will be out here with a long list to keep me busy.'

Mark chuckled. 'You have my word. Shall I say that the team spend every waking hour catering to the holidaymakers' every whim and don't get a minute to sit and drink cocktails. That is a cocktail you're drinking, isn't it? Let me get you another.'

Blossom giggled and gulped down the remainder of her drink. 'That would be great, thanks, both the comment and the cocktail. I'll have another 'screaming orgasm' please.'

Mark raised his eyebrows and his mouth curved into his lopsided grin. 'And what would you like to drink?'

'Very funny,' Blossom said. 'But surely ... howling is your speciality?'

'I do what I can,' he said. 'I aim to please.'

'Oh, I bet you do, Mark. And from what I read, Candice Cornwell was very pleased.'

Mark let out a long sigh. 'That was all rubbish you know.' He attracted the waiter's attention and held up Blossom's empty glass. 'May we have another one of these please and a beer for me? Thanks.'

'Yes. Willa told me you said that. Although she also said that most of it appeared to be true from the conversation you had on the way here on Saturday.'

'Oh? What else did she say?'

Blossom grinned and leant forward. 'Willa and I have very few secrets, Mark. We've been friends and colleagues for several years now and this is our twelfth summer season together, although her brother Daniel or her dad are usually hanging around or popping in and out. Anyway, when you do this job and share an apartment too, you learn exactly what makes the other person tick and you don't get much privacy. We tell each other almost everything.'

'Almost everything?'

'We keep some of the more ... intimate stuff to ourselves.'

'That's a relief – not that there's anything to tell on that score ... yet.' He beamed at Blossom and took a large swig of the beer the waiter had just put on the table.

'And if you don't patch things up with her pretty quickly, there won't be – at least, not with you. If you want something to happen between you and Willa, Mark, you'd better get your skates on, although I feel I should warn you, there's a bit of a queue. But I get the impression that you already knew that.'

CHAPTER THIRTEEN

Willa was more convinced than ever that there was something very odd going on involving Aristaios, Harry and Mark, and Blossom clearly had some idea what it was. She was spot on when she'd said Harry was on his way to ask Willa out. That was exactly what he was doing and Willa wondered whether someone had put some strange ancient love potion in the water because Harry, it seemed, also thought she bore an uncanny resemblance to Aphrodite.

'Are you busy, Willa, only I was really hoping that you'd go out to dinner with me – tonight – at Demeter's? I really like you and I think I may be able to give you some help regarding your advertising campaign if you do.'

'Oh! I ...' Willa was lost for words. There was no preamble with Harry it seemed. He got straight to the point. She wondered precisely what he meant by that remark though. Was it a sort of bribe? *If you have dinner with me, I'll help you with your advertising.* Well, that didn't make sense. What was in it for him?

'I've been thinking about it since yesterday morning when I saw you on the Hobie with Mark,' he said. 'You looked like a goddess and that got me thinking. I can visualise the advert, now. Aphrodite would be sailing one of the dinghies, only it would be shaped as a scallop shell and she would be standing up, wearing a scanty Grecian robe. There would be a throng of young Adonises waiting for her on the shore and as she raced towards them, hair flying and robe billowing, there would be rousing music. Then as she landed, she would appear as a modern day woman in a skimpy bikini and she'd say in a voice oozing sex, "Daventry Travel's Sailing Solo Holidays – the number one choice for gods and mortals." What do you think?'

Willa felt her jaw drop. 'Um,' was all she could say.

'I know it needs work but I think it captures the spirit of adventure and excitement and, of course – sex. Let's face it, nothing attracts single people to a holiday so much as the thought of having sex – especially with someone who resembles a god – or goddess in this case. And it has that fun, tongue-in-cheek quality, don't you think?'

Willa thought it had more of the 'finger down throat' quality but she didn't say it.

'It definitely has something, Harry but I really don't have the budget for a TV advertising campaign. I'm currently advertising in a couple of the travel magazines and one or two of the women's and men's mags. We're not a huge company, you know.'

'I wasn't thinking about TV either, although I do know a lot of people so I could get you a really good deal but no, I was thinking more of some of the social media sites and having a video on your company's website. That sort of stuff really appeals and quite truthfully, the tackier the better to get it to go viral.'

'Oh, that does sound quite good then,' she said, thinking that perhaps he knew what he was doing after all, although she wasn't completely convinced.

'So, are we on for dinner tonight then to discuss it?'

'I'd love to, Harry but the thing is, Aristaios has already asked me to ... meet him and I've agreed. I could do it tomorrow, if you like.' She saw his face fall and wondered again what these men were playing at.

'Okay,' he said. 'Tomorrow it is then. You'll probably want an early night tonight anyway, what with your sore toes and all.'

'And all?'

'Er ... Aristaios told me about the row you had with Mark. He heard every word because he was in his office next door and he said you were very upset. He was going to see if he could ... do anything to ... comfort you, I think he said. That must be why he's taking you to dinner, although that's odd really because I was sure I heard him ask Suki Thane what she was doing later. I'm obviously mistaken but I'm sure she said she was seeing Mark or something. I don't know. I can't keep up with those two. Right. I'll leave you in peace then. Until tomorrow, that is.' He winked and was gone.

Willa's head was spinning. Had Harry just said that it was Aristaios who'd told him about her row with Mark? That was odd because Aristaios had said that it was Mark who was telling Harry about it. And was Harry telling her, in a roundabout way, that Aristaios had asked her out because Suki was busy – with Mark of all people? So much for Aristaios proclaiming to be in love with her. Not that he had actually said that. Not in so many words, anyway.

She needed a headache tablet. She shouldn't have drunk so much wine at lunchtime. She had no idea how she was going to get through this evening and her date. Perhaps she'd better go and have a quick lie down whilst it was quiet. She'd just Google Harry Bullen first though, and read what the internet had to reveal about him.

***

Mark and Blossom were still on the terrace and Mark called out to Harry as he appeared from the reception area.

'You're looking pleased with yourself,' Mark said as Harry came and joined them.

'I am pleased with myself. Willa and I have just been ... discussing her advertising campaign.'

Mark sat up. 'I didn't know Willa was planning an ad campaign,' he said, looking from Harry to Blossom.

Blossom nodded. 'Her dad's given her an advertising budget but it's not huge. That's why she had that magazine, *Only The Best Will Do*. She'd placed an ad in there because they gave her a very good deal. She's also got a couple of ads in other magazines, including a lads'mag. I want her to get more men out here,' Blossom said, winking.

114

Mark grinned. 'Now why doesn't that surprise me?'

'I'll be giving her a good deal too,' Harry said, sitting down beside Blossom and grinning broadly. 'Well that and my expert ... touch.'

'Oh really?' Mark said drily.

Harry beamed at him. 'Well what can I say – the woman needs me. We're having dinner tomorrow night to ... discuss it. So, what are we drinking?'

Blossom smiled and leant towards him, brushing her hand against his leg. 'I've just had a screaming orgasm, courtesy of Mark,' she said provocatively. 'But I'm very happy to have another if you're offering, Harry.'

He coughed lightly and swallowed. 'I'll do better than that,' he said. 'I'll make it a double.'

'You should come with a health warning, Blossom,' Mark said. 'That would have given some men a heart attack.'

'Well, it's always better to sort the wheat from the chaff,' Blossom said. 'I don't want to waste my time on a man who can't ... keep up.'

Mark gave her a sideways glance and said, 'Speaking of keeping up. I've got something to attend to. I'll see you both later.' He got up from his chair and sauntered into the hotel reception, whistling the tune to the Billy Ocean song, 'When the Going gets Tough'.

***

'Bugger!' Willa said, prodding her keyboard with her forefinger.

'What seems to be the problem?'

Willa's head shot up at the sound of Mark's dulcet tones and she slammed down the lid of her laptop.

'Nothing,' she said, feeling her cheeks redden and her heart pound at being caught in the act.

'Really? Let me see if I can help. I'm quite good with hardware.'

115

'I bet you are,' she said, 'but it's fine thank you.'

He marched towards her and reached out for her laptop but she grabbed it from her desk. Unfortunately, she didn't have a secure hold on it and it shot out of her hand and landed on the chair to the left. She made a dash to get to it before he did, but he got there first and they both ended up face to face, only inches apart.

He gazed into her eyes for a moment. 'What are you hiding? Male porn or something?' he said, grinning.

He lifted the lid and hit a key and in that split second, Willa knew how Pandora must have felt when she opened that box. She watched his grin fade and his brows knit together. Then she saw a glint in his eyes and his lips twitched into a broad smile.

'Oh,' he said, 'you seem to be stuck on *me*.'

Willa tutted and walked back around her desk. 'Well, if you really are any good with hardware, perhaps you could get me *unstuck*.' She flopped into her chair and moved papers from one side of her desk to the other.

'And why would I want to do that?' he said. 'The hardware's not the problem but I can sort it for you. I see that you decided to Google me after all. Did you find anything interesting?'

'Nothing at all. I was Googling Harry actually and then I remembered you rebuking me for not Googling you – so I did. And what happens? The bloody thing crashes.'

He pressed a few keys, still looking like the cat that got the cream when he handed her laptop back to her.

'If that happens in the future, just turn it off and turn it back on again and it'll be fine. A bit like our relationship really. And I've taken you back to the start so you can begin again, if you want to.'

'Thank you,' she said, 'but I've seen enough.' She pressed the shutdown button and closed the lid. 'And what do you mean, a bit like our relationship? We don't have a relationship.'

'Not even a business one?'

'Well yes. I suppose we do have that. Actually...' she said, remembering that she had meant to apologise to him the next time she saw him, not snap his head off and that just because he'd caught her reading about him, it didn't change the fact that she needed to be ... pleasant.

'Actually ... what?' he said.

'Er ... I think I owe you an apology.'

He looked surprised.

'You do. But I owe you one too, so why don't we both just take it as read and forget the whole thing?'

'Oh!' It was her turn to be surprised. For some reason she'd thought he might make her grovel.

'Friends?' he said, holding out his hand to her.

'Friends.' She took his hand and they shook on it.

He sat down on the chair Blossom had occupied earlier and stretched out his long legs. He leant back, raising his arms and linking his hands behind his head.

'I see you've found the perfect place to file the magazine,' he said, casting a quick glance at the waste bin beside him.

'Actually, Blossom did that but you're right. It is the best place for it.'

'And only the best will do for *Only The Best Will Do*,' he quipped. 'Speaking of which, I was wondering if you'd have a drink with me one evening this week.'

Willa felt herself tense. 'Are ... are you asking me out?'

'For a drink, yes.'

'On ... on a date, you mean?'

His eyes held hers and he gave her a confused look. 'On a date? Now why would I ask you out on a date?'

She felt her backbone stiffen and she straightened herself in her chair. 'You wouldn't, of course. I'm sorry.'

'There's no need to be sorry, Willa. I would be happy to go on a date with you if you want me to. You only have to ask.'

'*Me* ask! Of all the ...' She stopped just in time. She had to be pleasant she reminded herself. 'I think there's been a

117

little misunderstanding. I thought you were asking me out on a date because ... well, it doesn't matter why, but you weren't, so that's fine because I didn't want to go on a date with you and I have no intention of asking you out on one.'

'Yes, I think you said as much earlier. No. Earlier you said that I had no chance of getting you into my bed, didn't you and that's a different thing entirely, isn't it? Why did you think I was asking you on a date though? I'd be interested to know.'

Willa's cheeks were burning hot and she desperately wanted a glass of water – or something stronger – but she took a few deep breaths and tried to stay calm.

'It really doesn't matter.'

'It does to me. Humour me, please.'

She tutted. 'Okay. Because Aristaios and Harry have both asked me out to dinner and I thought ... I thought ...'

'You thought I would too. Well I have to say, Willa, that I think you're the one being a little arrogant now. Sorry, I'm being facetious. You're a very popular young lady, I can see that and rightly so. After all, you do look–'

'*Please* don't say I look like Aphrodite. *Please*!'

'Why on earth would I say that? You look nothing like Aphrodite.'

'Thanks!'

'Don't get cross. You said you didn't want me to say you looked like her but when I do say that you don't look like her, you get angry. I'm utterly confused. Perhaps you could explain to me what's going on.'

'Nothing's going on! Well, I think something *is* but it seems it has nothing to do with you after all, so it doesn't matter.'

'Whatever you say. Oh, and by the way, I was going to say that you look ... lovely, particularly now, with your eyes sparkling with barely contained ... anger and your cheeks flushed. So. That drink. Is it a yes? I need to ask you a few questions to help me write the review and I thought it would be ... friendlier over a drink.'

She held her tongue and scanned his face but she couldn't tell what was going through his mind although she had the strangest feeling that she was being manipulated in some way.

'You can ask me questions now, if you like. I promise I'll be ... friendly.'

'I could,' he said, getting to his feet, 'but I have a prior engagement and besides, I'd rather do it over a drink.'

She bristled at the mention of him having a prior engagement and wondered whether it was with Suki, Susan or Sonia, or perhaps all three.

'Then please don't let me detain you.'

'You're not. So, how about tonight?'

'I'm going to dinner with Aristaios.'

'Ah yes. The date. And I assume you're having dinner with Harry tomorrow night?'

'Yes.'

'What about Thursday then?'

'Thursday? Don't you mean Wednesday? It's only Monday today.'

He raised his eyebrows. 'I know it is,' he said, his lopsided grin reappearing. 'I see. You meant that you don't have a date for Wednesday, so we could go for the drink then.'

'Well, I wouldn't put it like that exactly,' she said, shuffling papers and wishing that he would just go because she was getting more flustered by the minute.

'I'd love to make it Wednesday,' he said. 'But unfortunately, I can't. You see, I do have a date, of sorts, on Wednesday.'

'Oh!' She knew her shock and disappointment must have been written all over her face and she hastily averted her eyes. Her breath seemed to catch in her throat and she was having trouble swallowing.

'I'm sorry,' he said. 'But a commitment is a commitment and ... well, I'm sure you understand that. After all, you're committed to having dinner with both Aristaios and Harry, aren't you?'

Her head shot up and their eyes met for what felt like several minutes but was, in reality, just a few seconds.

'Yes, I am.'

'Yes, and you wouldn't cancel those ... dates any more than I would cancel mine ... with Blossom.'

'Blossom! You ... you've asked Blossom out on a date?'

'Don't look so horrified, Willa. We're both, young, free and single. I hadn't meant to actually but she was having a screaming orgasm and–'

'What!'

'The cocktail – a screaming orgasm cocktail. Oh! Surely you didn't think I meant ... Willa, really. I'm not the man you appear to think I am, you know. Blossom was having a ... cocktail and I mentioned a little bar I know a few miles from here that serves the best cocktails on this peninsula. She said she'd like to go there and I offered to take her. Actually, you can come too, if you like. I'm sure she wouldn't mind.'

Willa hung her head and pretended to be leafing through a file. 'No. That's fine, thank you. You go with Blossom and I hope you both have a great time.'

'I'm sure we shall. Right, so what about us?'

'Us?' Willa shot him a glance. 'There is no "us".'

'I meant what about us going for that drink on Thursday? Or we could go sailing. I've heard about a small island just outside of the bay in the Gulf of Argolis I'd quite like to take a look at. I haven't seen it before and it sounds idyllic.'

'I ... I'd prefer not to go sailing.'

'But it could make all the difference to my review, Willa.'

She raised her head slowly and glared at him.

'That's blackmail!'

'That's negotiation. I'll meet you in the hotel bar at six-thirty. We can get a bite to eat somewhere too, if you like – but don't worry, this isn't a date, Willa, remember that. So,

Thursday it is then. Yes?'

'Yes,' was all she could say; she felt positively exhausted.

CHAPTER FOURTEEN

'You rang?' Blossom said, strolling into Willa's office.

'Mark has just told me you're going on a date with him on Wednesday night,' Willa said.

Blossom's brows knit together. 'Well, I wouldn't call it a date, exactly. I was having a screaming orgasm and he–'

'Yes, he told me about the drink and the cocktail bar. So what would you call it … exactly … if not a date?'

Blossom eyed Willa for a few seconds before answering. 'I'd call it none of your business it if wasn't for the fact that you're my friend – and my boss. What's got into you? We had this conversation yesterday, after you kissed him. Do you honestly think that I'd go on a date with him after that? I know you like him – although I have to say that you're making a complete dog's dinner of it – but anyway, you like him so he's off limits as far as I'm concerned. So don't get stroppy with me. And ... let's not forget that I told you I liked him yesterday morning but that didn't stop you from kissing him yesterday evening, so before we start throwing stones, let's check our own glasshouse, shall we?'

They glared at one another and then Willa sighed heavily.

'I'm so sorry, Blossom,' she said, shaking her head. 'You're right, of course. I am really, really sorry about yesterday. You know I am. And it is none of my business who you go on a date with, so I'm sorry about that too. I seem to be losing my cool lately and I have no idea why. And you're right, I am making a mess of things. Please don't be mad with me.'

Blossom tutted. 'I'm not mad with you,' she said, smiling, 'but I would be really cross if you let your feelings for a guy you've only known for a couple of days come between our friendship.'

'That won't happen, I promise you,' Willa replied. 'And

'... Oh, I was going to say that I haven't got feelings for Mark – or anyone else for that matter – but I guess that's not really true, is it? I am behaving like a complete idiot, aren't I?'

'In a word – yes,' Blossom said, sitting on the edge of Willa's desk. 'So ... is that why you rang me and asked me to come in? So that you could bite my head off? I thought you rang to tell me that Mark had asked you out to dinner too – as well as Aristaios and Harry, I mean – not as well as me, before you jump down my throat.'

Willa smirked. 'I knew what you meant but no, Mark didn't ask me out. Well, he sort of did – for a drink – but he made a big thing about it *not* being a date. It's purely business. He wants to ask me some questions for the review.'

'Well, that's weird. I really thought he'd ask you out too, especially with what Loukas said at breakfast.'

Willa sat up. 'What did Loukas say at breakfast?'

'I thought I told you. No? Well, Aristaios said he was coming to check you were okay after I told him you had injured your toes and Harry and Mark both jumped up and said they'd come with him. I asked Loukas if they all had a thing for you or something and he said they did. Well, he actually said something like 'you could call it that' and I did wonder what he meant but something else happened to distract me and I forgot to ask him.'

'What *did* he mean, do you think?'

Blossom looked thoughtful. 'I assume he just meant they all fancy you but that must also mean that they all know they all fancy you, if you see what I'm saying, because otherwise, how would Loukas know?'

'What? You mean they've discussed it? I don't think I like the idea of that.'

Blossom sniggered. 'Why not? Haven't we been doing exactly the same thing? And don't we always – discuss fancying some guy, I mean, so I really don't see the difference.'

Willa fell back against her chair. 'No, I guess not. It just seems different somehow, with men, I mean. It's almost ... well, like they're in competition or something whereas you and I discuss it and if we know the other person fancies someone, we back off – or we should do unless we're absolute shit friends like me and then we kiss the guy without even realising we're doing it! I still feel awful about that.'

'Oh, stop going on about it. I really don't care about Mark. But it is interesting that you should mention a competition – between the men I mean – because that is exactly what it does feel like, doesn't it?'

Their eyes met and both sets opened wide.

'You don't think ...?' Willa gasped.

'They wouldn't, surely?' Blossom asked.

'That would be too awful for words.'

'That would just be plain nasty.'

'That would be ... typical of men on holiday, though,' Willa declared. 'And, it seems highly unlikely that all three of them would fancy *me*. I mean it's not like I'm ... Aphrodite or anything even though Aristaios and Harry said I am.'

'But ... if that were the case then Mark would have asked you out on a date too – and he didn't.'

'That's true,' Willa said after a moment's consideration.

'Did ... did Aristaios really say you look like Aphrodite?'

'Yes. And Harry did too but not Mark. In fact, he said that I look nothing like her – although he did say I looked ... lovely. I think he was being sarcastic though because I was cross and he pointed out my red cheeks. The other odd thing about all this, now that I think about it, is both Aristaios and Harry made comments about each other and Mark, sort of chasing other women – as if the others were rogues or something but Mark didn't. In fact, Mark made *himself* sound like a rogue and he said nothing about Aristaios and Harry.'

'A rogue!' Blossom said, giving Willa an odd look. 'Which time dimension are you currently trapped in? A rogue, for God's sake! I assume you mean a bastard?'

Willa smirked. 'I've been talking to Dad too much over the last few days, obviously. Yes, I mean a bastard. A deceitful, arrogant, womanising bastard, to be precise!'

'I'm glad we've cleared that up,' Blossom said, grinning. 'It is the sort of thing guys might do if they did fancy someone though. Try to put you off the other guy I mean, by making him out to be a ... rogue.' She giggled. 'I quite like that actually. I think it'll be my word of the day.'

'Yeah, yeah. Have a laugh at my family's expense, why don't you? Anyway, it's also something a guy would do if he wanted to win a bet. Try to remove his competitors.'

'Aristaios just doesn't strike me as the sort of guy to do that though. I have no idea about Harry but I'll never trust a man who wears budgie smugglers, so I wouldn't put it past him. And surely Loukas wouldn't let them do it? No. I think it must just be that both Aristaios and Harry fancy you and I'm sure Mark does too but maybe he's playing it cool.'

'I still find it hard to believe,' Willa said. 'Perhaps they've all had too much sun and they're suffering from delirium.'

'Too much alcohol more like. You should have seen them at breakfast. Mark and Harry looked really rough.'

'We're obviously wrong about it being some sort of competition though, which is a relief. I don't know what I would have done if I'd discovered I was the *prize* in some seedy wager.'

'I know what I'd do,' Blossom said, jumping down from her perch on Willa's desk. 'And it would be a very long time before any of the participants would want to enter into one again, believe me. I'd better get back to the guests. See you later.'

'Yeah. See ya.' Willa watched Blossom march towards reception – and she did believe her. She pitied the man who would dare to invoke Blossom's vengeance.

Willa couldn't stop thinking about her conversations with Mark and with Blossom. She went over and over them in her head right up until the minute she was getting ready for her date with Aristaios.

Mark had told her that she looked lovely but he made a point of specifically *not* asking her out on a date. That was perfectly reasonable; after all, she had told him that she would never go to bed with him, so perhaps he thought she didn't like him in that way and there was little point in him pursuing her.

But he had asked Blossom out and although both of them had said it wasn't really a date, Mark had called it a 'sort of' date, so had he now decided that it was Blossom he wanted to spend time with and not her? And why did it bother her so much anyway? She liked him, she'd admit that but she knew it wouldn't go anywhere, so why did it matter?

'No', she said out loud as she slipped into a v-necked, cotton dress in a blue and white floral print design with a fitted bodice and a flared skirt. 'I am going to stop thinking of Mark Thornton in a romantic way and concentrate on having a good time with Aristaios and Harry. Blossom is right,' she continued, studying her reflection in the mirror. 'You need to have some fun and see if you can get Aristaios to discuss a new deal for next season and, Harry to elaborate on his suggestions for an ad campaign on social media sites.' She smoothed down the front of her dress and did a half twirl to check the back.

'Yes, oh Queen, you are the fairest of them all,' Blossom squeaked from the doorway of Willa's room.

Willa spun around in surprise. 'Very funny,' she said. 'I don't suppose there's any wine open is there? I could murder a drink before I go. I don't know why but I'm feeling really nervous.'

'Well, it just so happens that there is,' Blossom said. 'I'm feeling really fed up, so I thought I'd have a drink.'

She held up the bottle and the two glasses she was holding.

'Some day, you'll make one lucky man very happy,' Willa said. 'Are you really feeling fed up? That's not like you. I can cancel this date and stay here and chat if you like.'

'No! I'll be fine. And what are you talking about? I make men very happy *every* day. Haven't you seen them ogling my boobs in my Pilates class? I swear that's why so many of them stumble about all over the place. They're too busy staring at my boobs or my bum and not paying enough attention to what they're doing.'

Willa chuckled, remembering that first day when she and Aristaios had sat and watched the morning session. Harry had fallen all over the place and so had some of the others, now that she thought about it. But not Mark, although Suki Thane had thrown herself at *him* more times than Willa had thought possible.

She shook her head. Stop thinking about Mark she silently reminded herself.

'That's true,' she said. 'I wonder whether we should monitor their blood pressure before allowing them to join one of your sessions. Men do seem to constantly fall at your feet.'

'And yet you're the one going out on a date and I'm the one left sitting at home,' Blossom said, handing Willa a glass of the wine she'd just poured out.

Willa took it and studied Blossom's face. 'Is everything okay, Blossom? You sound ...' her voice trailed off. She couldn't think of the word. It was almost 'jealous', but surely not?

'Jealous?' Blossom said, voicing Willa's thoughts.

'Well ... a little perhaps. You're not, are you? Jealous, I mean. Not really?'

Blossom let out a long, sorrowful sigh. 'Now why would I be jealous? You're only going on dates with the three hottest men here. Why would I be jealous of that?'

Willa was worried. She'd never known Blossom to feel

resentful in all the time they'd been friends but that was how she sounded.

'I'm going to call Aristaios and cancel. You and I need to talk.'

'No!' Blossom said. 'Don't mind me, I'm fine. It's just been a weird day, that's all. I'm tired and to tell you the truth, I think I had a few too many screaming orgasms today.'

'Lucky you!' Willa joked.

'Yeah. I wish. Anyway, you fall asleep when you've had too much to drink. Me, I get bitter and jealous. Don't give me that worried mother look. I'm fine, honestly. It'll pass. You go and have fun with Aristaios.'

'Are you sure, Blossom? Really sure? I don't mind cancelling. Really I don't.'

'I'm sure. Perhaps I'll go up to the bar and see if anyone's around. What time are you meeting Aristaios?'

'Seven-thirty. What's the time now?'

'It's time you found your watch.' Blossom glanced round and looked at the clock on the wall. 'It's seven-thirty.'

'God!' Willa said, knocking back the contents of her glass. 'I'd better run. Are you sure you're okay?'

'Are you sure you can run?' Blossom replied, nodding towards Willa's still swollen toes and grinning. 'I'm fine, woman! Now go. But don't do anything I wouldn't do.' She took the empty glass Willa handed her.

'That's means I can do just about anything I want then,' Willa said, racing out of the door.

***

As Willa approached Aristaios she had to admit that he looked particularly gorgeous. He was sitting at the best table at Demeter's, and she had to stifle the 'Phwoar!' she could feel was about to burst from her lips when he rose to greet her.

128

The black slim fit trousers he was wearing clung to his thighs and his black shirt enhanced the rich olive hue of his clean-shaven face. His black wavy, shoulder length hair shone in the glow from the multi-coloured lights strewn around the terrace of the restaurant and his eyes were the colour of Cadbury's Dairy Milk – her favourite chocolate. Perhaps I shall enjoy this evening, after all, she thought.

'Willa!' His eyes travelled the length of her body and lingered, as usual, on her cleavage. 'You are beautiful. Aphrodite will be jealous, I think.'

Or perhaps not, Willa told herself.

'Thank you, Aristaios,' she said, taking a seat opposite him. 'You look pretty good yourself. I'm so sorry I'm late. I was chatting to Blossom and I hadn't realised the time.'

'There is no need for apologies or explanations between you and me, Willa. I have told you this before.' He poured her a glass of wine and raised his in a toast. 'To you, Willa, and may this night be blessed by the gods.'

Willa grabbed her glass and took two very large mouthfuls. For some reason, she felt this night was going to be anything *but* that and as Aristaios reached out for her hand, she made a decision.

'Thank you for inviting me,' she said, hastily removing her hand from the table. 'I ... I think it's lovely that we can spend some time together – as friends, and get to know one another a little better but I've had time to think about this since you asked me and, well, I'm sure you realise that nothing can happen between us.'

She saw something in his eyes; a mixture of disappointment and annoyance she thought but he smiled and cocked his head to one side.

'I realise nothing of the sort,' he said, reaching out and stroking her other hand, which was holding her wine glass. 'We are adults, Willa. Yes, we have a business relationship but why can we not have a personal one too? Or if not that, then why should we deny ourselves a short time of ... excitement? Of ... passion? Do you deny that you find me ...

129

attractive?'

His eyes met hers and a lump came to her throat. She shook her head.

'No, I don't deny that. You are a very attractive man, Aristaios but ... I'm not very good at ... short-term relationships, shall we say and I would hate for us to do something that we might regret later.'

He studied her face for a moment. 'I should not regret it, Willa. Of this, I am certain. And I do not think you would either. We Greek men know a thing or two about love.'

Willa snatched her hand away from his fingers and gulped down the contents of her glass.

'I don't doubt it,' she said, holding out her glass for a refill.

He looked surprised but he poured her another glassful and smiled.

'You are a little afraid of me, I think,' he said. 'Willa, there is no need to be. I will not hurt you. This I can also promise you.'

'I'm not afraid of you and I don't think you would hurt me intentionally, Aristaios. But as I said, I'm not good at short-term ... stuff and the last thing I want is to get emotionally involved with someone I work with. I know myself, and I really wouldn't handle that well. I *would* get hurt and then we'd fall out and then what would happen to Daventry Travel's Sailing Solo Holidays?'

She saw his dark brows knit together and the smile fade.

'It would be so bad?' he asked.

Willa nodded. 'It would be like living in Hades, and neither of us would want that, especially as we need to discuss next season and renegotiate the deal my dad's company has with you and Loukas.'

'Ah,' he said. 'I had not thought this thing through. Yes. I can see that if I should hurt you, unintentionally, of course, it might affect our business dealings. You are right. Neither of us would want that, especially as things seem to be going so well, so far.'

Willa nodded. 'Precisely. And if Mark gives the holiday a good review, things will go a whole lot better.'

Their eyes locked but neither spoke for several seconds.

'Yes,' Aristaios said. 'I can see that a good review would benefit us both. I had not thought of that, either. We shall have to see if there is anything we can do to ensure that Mark's review is good.'

'Well, I'm not sure that there is anything we can do other than making certain the holiday exceeds his expectations – which I get the distinct impression aren't actually very high. I don't think he's a fan of singles holidays. I also don't think he's easily swayed. In fact, I think he's the sort of guy who makes up his own mind and won't be influenced by anyone, or anything, in any way. I think he just says and does whatever he wants and if you don't agree with him, that's tough.'

'You think so? I got the impression that he is a very easy-going, very friendly, sort of person.'

'Oh he's easy-going and friendly, all right. Just ask Candice Cornwell. Sorry. I think he behaves very differently with men than he does with women.'

'Don't all men?'

Willa spotted the curious look he was giving her and realised that perhaps she was saying a little too much about Mark and what she thought of him.

'You're right,' she said. 'And I think I need another drink.'

CHAPTER FIFTEEN

'All alone?' Mark said, seeing Blossom sitting at one of the tables on the top terrace, nursing another cocktail.

'Hopefully not any more,' Blossom said, grinning at him and pulling out a chair for him to sit. 'Will you join me for a bit?'

Mark raised his eyebrows in mock surprise. 'Is that where I ask, a bit of what? Or is that just too corny for words?' He smiled and sat on the chair she'd offered.

She gave him a sideways glance. 'If you did, I'd say, anything you like – or at least I would, if I didn't think you fancied Willa.'

'Who told you I fancy Willa?'

'Loukas. Although not in so many words. But let's not forget I saw the two of you kissing, so unless you usually go around kissing women you don't fancy, I'd say that said it all.'

'Oh, yes, I'd forgotten you saw that. Would you like another ... of those?' He pointed to her cocktail and grinned.

'A screaming orgasm, you mean? Yes, please. Were you afraid to say the name again in case I thought you were offering your services?'

'Something along those lines, I guess. We had a similar conversation at lunchtime and I thought you'd think it was a terrible chat-up line. Not that I'm trying to chat you up, of course. I didn't mean that.'

'Of course you're not. I'm not Willa after all, am I?'

He studied her face and wondered how many she'd consumed before he'd arrived. She sounded a little bit tipsy, he now realised.

'Are you okay, Blossom?'

'Yep! I'm absolutely fine. Willa has you, Harry and Aristaios all chasing after her and I'm sitting here alone.

Why wouldn't I be fine?'

'You're not alone, Blossom. I'm here,' he said.

He regretted it almost immediately but it was too late. He hadn't meant anything by it but he could see by her eyes that she'd taken it the wrong way. Within a split second, she had flung her arms around his neck and kissed him smack on his lips. It took him at least twenty seconds to pry himself free and as he did, he saw Harry and Suki Thane standing at the top of the steps, staring at him and Blossom.

'Blossom, we've got company,' he said, hoping that would encourage her to back off.

Her arms still wrapped tightly around his neck, she turned and looked at Harry and Suki.

'Hi,' she said. 'Come and join us. I'm going to have a screaming org–'

'A cocktail,' Mark interrupted, loosening her hold on him. 'I think that double entendre's been done to death now.' He smiled at Suki and Harry. 'What can I get you two? Beer, Harry? Suki, would you like a cocktail?'

'Don't let us interrupt anything,' Harry said, grinning from ear to ear.

'You're not, believe me.'

'I'd love a cocktail,' Suki said. 'What's that you're drinking, Blossom?'

'I'm having a screaming orgasm,' she said before Mark could stop her.

He sighed and closed his eyes, waiting for the inevitable.

'So we could see,' Harry said. 'And young Mark here seemed to be enjoying himself too, didn't he, Suki?'

'He certainly did,' Suki replied. 'Mark, may I have a screaming orgasm too, please? If you have the stamina, that is.'

And there it was, he thought. He also had a dreadful feeling that, just like the Candice Cornwell article, he was going to hear a lot more about this – and Willa probably would too. He felt that Harry would make sure of that.

He was right. Harry spent most of the next hour telling

him that he was a lucky man and Suki said more than once that he and Blossom made a lovely couple, although she didn't sound very pleased about it, for some reason that he couldn't fathom.

He repeatedly said that it wasn't what it had looked like but they ignored his protestations, so eventually he decided to just give up. He was relieved when his mobile rang and he could make an excuse to leave the table.

'Mum? What's wrong?' he said, a mixture of panic and dread seizing him. The only times his mother ever called him were when someone had died, was dying or she wished they were dying because she'd had an argument with them and really needed to talk to someone about it.

Apart from twice. Once when she'd rung him just before his twelfth birthday to tell him she was leaving him and his father and would he please tell his dad because she couldn't. And the second time, when she'd rung to tell him she was getting married.

He tensed expectantly. Then he realised she was probably phoning to ask about the holiday. After all, he was here as a favour to her.

'Don't sound so shocked, darling. Nothing's happened. Can't a mother call her only son just to say hello?'

'Well, there's a first time for everything, I suppose.'

'Don't be facetious, Mark. You sound just like your father when you take that tone. Sorry, darling. Mummy didn't mean to snap. It's just been one of those days. You know the sort, darling. No matter what one does, nothing seems to turn out as one planned.'

'Tell me about it,' he said, thinking he was having a bit of a day like that himself.

'Were you being facetious again, Mark or do you really want to hear about it?'

He took a deep breath. 'No, I wasn't being facetious. I meant my day's been a bit like that too. And yes, nothing would give me greater pleasure than to hear how your new husband bought you a diamond brooch when you specifically told him that only a diamond and sapphire one would do or that the painter – sorry, the interior decorator – painted the toilet – sorry, cloakroom, blue when you made it clear that you wanted lavender.'

After exactly six seconds of silence she spoke, 'I should never have left you with your father, Mark. You get more like him every day.'

'I'll take that as a compliment. And you didn't have to leave. It was your choice.'

Again, he counted the seconds of silence in his head and knew that when he got to six, she'd speak. He wondered if she counted them too or whether she just did it automatically. It was always the same when he said something she didn't like or he had upset her in some way.

'I ... I thought we'd got over all that. I thought we were ... friends now.'

'Friends? I thought I was your only and much beloved son whom you unfortunately had to abandon to go and live in Spain with some guy who owns a disco because you couldn't stand being left alone while your otherwise doting husband went out to work to keep you in the style to which you wanted to become accustomed. But yes, mother. We are *friends* now. I'm sorry, as I said, I'm having one of those days too.'

Silence. Then, 'Well, I didn't call to have an argument so I might as well ring off.'

'Mum. Wait. I'm sorry. What's wrong? Tell me. Or did you just call to see how the holiday is going?'

'Well, I did call to see how it was going, of course, but I also called because I read an article about you in one of those posh travel magazines, *Only The Best Will Do*. All the ladies at my spa read it, you know, and I just wanted to tell you how proud Mummy is of you, darling. You saved those lovely young ladies from that terrifying bear and a pack of wolves and then dived into the rapids to save the one who was drowning. I told them all that you are my son.'

The irony wasn't lost on him. 'I didn't realise you were

interested in travel magazines, Mum. You certainly never used to be. How long have you been reading, *Only The Best Will Do?*'

'Oh, I don't read it, darling. The ladies at my spa do and ... well, to tell you the truth, Mark they were all making suggestive remarks about you. I didn't know it was you at the time, of course. That would be too weird – and I said, "Ooh, let me look, I like a hot man." Imagine my surprise when I saw it was you!'

Mark could imagine it, but he didn't want to.

'And when one of them read out loud the part about the night of passion, well, I was as red as a beetroot. You are a devil, Mark, aren't you?'

'Don't tell me. I'm just like my father.'

He wished he hadn't said that. He could have done without that image in his head especially when, after the usual six seconds of silence, his mother spoke.

'As loathe as I am to admit it, yes, your father was ... very good in that department.'

Mark was genuinely stunned. That was the first nice thing he had ever heard her say about his dad.

CHAPTER SIXTEEN

Willa just wanted to go home. Her toes were throbbing – she'd foolishly crammed her feet into high heeled sandals – and her head was spinning. She wasn't sure if it was because of the wine she'd drunk or the pain in her feet but she didn't think she could last much longer without yanking off her sandals and collapsing onto her bed.

'I've had a lovely evening, Aristaios,' she said, 'but it's late and we've both got busy days tomorrow.'

'The night is young, Willa. We may just be friends but we could still go for a moonlit sail, could we not? There is something I particularly want to show you.'

'That sounds lovely but, to tell you the truth, my feet are killing me. I stupidly wore sandals tonight and my toes have been throbbing for the last half an hour. Can we do it another time? I'll be here for another twenty weeks or so, so there's plenty of time.'

'Willa! You should have told me you were in pain. Is there anything I can do?'

He looked genuinely concerned and she smiled in reassurance.

'No. It's not that bad really. I'll live but I'm dying to get these shoes off.'

'Then do so. I will carry you to your bed – as Mark did on Saturday night. You are as light as a feather, I am sure.'

She giggled. 'Not after what I've just eaten, I'm not. I'll be okay to walk but it'll have to be barefoot.'

She removed her sandals and carried them in her hands as they headed back towards the hotel and the apartment she and Blossom shared in a three-storey building in the hotel grounds.

'Thanks again for this. I've really enjoyed it,' she said as they strolled through the gardens.

'As have I, Willa. It is a pity that the evening has to end

137

here, but we must get you and your sore feet home,' he said.

'What was it, anyway?' she asked.

'What was what?'

'The thing you particularly wanted to show me.'

'Oh. Nothing of great concern. As you say, we have plenty of time to see it. We can go another time – if someone else does not take you there first.'

'Now I'm intrigued,' Willa said. 'Who else might take me?'

Aristaios met her eyes and she could see from the glow of the moonlight that he was clearly mulling something over in his mind, but the look on his handsome face revealed nothing.

'Loukas might,' he said. 'Or someone else. Ah, look, there are Harry and Suki. Oh … and Mark ... and Blossom.'

He didn't sound pleased and when Willa saw Blossom with her arms wrapped around Mark's neck, neither was she.

'Hello you two,' Harry called out, being the first to see them approach. 'Look, Mark here's Willa and Aristaios. Where have you two been?'

Mark seemed to jump up from his seat and Blossom almost fell out of her chair as he did so. Willa saw him reach back to steady her but his eyes appeared to be focused on Aristaios.

'We have been to dinner at Demeter's,' Aristaios said. 'I'm sure I told you earlier, Harry.'

'Oh yes. It completely slipped my mind,' Harry said.

Willa saw the odd look pass between them and her doubts about whether there was something going on, resurfaced.

'We were going to go for a sail in the moonlight,' Aristaios said rather loudly, 'as it is such a beautiful night, but sadly, Willa's toes are still painful so I am escorting her home.'

Blossom's head shot up. She was clearly trying to focus

as she kept opening and closing her eyes but finally she gave up and closed them instead.

'That's a shame,' Harry was saying. 'It definitely is a lovely night. Mark was just saying the same thing, weren't you?'

'I said that it was the perfect sky for sailing under the stars, yes,' Mark said.

'Yes, unfortunately Blossom's had a few too many screaming orgasms so she wasn't up to it,' Harry said, grinning.

'I wasn't asking Blos ...' Mark began but his voice trailed off and he took a swig of his beer instead.

'Are you going to join us?' Suki asked.

'No, sorry,' Willa said. 'My feet are killing me I'm afraid and all I want to do is go to bed ... alone! Not that I'm saying anyone had any intention of ... that is ... I think I've had a few too many wines, myself.'

She giggled and tried to make light of it but she saw the look in Mark's eyes and she hoped he understood what she was telling him. That she hadn't asked Aristaios to take her to bed – as she had when she'd been in Mark's arms that first night. Although, why she should care what he thought when he was clearly flirting with Blossom was beyond her.

'And I think I'd better get Blossom home too,' she continued, 'but someone may have to help me carry her.'

She expected Mark to offer immediately and was surprised when Aristaios stepped forward.

'Allow me,' he said.

He lifted Blossom in his arms in one smooth motion and she threw her arms around his neck and snuggled in close.

'You smell delicious,' she said.

He cast his eyes down to look at her. 'Thank you,' he said in a rather odd voice. 'Good night, everyone. I hope you all sleep well.' Then he turned and walked in the direction of the apartment.

'I'm sorry to have to tell you this,' Mark said quietly to Willa just as she was about to follow them, 'but unless I'm very much mistaken, I think young Aristaios has a bit of a thing for Blossom.'

Willa's head shot round and she looked him full in the face. 'Oh God! I really hope not.'

She saw Mark stiffen.

'Well then, you'd better get after him and make sure he knows what he'll be missing. Good night,' he said. He turned away from her. 'Goodnight Suki, Harry. I'll see you both in the morning.'

'Excuse me!' Willa snapped a few seconds later. Then, completely ignoring Suki and Harry, she hobbled after Mark as he entered the marbled floored reception area. 'What's that supposed to mean?'

He turned to face her, his surprise evident from his expression. 'What?' he said.

'You know full well what. That I'd better go after Aristaios to show him what he's missing!'

'Oh that. I would have thought it was quite clear. As I said, I think Aristaios likes Blossom more than anyone realised – including himself, and, if you don't want to lose him to your friend, you'd better make him see what's on offer.'

'What's on offer! What the hell do you mean by that? Am I supposed to be some sort of special deal or something? Nothing's on offer. And he knows that. I made it quite clear over dinner.'

'Really?'

Mark's lopsided grin appeared and he took a step towards her.

'Yes. Really,' she said. 'Not that it's any business of yours.'

'None at all,' he said, taking another step closer. 'The date didn't go quite as well as you'd hoped then? Or did you mean that you don't sleep with a man on the first date, and you told him so?'

'No! I mean, yes. I mean. Don't come any closer!'

'Why not, Willa? I thought you said you weren't scared

of being alone with me.'

'I'm not. But I am scared of you treading on my toes. Stop!'

He stopped and the grin turned into a broad and very sexy smile. 'I won't tread on your toes, I promise.'

'I don't know what you're playing at and I'm not sure I want to, but if you think you can keep chopping and changing, one minute flirting with me, the next with Blossom, the next with every woman here and then back round again, you can think again.'

He raised his eyebrows and for a moment the smile vanished but something flashed across his eyes and the smile returned.

'I'm not flirting with anyone, Willa.'

'Oh really?'

'Yes, really. I'm just here to write a review and have a good time.'

'Well you're certainly doing *that* from what I've seen. And I fail to see the difference. So why did you kiss me, yesterday then? Because you wanted a good time? Not because you were flirting?'

'Honestly? I'm not sure why I kissed you. I hadn't intended to. It just ... sort of happened. And I sincerely apologise for that, although I'm very glad I did it. But you've made it perfectly clear that you're not interested in me in that way and I respect your decision. It won't happen again.'

'Oh,' she said.

His eyes held hers and they stood just inches apart.

'Unless you want it to, of course, in which case, you only have to ask.'

She felt her mouth drop open. 'Of all the ... I can assure you, *that* I will never do. Goodnight!'

She turned on her heel and marched off, ignoring the shooting pains in her toes, which were causing tears to well up in her eyes. At least, she hoped it was the pain in her toes.

141

CHAPTER SEVENTEEN

'God! I feel like death warmed over,' Blossom said, holding her head in her hands and slumping over the kitchen table.

'You look like it,' Willa replied. 'I take it you'll be cancelling your break of dawn Pilates class.'

'Shit! I'd forgotten about that. I still haven't got used to having guests here and actually having to do some work.'

'Well, it is only Tuesday. I'll call reception and tell them.'

'No. The show must go on. I'm sure I'll be fine. I just need lots of coffee and a shower. Um ... I think I may have done something really stupid last night. Although it can't have been that stupid because I woke up in my own bed.'

'What makes you think that?' Willa poured Blossom a mug of coffee and slid two headache tablets across the table.

'Thanks. Because I have this awful feeling that I was ... kissing someone.'

Willa's head shot up. 'Oh? Can you remember whom?'

'Nope. I can't even remember coming home.'

'Aristaios carried you home,' Willa said, jumping back to dodge the mouthful of coffee Blossom spat out in surprise.

'Sorry! Did you say Aristaios carried me home? Like, in his arms, carried me?'

Willa nodded. 'Uh-huh. And you told him that he smelt delicious.'

'I ... did ... what? Oh my God. What did he say?'

Willa grinned. 'He said, "Thank you", wished everyone a goodnight and carried you home.'

'And?'

'And nothing. That was it. Well, I assume that was it. I got delayed and by the time I got here – only a few minutes

142

later, so don't panic – he was standing over your bed looking down at you. He'd covered you up with your sheets. Do ... do you not like him at all, Blossom? In that way, I mean?'

She furrowed her brow. 'In which way? Sexually, you mean? God no! He's good to look at – very good in fact, but I wouldn't want to get involved with him. Why? Oh, shit. You're not trying to tell me that it was Aristaios I was kissing, are you? Please God. Not him.' She took a large swig of coffee in an obvious attempt to calm her nerves.

'No,' Willa said. 'I think if you were kissing anyone, it was more than likely, Mark.'

This time Willa wasn't quick enough to avoid the jet of coffee from Blossom's mouth.

***

How Blossom made it to her Pilates class, Willa had no idea, let alone how she managed to provide the full hour's workout. Willa watched her in amazement as she stretched and bent and twisted her supple body.

'Good morning, Willa,' Suki said. 'I see Blossom is none the worse for wear. How on earth does she do it?'

'Good morning, Suki. I was just thinking the same thing to be honest. How are you today? Are you having breakfast? You're welcome to join me, if you'd like to.'

She rather hoped Suki would because she wanted to see if she could prise any information out of her about last night.

'Thanks,' Suki said, sitting opposite her. 'I feel surprisingly okay but then I didn't have as much to drink as the others did. At my age, I can't take it like I used to.'

'I know the feeling,' Willa added.

'Yes, but I'm a lot older than you. Sadly, I won't see the right side of forty again.'

'But you look sensational!'

Willa meant it. She knew Suki was around forty-five and

whilst she'd made an unpleasant comment or two about her being old enough to be Mark's mother, she knew that wasn't true. More to the point, Suki didn't look that much older than Blossom or herself and that was a rather depressing thought.

'Thanks, honey,' Suki said. 'I was a bit worried about coming on this holiday. I thought I'd be the only old trout in a sea of fingerlings but everyone is so laid back and friendly and I'm having the time of my life.'

'I'm glad. Er ... what's a fingerling? I haven't heard that before.'

Suki helped herself to coffee, and sneered. 'Blame my ex-husband for that. Sorry, honey. He was a fisherman. Not the sort who goes out in boats for Bird's Eye or the like, I don't mean. He was the, sit on a riverbank for days on end, type. A fingerling's a young fish, a trout or salmon mainly, past the fry stage but not yet an adult.'

'That's interesting.'

Suki gave her a sardonic smile. 'No, it's not. Not unless you're into fishing. Fishing facts can be bloody boring. Just like sitting on a riverbank for hours on end.'

'Oh. So ... you went with him then? Fishing I mean.'

'Yep. From dawn to dusk and several hours either side. I'm amazed my arse isn't as flat as a pancake.'

'It's none of my business of course, but do you mind me asking why you went then?'

Suki sipped her coffee and peered out of the open French windows towards Blossom and her class. 'Because I loved the silly bugger. And I quite enjoyed it, to be honest. I bought myself a camera and I'd sit and take photos while he sat and fished. It worked really well and we were both happy. Until he dumped me for a younger model, that is.'

'I'm so sorry, Suki.'

Suki shrugged. 'It doesn't matter, honey. I'm over it now. He left me two years ago. The decree absolute should be landing on my doormat any day. That's why I'm here. I didn't want to be sitting at home staring at a piece of paper telling me that my twenty-five years of married life were now a thing of the past.'

'I think I'd do the same,' Willa remarked. She didn't know what else to say and they both watched the Pilates class in silence for a few minutes.

'Good morning, ladies!'

It was Aristaios.

Willa had been miles away and the sound of his voice made her jump.

'Oh! Good morning,' she said at the same time as Suki.

'I see Blossom is her usual self this morning.'

Willa stole a glance at his face and she realised that Mark may have been right last night. There was something about the way Aristaios was looking at Blossom. There was a sort of softness about it. Tenderness perhaps, she thought with some alarm. Things were getting complicated enough this week without Aristaios mooning over Blossom, especially since she had made it clear that she had no interest whatsoever in having a relationship with him.

'Yes, she's back to normal. Nothing can keep Blossom down for long,' Willa said.

She saw his jaw clench and wondered why what she'd said would make him cross but then he smiled.

'Well, I shall see you both later. There are one or two things I need to attend to. Enjoy your day.'

'I may be wrong,' Suki said, giggling. 'But I think that man has got the hots for Blossom. Cor! She certainly knows how to pull them, doesn't she? Last night, Mark. Then Aristaios, and Harry's eyes are on stalks every time he gets within three yards of her. I wish I had some of what she's got.'

'Yes,' Willa said, picking up the mention of Mark and last night. 'What was going on between Mark and Blossom last night? Her memory seems to be a little ... vague.'

Suki chortled. 'Well, let's just say she was draped around Mark like a jumper.'

'Oh! Um, that's something else I haven't heard. What

does it mean – exactly?'

Suki tutted and grinned. 'She was draped around his neck. You know, when people tie the sleeves of their jumpers in a knot around their necks.'

'Ah, I see.'

'And when we first saw them, they were kissing. Oh! Be careful! You're spilling coffee down yourself.'

Willa leapt up from her chair, grabbed a napkin and tried to mop up some of the liquid before it soaked into her blouse but it was a hopeless task.

'I don't know what is wrong with me this morning,' she said. 'I'm so sorry, Suki. Will you excuse me? I'll have to go and get this cleaned up.'

'Of course.'

Willa dashed out of the dining room into the kitchen and dabbed at the stain with a wet cloth but all that did was water it down and make it spread.

Cursing under her breath, she marched into the reception area and made her way towards her office. She remembered she'd got a spare blouse in there which had been returned from the laundry yesterday, and she'd forgotten to take home. She'd have to put that on.

She was still dabbing at the stain with kitchen towel and didn't see Mark heading in her direction. She would have bumped straight into him if he hadn't avoided her but she still knocked against his arm. She cast startled eyes up to his amused, although slightly concerned ones.

'Hey,' he said. 'Where's the fire?'

'Sorry, I didn't see you.'

'Evidently.' His eyes followed the stain. 'That's an unusual pattern. Is it all the rage this season?'

'Very amusing,' she said, 'but if you'll excuse me I'm in a hurry.'

'So I see. What happened?' He nodded at the watery brown mark.

'I spilt my coffee. Excuse me.' She went to walk past him but he stood in her way.

'Are you usually this accident prone? First your toes and now your coffee. It isn't your week, is it?'

She gave him what she hoped was an icy stare but he just threw his head back and laughed.

'You'll have to do better than that,' he said. 'Remember, I've faced bears and wolves without fear, so glowering at me like that isn't going to have much effect.'

'I'm so glad that you find my mishaps entertaining,' she said, stepping to the side and making a dash for her door.

He was beside her in a second. 'I'm sorry, I shouldn't have laughed. I take it from the speed you just dashed past me, that your toes are recovering nicely.'

'My toes are fine, thank you. Now if you don't mind.'

She opened her door and strode into her office, turning to close the door behind her but he had stepped inside before she had a chance.

'Mark!' she snapped. 'Will you please leave me in peace? I need to take this blouse off.'

'Don't let me stop you,' he said, his eyes glinting with devilment. 'Perhaps I may be of assistance. As you know, I'm very good at helping beautiful women in distress.'

'Stop it! Just stop it!'

She saw the look of surprise on his face and remembered too late that she was supposed to be trying to be pleasant to him. The problem was he just made it so bloody difficult.

'I'm sorry, Willa. Are you okay? Has something happened? I didn't mean to upset you.'

He appeared genuinely concerned and she took a few deep breaths and tried to regain her composure.

'No. I just ... I can't do this, Mark. I can't play these games. I told you that yesterday. In fact, I told you that the first day we met. I'm not like you. I don't have one-night stands and I don't flirt with dozens of people at once to see which one comes up trumps.'

She saw the confused look in his eyes followed by the anger.

'Is that really what you think I'm doing? That's really

what you believe?'

'Well, aren't you?'

His eyes scanned her face.

'No. No, it's not. In fact, you couldn't be more wrong about it if you tried.'

'Oh really? So you didn't flirt with me on the way here from the airport then? And you didn't kiss me the next day? And then you weren't picking figs for every female here? And you weren't feeding Suki, Sonia and Susan olives by hand? And, most importantly of all, you weren't locked in a passionate embrace with Blossom last night? I'm wrong about all those things, am I? I'm sorry, Mark but I don't want to be the next woman whose name you can't even remember.'

His nostrils flared, his eyes flashed with fury and his lips formed a tight hard line. He stared at her, his breathing heavy and she got the distinct impression that he was holding himself back.

A flicker of fear shot through her and she wondered for a split second if he was going to lash out at her. The idea shocked her to her core. A moment later, she saw something in his eyes and she knew that she was being ridiculous. Mark Thornton may be a lot of things but she was somehow certain that he wasn't the sort of man to ever raise a hand to a woman. He hadn't done so with Candice after all, and she must have made him very angry over the whole wild animal situation. No, Mark Thornton was the sort of man who would rather make love than war, of that she was sure.

'My God,' he said, his voice just above a whisper. 'You were actually frightened of me just then, weren't you? I may be a lot of things, Willa but I can honestly say I have never, nor shall I ever, strike a woman. No matter how infuriating she may be. You really do have a very low opinion of me, don't you? I won't bother you again. You have my word.'

He turned to leave and without thinking, she reached out

for him, catching his arm in her hand. He glanced down at it and then up at her face with a questioning look in his eyes.

'I know you wouldn't physically hurt a woman,' she said.

His eyes held hers and she felt him relax a little. Her fingers slid down his arm and he caught them in his hand.

'But I would emotionally, is that what you're implying?'

She shook her head but her eyes remained fixed on his. 'Perhaps not intentionally, no. But not all women are like you, Mark.'

'You seem to think that I play games and to hell with the consequences. That's not true, Willa. I don't. I have never led a woman on or lied to one just to get her to sleep with me. I ... I may have been flirting with you but that wasn't to get you into bed. It was because I really like you.' He pulled her towards him and brushed a loose tendril of curl from her eyes.

She felt her breath come in short sharp gasps and she knew she had to stop this – now.

'I want to believe that, Mark,' she said, 'but unfortunately the evidence goes against you. You were flirting with Suki and Sonia and Susan. You may not call it that but believe me, all of us women do. And last night, you were seen in a rather passionate embrace with Blossom. Are you going to deny that?'

His eyes half closed as if he was reliving a painful memory and then he let her go and stepped back.

He shook his head. 'There doesn't seem much point, does there? You had made up your mind about me before I even arrived and you've made up your mind that I was kissing Blossom, so let's leave it at that. We seem to be going around in circles. I'm truly sorry if you think I've been playing games with you though because I haven't, not in the way that you seem to think, at least.'

'But surely you're not going to try to deny kissing Blossom? You were seen, Mark. Suki Thane saw you. She told me this morning. And even Blossom knows she was kissing someone, she just couldn't remember it was you.'

Mark smirked. 'It seems I'm not the only one who kisses and forgets someone then. But actually yes, I do deny kissing Blossom. It takes two people to kiss, especially passionately, and I can promise you on my life that I was not kissing Blossom, no matter what anyone may have said, or thought they saw. I will, however, admit wholeheartedly to kissing you and I'll accept that perhaps I shouldn't have. I'll also admit that I was rather hoping to do it again but I'll accept that that would probably be a very bad mistake. I'll leave you to get changed.'

This time he was gone before her hand could reach him.

CHAPTER EIGHTEEN

Willa wondered how she would get through the day. Her head was spinning with thoughts about Mark and what he could have meant. A part of her wanted to ask him but it seemed to her that every time they had a conversation, it ended in some sort of drama, so she thought better of it.

Not that she could have talked to him anyway. He appeared to be avoiding her again. On the two occasions she got within shouting distance of him, he either dived into the swimming pool or jumped into a boat and set sail before she could open her mouth.

She was taking some of the guests on a day trip to Nafplio and hoped, although she had no idea why, that he might join them. She went down to the beach to round up a couple of missing participants before the coach departed at nine-thirty and saw Mark heading towards the boats. She reminded herself that he knew the area well and had probably seen the city at least once already but she was disappointed all the same.

Blossom would normally have accompanied the day trippers but she had covered the sailing yesterday when Willa's toes were painful and she wasn't really up to a day sight-seeing, no matter what she said about the show having to go on. Instead, Willa insisted on going in her place. She was looking forward to it – or at least she had been.

According to the brochures she handed out, Nafplio was one of the most romantic and beautiful cities in Greece and as soon as Willa descended the coach steps, she realised the brochures had not lied. She wandered around the narrow cobbled alleyways of the Medieval Old Town and admired the neoclassical mansions. The scent of bougainvillea hung in the air from the many trees in their courtyards and mixed with the smell of strong black coffee wafting from the cafés and tavernas dotted around.

She climbed the nine hundred and ninety-nine steps carved in the rock leading up to Palamidi Castle. From here she could not only see for miles around but also the rocky islet of Agioi Theodoroi and the famous Venetian fortress of Bourtzi in the bay far below.

The view was spectacular but she was surprised that oxygen wasn't on offer. She was young and fit but was out of breath by the last step. That may have been due to the heat though. The morning sun was melting her skin and the clean white blouse she'd changed into earlier was now sticking to her back. She was glad two of the party had decided against the trek to the top and gone off in search of a postcard of the castle instead. They didn't look terribly fit despite the fact that they had come on a sailing holiday.

After a long and leisurely lunch, she and several of the party took a ride on the tourist train and then marvelled at the many treasures, mainly Mycenaean, housed in the Archaeological Museum which was based in a Venetian warehouse, surprisingly.

All the while, she found herself wondering if Mark had seen and done all these things. She had to tell herself to 'stop it' more times than she cared to remember. Somehow, the man had got inside her head and she had to find a way to get him out or she would bitterly regret it; of that she was sure.

By the time the coach arrived back at the hotel at seven p.m. all Willa wanted to do was have a large glass of cold white wine and flop onto the sofa with her feet up. Unfortunately, on the return journey, she remembered her date with Harry and instead of a leisurely evening doing nothing, she had to rush in, shower, dress and rush back out to meet him within the space of thirty minutes.

She was astonished to find she was only ten minutes late, although her hair was still dripping at the ends and the only make-up she'd had time for was a swipe of mascara and lipstick.

Like Aristaios, Harry had suggested dinner at Demeter's

and she wondered whether Loukas was giving out vouchers or something. She was tempted to call Harry's room and ask if they could have dinner at the hotel instead. She wouldn't have to walk so far then and although the restaurant was only a ten-minute walk from her door, that was still ten minutes on top of the several hours she'd walked today.

'I'm sorry I'm late, Harry,' she said as she joined him at their table. 'I've been in Nafplio all day and I only got back half an hour or so ago.'

'Don't worry about it,' he said, smiling warmly. 'Loukas has been chatting to me so I haven't been sitting here like a wallflower. Would you like a glass of wine?'

She was about to say that she would murder for one but he was already pouring it. She just smiled and said, 'Thanks, I've really been looking forward to this.'

His eyes lit up and she realised too late what she'd said.

'So have I, Willa. I don't usually make a habit of asking holiday reps out on dates – it's too tacky for words – if you get my meaning. Not that I'm saying you're a holiday rep. I know it's your family's travel firm. Oh! And I'm not saying you're tacky, of course. It's just the whole 'single guy on holiday chats up the reps', sort of thing. But there is just something about you, Willa. I don't know what it was but from almost the very first day, I knew I had to get you to go out with me.'

She smiled. 'I'm flattered, Harry, really I am and I know what you mean about the whole 'tacky' business. It goes against all my own rules too but ... this isn't a 'real' date is it? I mean, it isn't the boy meets girl, boy asks girl out because he fancies her, kind of date. I thought we were going to have a chat about the possibility of doing an ad campaign. I hope I didn't get the wrong end of the stick because I'd hate you to think that ... well, you know.'

His eyes narrowed momentarily and the muscles in his face seemed to tighten. Then the smile reappeared.

'Well, I must admit that I used the ad campaign as a bit

153

of a carrot. I thought you'd say no if I asked you outright – which you've as much as said you would have done as it goes against your rules. I really like you and I think, well, who knows where it could lead?'

Willa wasn't sure she'd ever seen such a self-assured expression on a man's face – not even Mark's and it irritated her that he just assumed he could win her over.

'I'm sorry to say this, Harry, but I do,' she replied, giving him what she hoped was her sweetest smile. 'I know exactly where it could lead and as I've said, dating guests goes against my rules.' She saw that he was about to argue. 'No. Please don't say anything to try to make me change my mind. It won't work. I'm very, very stubborn. Just ask Blossom – or my father. When I make up my mind about something, nothing will change it. Sorry.'

'Not even a free advertising campaign?'

She wasn't sure whether he was joking or not. 'No, not even that.'

He let out a long sigh. 'You might change your mind if you got to know me. We could see how this evening goes and decide from there. We don't have to make any rash decisions right now, do we? Decide in haste, repent at leisure.'

'I think that refers to marriage, Harry, not dating but no, I'm certain I won't change my mind. You're a very handsome man, and you're great company. I'm sure you'll make one very lucky woman the perfect boyfriend – but that isn't me, I'm afraid.'

'Do you always know whether or not you want to date someone when you've only known them for a couple of days? Sometimes things take a while to develop.'

Willa thought about it for a moment. 'Oddly enough, I'd have to say yes. At least, I have up to now. Every man I've ever dated, I've known almost from the very first day that I've wanted to. Sometimes it took a while for them to ask me but I've always known I'd say yes. I've got a few male friends who have never been or never will be, anything but friends and I've known that since I met them. I haven't been wrong so far.'

'So ... you knew when you met me that we'd just be friends then?'

'Well, this is slightly different because you're here as a guest so I didn't even think about you in that way, but yes, or no, I guess I should say, I didn't think we'd be dating or anything.'

Harry refilled her glass and looked her straight in the eye. 'And Mark?' he asked.

She felt something catch in her throat and she sounded like a mouse when she answered.

'Mark? What ...what do you mean?'

'I mean,' he said, his eyes firmly locked on hers, 'what did you feel about Mark when you first met him?'

She tore her eyes away and gulped down a few mouthfuls of wine.

'Nothing,' she lied, staring at the table. 'Absolutely nothing.'

'Well then. It looks like we'll all be losers.'

Her head shot up at that. 'Losers? What do you mean, losers?'

'N–nothing! I meant that I think all three of us wanted to go out with you and clearly none of us will be, that's all. So we're all losers – as in, we don't stand a chance of getting you, not as in, we're all saddos or something.'

'Getting me?'

'Sorry, that wasn't the right word. Dating you, I should have said. We've all asked you out on dates and you're not interested in dating any of us, that's what I meant.'

'All? I assume you mean Aristaios, yourself and Mark by that?' She saw him nod. 'But ... Mark hasn't asked me out on a date. In fact he made it very clear that it *wasn't* a date.'

'Perhaps he was trying to play it cool and hoping he could get you there another way.'

'Get me *where*, Harry?'

155

'Er ... out on a date. Perhaps he was hoping to get you out on a date another way.'

Willa studied his face. For a guy in the advertising business he wasn't a very good liar.

'I see,' she said, watching his eyes. 'I thought you meant it had something to do with a silly bet.'

'Bet? W ... what bet? Who said anything about a bet? There isn't a bet.'

She was right then. There was a bet and Mark was in on it. No wonder he'd spent so much time flirting with her. The bastard! The absolute bastard! She was furious but she had to keep calm.

'No? That's good. I thought Blossom may have said something to you. She's always saying I shouldn't worry so much about mixing business with pleasure and that she'd bet that one day I'll let my hair down and have some fun. I thought perhaps she'd asked you all to ask me out to encourage me to do just that. Obviously not though, so forget I said it. Shall we order? I'm starving.'

CHAPTER NINETEEN

Willa had to find Blossom – and fast. She'd forced herself to eat, drink and laugh with Harry, showing no signs of the anger boiling within her but if she didn't tell someone soon, she would burst. The fall out, she was sure, would make the eruption at Thira, around three thousand years ago, look like a champagne bottle popping its cork. After all, that one was only believed to have caused the end of the Minoan civilisation. The way she feeling, the fall out from her wrath would be far, far worse.

'Look,' Harry said as they came within sight of the hotel terrace. 'It seems Blossom and Mark – and the others, are drinking again. Shall we join them?'

'Yes, let's,' Willa said through clenched teeth. So Mark was obviously *not* flirting with Blossom again then, she thought.

She had no idea why she did it; she certainly hadn't intended to but she linked her arm through Harry's and as they reached the top of the steps, she stood on tiptoe and kissed him on the cheek. She could just see Mark's face out of the corner of her eye and he didn't look happy.

Harry gave her an odd look but he smiled, pulled out a chair for her and sat down beside her.

She leant provocatively towards him, glanced up into his eyes and in as sexy a voice as she could manage said, 'I think I'm going to have a screaming orgasm ... Harry.'

Mark choked on the mouthful of beer he'd just swallowed.

'That went down the wrong way,' he spluttered, slapping himself on the chest several times.

Willa ignored him and moved a little closer to Harry.

'Well,' Suki said, 'it looks as if you two have had a good time.'

'We have,' Willa said. 'Harry has been ... so helpful and

so generous both with his time and with his advice. I don't know how I'll ever repay him. I'll have to think of something very, very nice,' she said.

Harry gave her another odd look as did Blossom and Aristaios. Suki, Sonia and Susan all appeared to be smiling but Mark had something resembling a sneer spread across his lips.

'I ... I told you, Willa,' Harry said. 'I'll be happy to assist you in any way I can. You only have to ask.'

'And I think I very probably will ... ask you, Harry. I'm sure I'll be safe in your experienced hands.'

'Dear God!' Mark commented, his voice just above a whisper.

Willa heard it and she saw by Blossom's expression that she had too but no one else took any notice.

Mark stood up abruptly and in a rather sarcastic tone said, 'I'm going to bed. I'm suddenly feeling a little nauseous. Goodnight. I'll see you all tomorrow.' With a final glance at Willa, he marched into the hotel reception without looking back.

Willa immediately sat upright, no longer having a reason to flirt with Harry and only Blossom appeared to notice that too. Harry, it seemed, was too busy staring at Sonia's breasts as she bent over to adjust the strap of her sandal.

'I think I also need to go to bed,' Willa said. 'Are you coming, Blossom?'

'I think I may stay here a little longer. I'll see you in the morning. Pleasant dreams.'

'Fine,' Willa replied, feeling it was anything but. Now she'd have to stay up until Blossom got home and she had no idea how long that would be.

She bade the others goodnight and headed for home still feeling angry but a little less so. She may have been mistaken but she could have sworn that Mark was actually jealous. It could of course all be a part of his game playing or possibly because he thought he may be losing the bet. She was determined to find out exactly what this wager

158

involved, if it was the last thing she did.

***

Willa woke to the smell of coffee and the ring of her mobile phone. She glanced at her wrist but realised that she still hadn't found her watch and she had to check the time on her mobile instead. It was seven-thirty which meant that both she and Blossom were running late. She leapt out of bed at the same time as answering the call, which she could see was from her brother.

'Hi Daniel, what's up?' she said. 'I'm running a bit late today so unless it's urgent, can I call you back in half an hour or so?'

'Late night?' he asked, sniggering.

She could hear a slight inflection of concern in his tone though.

'I hope you haven't been showing that Mark Thornton too good a time, Sis. I saw the article about him in *Only The Best Will Do*. He looks just your type.'

'Don't start that again, Daniel! Did ... did Dad say anything?'

'Only that he should have checked the chap out before arranging for him to do the review. That he'd thought the chap would be older, and that he hoped you'd be 'sensible and professional about it'. You know Dad.'

Willa sighed. 'What did you say?'

'I said exactly the same thing I did last time he mentioned it. That you were a big girl now and you could handle pretty much anything so he shouldn't worry.'

'Thanks. But I really wish the pair of you would stop going on about it. Will I never be allowed to forget it? It was fourteen years ago, for God's sake. Enough is enough.'

'Okay, calm down, Willa. Shit! I was only saying.'

'Yes. Well. You shouldn't. And I really hope that's not the reason you called me. I'll be very disappointed if it is.'

'No, I was actually calling to tell you that the adverts

159

you placed in the magazines had the phones ringing off the hook. They brought in far more bookings than the earlier ads. Dad's over the moon about it.'

'But not enough to call me himself. Wow! I'm glad though it's had such a good response. I knew it was the right decision to have Blossom, Aristaios and Loukas in the picture.'

'Yeah. I think it helped that they weren't wearing much. Dad even pretty much admitted that you were right about that too, about refusing to go along with his suggestion.'

'Wow! Well, there was no way I'd have got Blossom to wear some sort of sailor outfit-cum-uniform let alone Aristaios and Loukas, so that really was a non-starter. Anyway, as lovely as it is to hear that, I really must go, Daniel. I'll call you later, okay?'

'Okay. And well done, by the way. I knew you could do it.'

Despite telling Daniel she was late, when she ended the call she sat on her bed and sighed heavily. Even after all this time, her dad still didn't think she could cope and he was still surprised when a decision that she made, actually worked and worked well. She was disappointed that he wouldn't even tell her she'd done well, let alone congratulate her.

More importantly though, he would clearly never stop thinking of her as the silly, naive eighteen-year-old girl who fell head over heels in love with a holiday rep on her first season. He'd panicked about Aristaios and now he was worrying about Mark.

She smirked, wondering what her dad would have to say about the present situation. She had been on a date with the hotel owner, a date with a holiday guest and had kissed the guy writing a review. Immediately, she realised her dad was probably right to worry. She had had a crush on Aristaios although she was over that now, and she couldn't seem to get Mark out of her head, no matter how hard she tried.

'Willa! I'm late. I've got to run. Are you up?'

Blossom's voice snapped her out of her thoughts.

'Yes! Don't go yet, I need to talk to you,' she yelled, dashing towards her bedroom door.

'I can't stop,' Blossom called back. 'I'll catch up with you at breakfast after the Pilates class.'

Willa heard the front door slam before she made it to the kitchen.

***

It was going to be another hot day and Willa decided that she would wear her favourite sundress to cheer herself up. She shouldn't be feeling down though, she kept reminding herself. She had made a good decision over those adverts and the fledgling sailing section of Daventry Travel was thriving because of it.

There had been a substantial number of bookings from the advertising her father had done, announcing the launch of the holidays, but not the steady stream they'd hoped for. With this new round of bookings, the sailings holidays stood a much better chance of succeeding. Now if she could just get a five-star review from Mark too, her dad would surely have to start taking her seriously as a senior player in the business.

That thought soured her mood again instantly. There was no way Mark was going to give her a five-star review even though he said what happened between them personally wouldn't affect his judgement on that score. She'd written those awful things about him in the magazine; had made those silly additions to his photograph; had had rows and temper tantrums because she thought he was flirting with her and because he'd kissed her. And finally, she'd pretended to like someone else to try to make him jealous. Her dad was right, she thought despondently. She was still a silly naive girl. But now, she didn't have the defence of being an innocent young girl of eighteen.

The restaurant was packed by the time she got there and

she decided to go and do some work until it quietened down a bit. Not that she could concentrate on work. She was still mulling over the situations with her dad, with Mark and now with this bloody wager. By the time she heard Blossom's voice heading towards the restaurant, she had only sent one email.

She dashed after Blossom but was too late to stop her joining Suki at a table beside the French windows. She had hoped to get her alone and yet again, had failed. Growing more irritated by the minute, she stomped over and asked if she could join them.

'Of course, honey,' Suki said. 'In fact, I think I need to have a word with you, with both of you.'

'Oh!' Willa said. 'Is there a problem? I hope it isn't regarding the holiday or the hotel. What can I do to help you?'

'You can sit down for a start,' Suki said, grinning, 'and no, it has nothing to do with the holiday or the hotel ... although, in a roundabout way I suppose it does.'

Willa exchanged confused glances with Blossom.

'Whatever it is, I'm sure we can sort it out,' Willa said, not sure of anything of the sort.

'It's a little ... delicate, honey and ... well, I've been wondering whether I should say anything or not. Boys will be boys after all and perhaps you won't mind. I'm sure being in the holiday business you're used to this sort of thing. But I know I would be furious, so I think it's best if I tell you and you can decide how you feel about it. First though, I need to ask you both a personal question and you can say it's none of my business but I do have your best interests at heart.'

'Now I'm really confused, Suki. Whatever it is, go ahead. Neither Blossom nor I have anything to hide.' That was a total lie, she thought but hey-ho. Needs must.

'Okay, do either of you have feelings for Mark, Aristaios or Harry? And by feelings, I mean the loved-up, want to rip his clothes off and have sex with him for the rest of your

162

life, kind. Not the ... he'll be a great shag for this week and next week I'll move onto someone else, kind.'

'Oh!' Willa said.

'I don't!' Blossom said emphatically.

'Then you kissing Mark the other night was just a bit of fun?' Suki asked.

Blossom was clearly horrified and she shot a guilty look at Willa. 'Kissing Mark! Oh my God. I wasn't. When? Oh shit. You were right, Willa.' She closed her eyes, reopened them and gave Willa a pleading look. 'I'm so sorry. Please, don't get cross. I didn't mean to do it. I can't believe I did. Did I really, Suki?'

Suki nodded. 'You were very drunk though. I did wonder whether it was one of those things you'd regret in the morning.'

'It's okay, Blossom. It doesn't matter.'

'It does,' Blossom said. 'But at least I suppose we're quits on the shitty friend scale. N ... nothing else happened, I take it?'

'No, because that was the night Aristaios carried you home,' Willa said.

Blossom let out a sigh. 'Oh well, I guess I should be grateful to Aristaios then.'

'And you, Willa?' Suki said.

Willa frowned. 'Me? Oh, you mean do I have any feelings for any of them? Er ... no.' She saw Blossom's raised eyebrows and sighed. 'Well, maybe I thought I did – for Mark. But I'm fairly certain I don't and even if I did, he doesn't feel the same about me so it really doesn't matter what I feel for him because it won't go anywhere and besides, I can't mix business with pleasure.'

'Wow, Blossom exclaimed. 'I don't think you took a breath throughout that entire spiel.'

'I'll take that as a 'yes' then,' Suki added.

Willa's eyes darted from one to the other. 'No! I just said I didn't.'

'Believe me, honey, that is *not* what you just said. And

163

that puts a different complexion on what I want to tell you. But why were you draped all over Harry like a jumper if you've got the hots for Mark? Okay, there's no need to answer that. It's obvious. You were trying to make him jealous. Bloody hell! You girls have a really complicated, mixed up love life.'

'I wasn't. And we don't. ... All right, maybe I was.' She hung her head and sighed again.

'So what is it then? That you need to tell us. Willa's a big girl. She can handle it. And so can I,' Blossom said.

'Okay. If you're sure.' Suki bent forward and did a quick recce of the room. Clearly satisfied that no one could overhear her, she continued, 'Last night before you arrived on the terrace, Blossom and long before you came back from dinner with Harry, Willa, Aristaios, Mark and Loukas were sitting chatting. I was just the other side of the French windows, about to come out and see if I could weasel my way into joining them when I heard Loukas say, "A bet is a bet Aristaios and Willa will never find out." Well, that stopped me in my tracks.'

'I knew it!' Willa said. 'I knew there was something going on. Blossom and I were discussing this only the other night and last night, Harry almost blurted it out! That's what I wanted to talk to you about last night and this morning, Blossom. I knew we were right. What else did they say? Is Mark involved? What am I saying, of course, Mark's involved. The bastards. The absolute bastards! I'll kill them. I'll bloody well kill them.'

Suki's perfectly shaped eyebrows shot up in surprise. 'Oh dear! Perhaps I shouldn't have told you.'

'No,' Blossom said. 'You were right to tell us. We suspected there was a wager or competition of some sort but then decided we must be wrong. Did you hear anything else?'

She nodded. 'I'm not sure I understood it correctly and I may have missed something but Aristaios then said, "Yes but things have changed. And what if she does find out?

She will not be pleased." Mark said something about how he didn't think they should have agreed to it in the first place because they were all so drunk. Then Loukas said that until they knew whether or not Harry had won they could do nothing but that if Harry couldn't get you to ... I think he said, Aphrodite's head – which I assume is a local beauty spot or something, then they could all agree to call it off if they wanted to. But they must *all* agree and would they rather not wait until after Mark's date to see if he could win?'

'I knew it!' Willa shrieked. 'So that's what he was up to. All that, "it's not a date, it's just a drink" nonsense was just a lie. A deception to put me off my guard or something. Ooh! That man is *dead*.'

'Okay, Willa. Calm down,' Blossom said. 'I can understand why you're fuming. I would be too, but don't forget you still need that review. You've got to be a little bit careful about what you say to him. And ... I think it's Aphrodite's Bed they were talking about.'

'What? They've all been trying to get me into someone else's bed! What kind of sick bastards are they? '

'Aphrodite's Bed isn't a bed,' Blossom said. 'It's a small privately owned island to be precise. It's in the Gulf of Argolis and it's called that because of its shape. I think there's a villa or something there. I heard Loukas mention it once, shortly after I arrived. It's very exclusive and incredibly expensive so if they were taking you there, someone must know someone or have a very rich friend.'

'Well that's probably Mark, isn't it?' Willa said sarcastically. 'He's bound to know someone like that.'

'So, were they just trying to get Willa to this island then?' Suki asked, 'or were they trying to get her to the villa? If that's the case, they may well have been trying to get you into bed, honey. And that's a really shitty thing to do as a bet.'

'But so bloody typical of arrogant men on holiday,' Willa declared.

All three of them nodded.

'But ... you heard this conversation last night before Willa and Harry came back from their date?' Blossom asked.

Suki nodded.

'So ... they now all know that Harry didn't get you to Aphrodite's Bed, Willa. Didn't you say, Suki that Loukas said they could call it off after they knew that?'

'Yes, he said they could, but that they might rather wait to see if Mark could win. Oh! I see what you're saying, honey. They could all now agree to call it off or they could let Mark have his turn.'

'Have his turn!' Willa said. 'What am I, some bloody computer game or something? Argh! I *so* wish there was some way I could play them at their own game and teach them a thing or two.'

'That's actually not a bad idea,' Suki said.

'What? How?' Willa looked from Suki to Blossom.

'I agree,' Blossom said. 'But I'm with Willa. How are we supposed to do that?'

'Well, first we need to know the exact details of the bet without letting them know we've found out.'

'How do we do that?' Willa asked. 'We can't ask one of them, so that only leaves Loukas and he won't tell us.'

'He might with a little persuasion,' Suki said.

Willa frowned. 'What sort of persuasion? Are you saying that one of us needs to ... use our feminine charms to try and get him to talk?'

'She means have sex with him,' Blossom said to Suki. 'She sometimes forgets she's only thirty-two and talks like she's a ninety-year-old.' She shook her head in amusement.

Suki grinned. 'I'm not suggesting we need to go that far – although personally, I wouldn't mind getting that man's kit off. I didn't tell you what my husband did, did I?'

'Yes,' Willa said, furrowing her brow. 'You said that he left you for a younger model. Oh, you didn't mean that part. That he was a fisherman? Sorry, I'm lost.'

166

Suki shook her head and giggled. 'Neither of those things – although they're both true. No, I meant what he did for a living. My lying, cheating, two-timing husband ... was a hypnotist – and a bloody good one at that.'

'Wow!' Willa said. 'Er ... but I'm not sure how that helps us.'

'It helps us because he taught me everything he knew,' Suki said. 'Although it didn't work when I tried to hypnotise him into believing he didn't want to leave me for some nineteen- year-old bimbo but then, he was immune to it – being hypnotised, I mean. Anyway, I could try to hypnotise Loukas into telling us the details. It is slightly unethical but we're not in the U.K. now and I won't tell if you won't.'

'You couldn't hypnotise Mark into giving the holiday a five-star review as well, could you? That might help. And falling head over heels in love with Willa too. That would be good.'

Willa tutted. 'I don't want him to fall in love with me. I don't want anything to do with a man who enters into a bet over a woman.'

'I couldn't do it anyway,' Suki said. 'Despite what people think there are limits to the powers of hypnosis. You can't make someone do something against their will or even do something in contradiction to their beliefs and values. A person's subconscious would stop that happening. They have to want to do it. Perhaps I could make Mark fall in love with you, come to think of it, honey. Anyway, I may not be able to get much out of Loukas if he believes strongly enough that it's wrong to divulge it. So I may need to try all of them individually and see which one gives in first. Do you want me to do that?'

Willa and Blossom exchanged looks of uncertainty.

Blossom nodded. 'I think we need to know the details. And then we need to think of a way to get even.'

CHAPTER TWENTY

Suki didn't need very long to discover which of the men was the best candidate for hypnosis. Just by asking a few questions and going over in her head the conversation she'd overheard, she decided that either Aristaios or Mark were the ones who were most likely to reveal the terms of the wager. After all, they were the ones who seemed to want to back out of it now, from what she'd heard last night. Then she had to decide which of those two would be most susceptible. In the end, she chose Aristaios, partly because she felt he might be easier to persuade and partly because he happened to be the first of the two men she was able to get alone.

'So what did he say?' Willa asked when she, Suki and Blossom met for a prearranged lunch at one of the small tavernas in the village of Kritiopoli.

'Quite a lot, actually,' Suki said. 'Mark showed them an article that you'd written something on – about him, Willa and it had made him livid. They were all very drunk and there seems to have been some debate as to whether you and Blossom were playing games and flirting to get a five-star review, amongst other things.'

'What other things?' Blossom said.

'I'm not sure, honey. It was all a bit mixed up. Anyway one thing seems to have led to another and somehow they decided they had to show you that men are better at playing games than women and that led to them being competitive and that led to the bet.'

'But what *was* the bet?' Willa said, not really sure she cared how they got to it.

'It was to see who could get a date with you. But not just any date. It had to start at Demeter's and then they had to get you to go to this Aphrodite's Bed place ... and the winner would be the one who could get you to stay there.

But don't worry. The bet wasn't based on whether you would have sex with one of them – although it does seem that at least Harry hoped you would. It was based on you not asking to come back for at least two hours.'

'So that's why you had to have dinner with Aristaios and Harry at Demeter's,' Blossom said. 'I thought it was odd that they should both want to go there although I guess, other than the hotel dining room, it's the only place to go without coming into Kritiopoli. Where are you meeting Mark for that drink tomorrow?'

'The hotel bar.'

'That's odd. Perhaps he isn't going to take part in the bet, after all,' Blossom said.

'Unless he thinks that you'll have drinks there, and then he can suggest going for dinner at Demeter's and it won't seem as if he's doing the same as the other two. It could be a clever little ploy, honey,' Suki added.

'Oh God!' Willa said. 'I've just remembered something. He said we'd meet in the bar but he'd like to go sailing because he'd heard of an idyllic little island that he wanted to include in his review. And ... he even said we could have a bite to eat somewhere. The absolute bastard! I am *so* angry. And all this because I drew a few things on a picture of him and wrote a silly piece which I did apologise for and it was before I met him.'

'I wonder why he took it so badly,' Blossom said. 'Although it wasn't very flattering, I guess and if he found the article when we think he did, he had just been kissing you. Ah, I can see why that would make him angry, actually, especially if he had feelings for you. But let's not forget the other two are involved now. What I want to know is how exactly they were planning on keeping you at Aphrodite's Bed for over two hours. With only a small beach and a villa I don't think we need to use much imagination to see what they all had in mind.'

'God! And Mark was okay with that. He couldn't care less about me, obviously. I mean, if you liked someone you wouldn't want to think of them having sex with someone else would you? Especially not for a bet. I've been a complete and utter fool yet again. I had actually convinced myself for a moment that he liked me!'

'I think he does,' Blossom said. 'Perhaps he joined in to stop the others from doing just that, even though he was furious with you.'

'What, by letting them take me out first, you mean? I don't see how that would work.'

'Perhaps he didn't have a choice, honey. If the others asked you first, what could he do? I didn't know that he'd kissed you though. When was that?'

'On Sunday. It ... it just sort of happened.'

'Suki's right,' Blossom said. 'And perhaps he was hoping that you liked him too so you wouldn't go to the island with either of them – and he was right – you do like him and you didn't go. You came back to the terrace on both evenings.'

'And then flirted with Harry,' Suki said.

'So what are we going to do? To get even for Willa, I mean? And, come to that, for all women. How dare they think they can make bets about us and get away with it!'

Willa shook her head. 'I have no idea but I do want to do something and to hell with the review – or what Dad will say if he finds out.'

'You could play them at their own game.'

Blossom and Willa exchanged doubtful glances.

'How?' Willa asked.

'Well ... if they think it's okay to lead women on and deceive them. You could do the same to them.'

'Yes, but how? Surely that would be falling right into their hands, wouldn't it?' Willa said.

'Not if we all pretended to be crazy about them.'

'The three of us, you mean?' Blossom said, looking unsure.

'Yes. We could all flirt with them and lead them on. I know I may look a bit old in the tooth but I think I've still

170

got a little something when it comes to seducing men.'

'By seducing, what do you mean exactly?' Willa asked.

'Have either of you ever seen a French farce?'

Willa and Blossom nodded.

'Well, I mean like that. We could each proposition the men and tell them to leave their doors unlocked. It's a good thing the hotel doesn't have self-locking doors and that's something I never thought I'd say. Anyway, one of us would turn up in one of the men's rooms, this evening say, and tell him how much we wanted him. Then the next one of us would arrive, so the first one would hide in the bathroom and then sneak out. Then the next one would turn up. It's a bit like a round robin. It's very silly but it could be fun and they'd get the shock of their lives thinking three women have the hots for them, only to find each one keeps slipping away.'

'I quite like the sound of that,' Blossom said. 'I'd like to do a bit of over-the-top flirting.'

'I'm not sure I do,' Willa said. 'I'm hopeless at flirting.'

'You seemed pretty good at it last night, honey. With Harry.'

Willa felt herself blushing. 'Yes. Well, I was angry.'

'So stay angry. Of course, in the case of Mark and Aristaios, their problem would be that they've got to fend off two women they're not interested in to be able to 'keep' the one they are, which is even more amusing. Then, when we've got them all believing they are onto a good thing, each of us will arrange to meet them at the quay. We could tell them we wanted to go to one of the secluded bays nearby. The three of us will go together to the quay. When each of them turns up, we'll tell them we know about the bet and we were playing them at their own game. Willa, you arrange to meet Mark. Blossom, you arrange to meet Aristaios and I'm fairly certain I can get Harry.'

'Oh! I'd rather you get Aristaios and I get Harry,' Blossom declared.

'Really, honey? I don't think you do. Not deep down.

And I'm not sure Aristaios would agree to meet me. In fact, I'm pretty sure he wouldn't. But Harry almost certainly would.'

'I don't know what you mean!'

'Blossom, honey, do you really want me to spell it out?'

Willa was confused. 'But Blossom doesn't really like Aristaios. She thinks he's gorgeous of course – everyone does but she doesn't fancy him in that way although I see what you mean. That's not the point because nothing's going to happen. Aristaios fancies her so he'd meet her. But Mark doesn't fancy me. Hang on, are you saying he'd meet me because of the bet? He still has his turn tomorrow.'

'You girls,' Suki said, shaking her head. 'I don't think you can see what's right in front of your own noses. Anyway, are we going to do this? It will need careful planning.'

'Just one problem,' Blossom said. 'How does the last woman get out of the guy's room? I mean, if there isn't another woman to replace her, surely she's stuck there? Why would she have to arrange to meet him somewhere else?'

'Ah! I hadn't thought of that,' Willa said.

'We wouldn't have to arrange it. I think the men will suggest going somewhere else. Don't forget, they'll each be wondering if the other two women are going to be coming back at any moment. They wouldn't want to be ... interrupted, would they?'

'What ... what if they don't suggest it?' Willa had visions of being alone with Mark in his room and she wasn't sure that was a good idea. As angry as she was with him, she didn't trust her own emotions at the moment.

'They will. The only one who might not is Harry. He might want to get rid of me in the hope that one of you two will return. Don't worry, I'll think of something. Now, if we're going to do this, we need to start flirting with the men this afternoon. You know. Laying the foundations, so to speak.'

'Er ... there's another problem,' Willa said. 'Blossom is going on a date with Mark tonight. He wouldn't cancel that to meet me. He even said as much the other day.'

'It's not a date, Willa. We're just going for cocktails. You can come too if you like, and you, Suki.'

Suki tutted. 'I think you'll find he will, honey. Especially if he thinks Blossom has the hots for him – and let's face it, you have already kissed him, Blossom, so he can't be sure. I think the man will be running scared.'

'Thanks. I'm not that bad,' Blossom said, pouting.

'You will be to him, honey, if he thinks he could lose the woman he's fallen for because of you.'

'Who's he fallen ...? Oh! You can't mean me?' Willa said in disbelief.

'As I said, honey, you can't see what's right in front of your nose. Right, let's have another bottle of wine and put this plan into action.'

***

To Willa's great surprise she found flirting with Aristaios and Harry much easier than she'd anticipated. Flirting with Mark was a different thing entirely. It had something to do with his eyes, she was certain. The way he looked at her when she smiled at him or when she 'accidentally' brushed his arm when she passed him in reception. She began to wonder who was the seducer and who was being seduced. The strange sensations darting around her body were like a computer bug – gone viral, and all rational thought data was rapidly being corrupted.

Suki seemed to be unaffected by any of it whilst Blossom just looked tired.

'I've ordered tea although I could do with something much stronger,' Blossom said when they met for afternoon tea at four-thirty on the terrace. 'I don't remember flirting ever being this exhausting and we haven't even got to the main event yet.'

'And it's not as much fun as I thought it would be,' Willa added. 'I feel as if I'm about to walk into the lion's den and he hasn't eaten for a month. I'll be glad when it's all over too.'

'Well, we can always start earlier than planned,' Suki suggested. 'Where are the men now? I haven't seen any of them for half an hour.'

'Aristaios in his office,' Willa said.

'Harry is sailing. I was flirting with him on the quay ten minutes ago. I thought he wasn't going to go out for one dreadful moment but Susan and Sonia appeared, thank God and I told him I couldn't be seen getting close to one of the guests so he'd better go.'

'And Mark?'

'No idea,' Willa said.

'Me neither,' Blossom said, shaking her head. 'But I did see him just before I went down to the quay. I tried to flirt with him but he looked ... preoccupied and he just smiled when I told him that I was really looking forward to having a few screaming orgasms tonight – and that I didn't just mean cocktails.'

'Blossom!' Willa said, blushing at the thought of saying that to Mark. Her imagination instantly ran wild at the thought of *doing* that with him.

'Well, we are supposed to be seducing them, aren't we?'

'You're doing a great job, honey,' Suki declared. 'Both of you are. Now the important thing is to make sure none of us are alone with any of them until this evening.'

'That shouldn't be too much of a problem,' Willa said. 'Tonight is 'Meze Night' so we'll all be seated on a long table on the terrace. It starts at six-thirty and ends around eight-thirty.'

'I think the bigger problem is how do we get them to go to their hotel rooms after?' Blossom said. 'If we're going to turn up at their doors, they need to be in their rooms.'

'Well, I think you can just tell Harry to go to his room and wait for you, Blossom. He'll go. Do the same to

174

Aristaios. Tell him to go to his apartment. I'm sure he will. And Willa, honey, you do the same with Mark.'

'He won't go. He'll say he's taking Blossom out for cocktails – or screaming orgasms, more than likely.'

Suki tutted. 'I'm sure he will, but okay, sit next to him at dinner and accidently knock a glass of wine over him.'

'Hmm. Nothing would give me greater pleasure. In fact, I may spill hot black coffee all over him.'

'That'll put a fire in his loins,' Blossom said, giggling.

'But it may dampen his ardour,' Suki said, grinning. 'You're better off using wine. It's still damp but at least it's not scalding hot. We don't want anything to stop him, shall we say, rising to the occasion. Although I don't suppose even burning liquid would stop him where you're concerned, honey. Anyway, he'll have to go and change and I can follow him up.'

Willa looked pensive. 'Actually, we need to decide which order we go in. Who gets whom, and when.'

'I'll be first with Mark. Then you, Willa and you last, Blossom. Aristaios gets you first, Blossom, then me, then Willa and Harry gets Willa, you, then me. Is that clear?'

'As mud,' Blossom quipped. 'Why in that order?'

'Because then Mark ends up with you and he won't want to risk that. Willa can hide in the loo before he opens the door to you, then sneak out. She can call him and tell him to meet her and he will because he won't want her to think he's staying in his room with you.'

'Okay, I get that bit.'

'I'm not sure I do,' Willa said. 'I do get Aristaios though. He'll want to be with Blossom so if she's first, he'll want to get rid of us so that he can be with her.'

'That's right, honey. Harry is the problem again so I think one of you two needs to call him when I'm there and ask him to meet you. That way, he'll make some excuse and get rid of me.'

'I think you're underestimating your charms, Suki. I'm not at all sure Harry will want to get rid of you,' Willa said.

175

Blossom agreed. 'But if you want someone to call, I'll do it.'

'I think it's best, honey. Just in case. It could go either way.'

Willa shook her head. 'I knew from the first day when I saw him in those budgie smugglers that the man would cause trouble.'

CHAPTER TWENTY-ONE

Willa was glad that she didn't see Mark again until six-fifteen that evening. She and Blossom were waiting on the terrace for the rest of the Sailing Solo party to join them for the Meze Night when he came up behind her.

'You look stunning,' he announced, 'and that's just from the rear view.'

Startled, she spun round to face him and saw the appreciation in his eyes as they took in every inch of her body. She was wearing a black chiffon v-neck dress, which tied at each shoulder. The bodice was figure hugging but the skirt was full and floated around her hips and thighs down to just above her knees. She wore black high-heeled strappy sandals and her brown curls were piled on her head in an 'up-do'.

He gave a low whistle. 'I take it back, you do look like Aphrodite – and that's not a chat-up line. Why aren't you wearing your glasses?'

It took her a few moments to find her voice. 'Contacts,' she said, her eyes scanning his body. Damn, she thought, it's going to be a shame to ruin those trousers. 'You look rather gorgeous yourself, Mark. That light blue shirt matches the colour of your eyes. I may have to take back what I said too.' She gave him what she hoped was a sexually inviting look but she couldn't be sure.

His eyes narrowed slightly and his lopsided grin appeared. 'Thanks. Which part? There were so many. The part where you said that I was arrogant or the part where you said you wouldn't ask me out?'

She leant in close to him and looked up into his eyes. 'The part where I said that you would never get me into your bed,' she whispered.

After a few seconds revelling in the obvious effect her comment had on him, she smiled, brushed his arm with her fingers, making sure her nails gently scraped at his skin, and wandered over to chat to some of the other guests. When she glanced towards him a few minutes later, he was standing in the same spot, his eyes firmly fixed on her.

Ten minutes later, everyone was on the terrace and took a seat at the long table, which was covered in large, white linen tablecloths. Willa had originally intended to sit next to Mark but she thought better of it. She didn't want to be that close to him. He wasn't the only one who had been affected by her words. Immediately, images flashed before her eyes and it took all her powers of concentration to converse with the guests around her.

Instead, she sat opposite him but that was just as bad, she soon realised. His intense blue eyes hardly left her face and even before the first dishes of tzatziki, houmous and taramaslata arrived, she was feeling like a rabbit caught in headlights. That wasn't the only problem. Having flirted with Harry for quite a bit of the afternoon, he took the opportunity to sit next to her and with Blossom seated at the other end of the table, things could get awkward. Thankfully though, Suki sat next to Mark so at least she'd help keep both of them occupied.

'There's bread coming,' Willa announced, 'and there's an eggplant dip and a spicy cheese one too. If any of you want to know what they're called in Greek, just ask one of the waiters or Aristaios who will be joining us for coffee and liqueurs later. We're also having stuffed vine leaves, meatballs, stuffed green peppers, spinach patties, whiting, tomato fritters and lots more besides. If you're unsure of what some of the dishes are, again, just ask Blossom or me. Please help yourselves and ... enjoy!'

She soon discovered that Harry had more tentacles than an octopus – another dish on the table tonight – and between trying to flirt with him but keep his hands at bay, and running her bare foot up and down Mark's shin and inner thigh a few times, she didn't have much chance to eat. She did manage to drink though. Well, she needed alcohol to steady her nerves, she told herself. Far from looking pleased by her amorous advances, Mark appeared to be scowling, so she put her sandal back on and poured herself another glass of wine.

By eight-thirty when dinner was over, she was feeling rather light-headed. She wondered how she was going to manage to pretend to seduce all three men, run between their rooms, which in Aristaios' case, meant either dashing up and down three flights of stairs or waiting for the lift and still be standing at the end of the night. She was nervous about the entire plan now and the thought of meeting Suki and Blossom on the quay to remove the veil on the men's little wager, seemed light years away.

Coffee and liqueurs arrived bang on time – along with Aristaios, and after taking one final look at Suki and Blossom, she gulped back a large glass of Metaxa and knocked a full glass of wine across the table and into Mark's lap.

He jumped up but not before a huge wet patch formed around his groin.

'Oh gosh! I'm so sorry, Mark,' Willa exclaimed, trying her hardest to look surprised and apologetic for what she'd done.

Mark studied her face for a moment before grinning sardonically. 'It's not a problem,' he said, 'I got a very definite feeling that you were trying to get me out of these trousers.'

Willa felt her cheeks flush crimson and as she averted her gaze, she could see that Harry appeared to be unsure whether to take Mark's comment seriously or not. When several of the other guests started laughing though, he did the same.

'Women will try anything these days,' Harry said.

'We don't need to spill wine over men's groins to get their trousers off,' Suki added.

Susan and Sonia cheered loudly and offered their services to assist Mark.

'Thank you,' he said, 'but I think I can manage. Excuse me.'

With a final glance in Willa's direction, he marched into the hotel.

Willa turned to Harry and whispered in his ear, 'I should have knocked that wine over you, shouldn't I, Harry? Or do I need to go to such extremes?'

Harry nearly choked on his coffee and when his eyes met hers, she could see that he wasn't sure he could believe his ears.

She whispered again, 'I'll meet you in your room in ten minutes ... unless you're not interested, of course.'

She ran her fingernails up his thigh, got up from her seat and headed towards Suki and Blossom who were standing near the other end of the table. When she looked over her shoulder and winked at him, he disappeared into the hotel, and she hoped he was heading for his room.

Timing was crucial if their plan was going to work.

'Remember,' Suki said, 'you must only be in each room for fifteen minutes before one of us arrives to take over. That doesn't give us long, so we'll have to make sure that each of the men gets a very clear message that sex is definitely on offer from all three of us.'

'I don't know about that,' Blossom said. 'With some of my past men, fifteen minutes has been enough time to make the first move, do the dirty deed and have a cigarette or drink afterwards.'

'Then you'll have to make sure they take things slowly, honey. We don't want the kettle blowing its lid before the teapot is ready, do we?'

'If I understood that, I might be able to answer,' Blossom said, grinning.

'Er ... there's just one problem,' Willa said. 'I still haven't found my watch.'

'Bloody hell, Willa! You'll have to use the alarm on your mobile then. You have got that with you, haven't you?'

Willa nodded.

'Let's not panic, girls,' Suki said. 'It'll all be fine. Good luck.'

'Let the mayhem begin,' Willa said.

She clinked glasses with Suki and Blossom. Then Blossom made a beeline for Aristaios. In less than one minute, he was sprinting towards his apartment on the top floor of the Argolis Bay Hotel and Blossom followed a few seconds later. Willa emptied her glass and headed off after Harry. Suki went with her in the lift on her way to Mark's room.

'Have you set your mobile alarm, honey?'

'I'll do it as soon as I get to his door,' Willa said. 'Good luck with Mark.'

'Thanks honey,' Suki said. 'I think I'm going to enjoy this.'

Willa gave her a sardonic smile. 'Yes, but not too much, okay?'

'Well, he is rather gorgeous,' she said.

'Tell me about it,' Willa said as they left the lift and she turned right whilst Suki turned left.

Willa set the alarm and knocked on Harry's door. It shot open and she was astonished to see Harry standing in the doorway, the look on his face akin to a child in an ice-cream parlour. He reached out and grabbed her, pulling her into his arms and holding her against him in a vicelike grip.

'I couldn't believe my ears, Willa,' he said, planting a kiss on her lips.

She managed to wriggle her hands up to his chest and push him away. Suki may not think fifteen minutes was a very long time but Willa had a feeling that Harry was like some of Blossom's past encounters.

'Slow down, Harry,' she said, easing herself out of his arms.

'I ... I thought you were the one in a rush,' he said. 'You seemed eager to get me up here.'

'I was, Harry, but we've got all night. Let's just take it

slow to start with shall, we? I ... I'm a little shy to be honest. I'd love a drink. Just to help calm my nerves.'

'There's nothing to be nervous about, Willa but I'll get you a drink, no problem.' He walked over to the mini bar. 'What would you like?'

'Gin and tonic, please.'

She sat on the bed but quickly realised that would be a mistake, so she jumped up and sat on the chair near the balcony and the sliding doors.

Harry handed her the drink and knelt down in front of her. He planted a kiss on her knees, teasing the hem of her skirt up and moving his lips higher.

Willa prayed for her mobile alarm to go off or for the sound of knocking on the door but the only sound she heard was Harry's heavy breathing as his other hand slid up her calf. In desperation, she grabbed him by his collar and lifted him up so that they were face to face. She kissed his chin and his neck, slowly teasing his shirt from his shoulders.

'Willa,' he whispered.

She could feel his arms reaching out for her so she yanked the shirt down so that it was half way down his arms effectively pinning them to his sides. He was trying to wriggle free of it and after a minute he succeeded.

He wrapped his arms around her and pulled her towards him, one hand reaching for her breast.

'No!' she said rather too loudly. 'I mean, not yet, Harry. Let me undress you first. Let me see you naked and then you can undress me.'

'What? You want to inspect the goods before you open the shop,' he said, leaning in to kiss her.

Willa was glad that she wasn't attracted to him. That sentence alone would have been a real passion killer as far as she was concerned. She held him at arm's length.

'I want to ... feast my eyes on your horn of plenty,' she said, cringing at the words, 'but first, I'm afraid I need to go to the loo. Sorry, Harry, I think I've had a bit too much to drink.'

She pushed him away and could see by the look on his face that he was becoming a little irritated but she managed to wriggle past him and she fled to the bathroom, locking the door. She leant back against it, took a couple of deep breaths and looked at her mobile. Just a few more minutes, she thought and then she'd be safe. Well, safe from Harry the octopus at least.

'Are you okay in there?'

'Fine thanks, Harry. I'm just coming.'

'Don't tell me you've started without me,' he said.

She counted the seconds to her salvation.

CHAPTER TWENTY-TWO

Mark heard the knock on his door and opened it, half expecting Willa to be standing there. He had no idea what she was playing at tonight but she was definitely playing at something and he'd really like to know what. For someone who'd told him that she wasn't any good at this sort of thing and couldn't handle a holiday fling or words to that effect, she'd done pretty well so far.

When he'd first seen her this evening before dinner, just looking at her from the back had made his heart skip a beat. When she'd turned round to face him, she'd taken his breath away and when she said that she might have to take back what she'd said about never getting into his bed, he was surprised that he hadn't had coronary failure on the spot. Blood must have stopped flowing to his heart; it was all heading for his groin. And when he'd felt her foot sliding up his inner thigh, how on earth he'd managed not to choke on the meatball he was eating, he still wasn't sure.

'Oh!' he said, opening the door to find Suki leaning provocatively against the frame.

'I thought you might need some help getting out of those wet trousers,' she said, diving under his arm and darting into his room.

'Oh,' he said again, wondering what the hell was happening this evening. 'Um. Well that's very kind of you, Suki but I've managed to get in and out of my trousers for many years now without any help, thanks. Do come in though.'

She smiled at him from where she was perched on his bed. 'Thanks. I will.'

'So, as you can see, Suki, I've changed my trousers and I'm ready to go back downstairs now.'

'What's the rush,' she asked, leaning back on his bed with her arms supporting her. 'I thought we could have a drink.'

'That's a very good idea. I could definitely use a drink. Let's go to the bar and have several. In fact, I'm meeting Blossom there very soon and we're heading off to a cocktail bar a few miles from here. You're welcome to join us. The more the merrier.'

'I'm more of a 'quiet drink for two' type of woman. Why don't we just stay here? I'm sure Blossom will be able to find someone else to entertain her. Like Aristaios or even Harry.'

'I'm sure she will, but I like to honour my commitments and I made a commitment to meet her at nine p.m. and it's eight forty-five now.'

'I can do a lot in fifteen minutes, Mark, believe me.'

'I don't doubt it. But you may have read that article which several people here have been talking about in *Only The Best Will Do*. If so, you'll see I'm more of an all night kind of man. It takes me more than fifteen minutes just to get warmed up.'

Suki smiled at him. 'Perhaps we could sit and talk for a few minutes instead then.'

'That I can do, and we'll have that drink while we're at it.' He strolled over to the minibar and peered inside. 'I can't offer you a screaming orgasm I'm afraid but you can have a G&T if you like.'

'At my age, Mark, I'll take whatever I can get. A G&T is fine.'

Mark had the strangest feeling that Willa wasn't the only one playing at something tonight. Unless he was very much mistaken, Suki was in on it too and when he heard the knock on his door around ten minutes later, he was sure of it.

'I'd better hide in the bathroom,' Suki suggested. 'We wouldn't want anyone to see me here.'

'Why not? We're both adults, we're both fully clothed and we're just having a friendly drink. Why should that be a problem?'

185

He opened the door before Suki had a chance to hide and when she and Willa came face to face, he could see genuine surprise on both their faces. Perhaps he had been wrong after all, he thought cursing himself for his arrogance.

'Ah! Willa said. 'I see you've got company. I'm sorry.'

'Don't mind me, honey. I was just leaving.' Suki slid under Mark's arm as he held the door open.

'Oh ... um.' Willa hovered in the corridor.

'You go in, honey' Suki said, giving Willa a gentle shove into the room and disappearing along the corridor.

Willa stumbled and fell against Mark's chest.

He grabbed her to stop her from falling and they stood looking into one another's eyes as if neither knew quite what was happening – which Mark thought in his case, was precisely how he felt.

'Come in,' he said. 'Er ... have you come to see if I need any help dressing myself?'

'What? Oh ...um ... no. I mean ...'

She gave a little cough and he watched her stand up straight, push her shoulders back and take a deep breath as if she were going into battle or something. She sashayed across the room and looked through the sliding glass doors.

'Quite the opposite actually,' she said, placing her mobile on the coffee table in front of her. She sat down, crossing her legs and leant back provocatively in the chair. 'I've come to see if you need any help *un*dressing yourself.'

Mark stared at her and felt his throat closing up. He wanted her more than he could ever remember wanting any woman in his life and if he'd thought for just one second that she meant those words, he'd have been over there like a shot. But he was pretty sure she didn't.

'Really,' he said when he could finally speak without his voice cracking. 'May I ask what I've done to bring about your sudden change of heart? It's just that until this evening, you really didn't seem to be that interested in me. In fact, you've told me several times that you are most definitely *not* interested in me – clothed or otherwise.'

He saw her eyes flash and had to force himself to stand his ground.

'That's not true.' She looked as if she meant it. 'I *am* interested in you. I have been since I saw you at the airport. It's just that ...'

'Yes. It's just that what?'

She lowered her eyes towards the floor. 'It was difficult ... complicated.'

'And it's not difficult or complicated now?'

Her eyes met his. 'Yes, it still is. But now that doesn't matter. Now I know exactly what I want and I'm determined to get it.'

He took a step towards her before faltering.

'And ... would that be a five-star review?'

'No!' She stood up and turned to stare out of the glass doors. 'I couldn't care less about a five-star review. You can give me one star for all I care. That's not what matters, Mark. What matters,' she said, turning to face him, 'is you.'

He felt a burning need to go to her, to take her in his arms and kiss her but something held him back. Some sixth sense warning him that he was about to get hurt and that his mum leaving him before his twelfth birthday would be a piece of cake compared to the pain he could be about to suffer.

'What's made you change your mind?'

Her eyes looked so sincere, so ... full of genuine desire that he was really struggling now and he could feel his breath coming in quick, sharp snaps.

'You have,' she said. 'Seeing you flirting with Suki and Sonia and Susan was bad enough but seeing you with Blossom made me realise how much I wanted to be in her place. How much I wanted to be with you. I tried to deny it because ...well ... because you make me so mad sometimes but every time I see you, Mark, my heart skips a beat. You said you'd go out on a date with me if I asked you. Well, I'm asking. Will you please go out with me, M–?'

He was in front of her and sweeping her into his arms

187

before she had finished her sentence.

'This had better not be some kind of joke, Willa,' he said. 'I don't think I could take that.'

She shook her head and her lips parted expectantly. 'What sort of person do you think I am, Mark?' she asked.

He kissed her with all the passion he'd held in check since that first kiss on Sunday, and that felt like a lifetime ago.

'Mark, I ...' she began when he finally relaxed his hold.

'Yes,' he replied, planting kisses on her eyes, her nose and her neck.

She didn't continue so he carried on kissing her, removing the hairgrips from her hair and letting it fall about her shoulders. He ran his hands through it and gently eased her head back, kissing her mouth again, deeply, longingly. He could taste her passion, hear her soft moans, feel her body lean into his so that they seemed to fit together in perfect symmetry.

He wanted to fondle her breasts, to kiss them and see them react to his touch. He wanted to slide his hand up her thigh, across her stomach and inside her panties. He wanted to feel his fingers touching her, teasing her, caressing her. He wanted to feel her naked flesh next to his, to feel the heat of her body and the longing he was sure she was experiencing almost as deeply as he was.

He could feel the excitement building fast and he knew he had to slow things down. As much as he wanted to make love to her right here, right now, to feel himself inside her and give her as much pleasure as she would definitely give him, he couldn't. He wouldn't. Not yet. Not just yet. He wanted to savour this moment. This need for her. This realisation that she meant the world to him.

But this made him want her more. He hadn't realised it at the time but the moment he'd seen her waiting for him at the airport, he'd fallen head over heels in love. He'd known he'd been stunned by her but until now, until this very second, he hadn't realised just how much.

This was real. This was incredible. This was intoxicating. This was love.

The knock on the door went unrecognised by him at first. Somewhere in his befuddled brain, he thought he heard it but he dismissed it. His hand slid slowly across to Willa's right breast and he cupped it in his hand.

'God, Willa, I want you so badly,' he said between kisses, pulling her body closer to his so that she could feel just how much he wanted her. He heard her gasp.'

'Mark!' she said, her voice hoarse.

The knocking grew louder and more persistent.

'Mark! It's Blossom. May I come in? We've got a date tonight.'

Willa pulled away from him as if she'd be stung by a thousand bees and he stared at her aghast, trying desperately to catch his breath and to fathom out what was going on. Desire still burned in her eyes, he could see that but there was something else. Fear? Shame? Shock? He wasn't sure. Her breathing was as laboured as his. She'd wanted him as much as he had wanted her he was sure of that.

'You'd better let her in,' Willa said, gasping for breath. 'I'll go.'

'No.' He reached out for her but she shot past him.

She yanked open the door and he saw the surprise on Blossom's face just as it had been on Willa's earlier. Something deep inside him mocked him and he had a dreadful feeling that he had just made a very big mistake.

'Willa, wait!' he said, but she was gone.

Blossom came into the room and closed the door behind her. 'I thought we had a date tonight, Mark. I've been waiting for you. Of course, this is even better. Why don't we just stay here instead?'

Mark dragged his hand through his hair and dropped down uncomfortably onto the bed.

'Okay, Blossom. What the fuck is going on? And please don't bother lying to me. I'm really not in the mood.'

189

CHAPTER TWENTY-THREE

Willa ran along the corridor despite the fact that she couldn't feel her legs. She wasn't sure she could feel anything other than the memory of Mark and being in his arms, his mouth on hers, his hand on her breast. Even though she was nowhere near him she still felt as if they were joined at the hip, as if in those minutes, those few precious minutes, they had shared some deep emotional connection, that somehow she had given him a part of herself and that she would never feel complete again unless she were with him.

She knew she was being overly dramatic and yet she felt the loss of him in the same way that amputees have reportedly felt limbs that have been removed and which, in reality, they can't possibly be feeling. She understood what people meant when they said they would die if they didn't see a particular person again. She was sure she would die if she couldn't be in his arms again.

This had started out as a game. A way to get revenge for a stupid bet and whilst she told herself that she should still be angry with him, what she felt was something else entirely. Why did he make that bet? she asked herself over and over again. If he hadn't, Suki wouldn't have heard the conversation and they wouldn't be doing what they were all doing now.

'Oh my God!' She suddenly remembered that she was supposed to be replacing Suki in Aristaios' apartment.

She didn't have the heart for it. She couldn't go to him and pretend to be seducing him when all she could think about was Mark. All she could see was Mark. There was nothing else for it. She had to call this off and call it off now. She dialled Aristaios' number. He sounded relieved to hear from her.

'May I speak to Suki please,' she said, 'and don't

pretend she's not there because I know she is. She'll explain in a moment. Just put her on the line please.'

He did what she asked.

'Suki, it's Willa. I need to call this off right now. Just tell Aristaios that we know about the bet and that I wanted to pay them all back but now I don't. Right now, I just want to forget it ever happened.'

'Is everything all right, honey. Are you okay? Where are you? I'm coming right there.'

'No. I'm fine, Suki. Please don't worry about me. There's something I need to do. I do need you to ask Aristaios to tell Harry about this too. I don't want him to continue thinking that all three of us have got the hots for him. Will you do that please?'

'Of course I will, honey. I'll be in the bar if you need me. I think I can guess where you'll be.'

Willa sighed. 'I may be in the bar sooner than you think. I'm not sure this is going to go well. I think instead of getting revenge and getting my own back, I've just made my life a whole lot worse. Wish me luck.'

'Good luck, honey.'

Willa pressed the end call button, took a very deep breath and made her way back to Mark's room. She knocked on the door and waited, feeling as if she were in the dock at court and was about to hear her sentence. One word from him would mean she would either live or die and as the seconds passed, she had a dreadful premonition that it was going to be the latter. When the door swung open and Mark stood glowering at her, his nostrils flared, his jaw rigid, she knew she was right.

'Did you forget something?' he asked.

His voice slashed her heart in two with the swiftness and accuracy of Achilles' sword.

'May I talk to you please, Mark?'

Blossom ran to the door. 'What's the matter? Are you okay?'

Willa shook her head. 'No,' she said. 'I've told Suki to

tell Aristaios what we were doing and asked him to tell Harry. She's going to the bar afterwards if you want to talk to her but for now, Blossom, would you leave me to talk to Mark, please?'

'I don't think we have anything to talk about,' Mark said, 'and frankly, I need a drink.'

'Please, Mark.'

'Um ... he already knows most of it.' Blossom grabbed her bag and eased her way past them. 'I'll leave you to it.'

Mark stood in the doorway and didn't move.

'May I come in?'

'I don't think so. There really isn't much point. You've done what you came for. Congratulations.'

'I know it was wrong and Suki, Blossom and I shouldn't have done it but you three did it first. We were only trying to get even. To get our own back. To ... to teach you a lesson.'

'Well, you've accomplished it. I have learnt my lesson and I will never do this again, believe me. Is that it?'

'No! How ... how can you be so ... so cold after what happened between us just now?'

'Me? Cold? That's fucking rich coming from you. And from what I can make out, the only thing that happened between us just now is that I got well and truly played. Well done, Willa. You're not just a talented writer and artist, you can also add actress to your many skills. You really had me fooled.'

'How dare you! How fucking dare you! Okay, it was mean and deceitful and when I came in here, all I was thinking about was the fact that you'd made a bet with Aristaios and Harry to see who would be the first to – effectively, screw me – and don't say it was just a date. Of course, it wasn't just a fucking date. Oh! Actually, that's exactly what it was. A *fucking* date! And that is far, far worse than anything I just did.'

'It was not! It was just to see who could get you to go to the island with them, that's all. It was entirely your choice whether you had sex with any of us. None of us would have forced you to do anything against your will.'

'Oh how very kind of you. But what if I had? What if I'd gone there with Aristaios and had sex with him? Or Harry? Because I wasn't to know it was just a bet, was I? I might have believed the lies they spun. I might have actually thought they liked me. Shit, I even thought you liked me. I might have had sex with one of you and then come back only to find the bet was won and I was dismissed. How do you think that would have made me feel, Mark? At least I hadn't planned to sleep with you. Any of you. All I planned to do was flirt and lead you on. I can't see how that is even half as bad as what you had planned for me.'

'I didn't have anything planned for you and I wasn't going to try to sleep with you. I only agreed to the bet to try to stop them winning and doing precisely that.'

'What? By letting them go out with me first? How was that going to stop them?'

'I ... I hadn't thought it through. They asked you and you agreed to go out with them. Part of me thought you might say no but you didn't. Then I guess, I wanted to see if you would go with either of them because if you did then ... well, I just wanted to know, that's all.'

'Then ... what? That would make me some kind of tart or something, would it? And not worth your attention anymore? You really are an arrogant shit, Mark.'

'No! It would mean that you preferred one of them to me, that's all. And that would have been your choice so I would've had to live with it.'

'Live with it! What's that supposed to mean?'

'It means that I– It doesn't matter. It's all irrelevant now, anyway. You're right. I totally accept it shouldn't have happened but we were all very drunk. I'd found that ... article you wrote. We'd just been kissing and I was ... angry. I couldn't understand how you could dislike me so much before you'd even met me. Then one thing led to another and somehow I'd got involved in something I knew was wrong but couldn't see a way out of. But that doesn't mean it's okay for you to turn around and do the same just to get your own back. To ... to pretend you wanted me, that you had feelings for me.'

'But it's okay for you to pretend to have feelings for me? God, you really are the limit! And as to not being able to see how to get out of it – you could've just come and told me about it and ... and apologised.'

'Me apologise? You kiss me back then run off and then I find that article. How do you think that made me feel? I was livid. I can't remember the last time I've been that angry.'

'I'm sorry! How many times do I have to say it? I ran off because I didn't want Blossom to be upset and I apologised for that and for the article. You said we were friends. I thought we'd got past that. And I wrote it because ... because. Well, it doesn't matter and I'm not really sure why I wrote it anyway. The point is. I wrote it before I met you. Before I ... knew you. At least I thought I knew you. It seems I was wrong about that too.'

'It seems we were both wrong about each other. How far would you have let me go? Just to fondle your breasts or would you have gone further?'

'No! I ... that wasn't meant to happen.'

'And did you let Harry do the same before you came to me?'

'No! I ... No!'

'Really? Well, let's leave it at that, shall we? I don't think there's any point in dragging this out any further. We've both done things we're not proud of and we both regret them. Okay. It's done. Let's forget it. We were both playing games with one another and we shouldn't have been. We'll keep things entirely professional from now on. You're the holiday rep. I'm the reviewer. End of story. Let's try to be civil to one another. Now may I please go and get a drink? You have no idea how much I need one. How much I need several, in fact.'

Without waiting for her response, he yanked open the

door and strode into the corridor.

Willa wasn't sure what had just happened. Had he just admitted that it had all been a game to him? All of it? Every last second? She couldn't believe it but that was what he'd said. She couldn't seem to get her feet to move. She wanted to run after him. To ask him if he meant that. To tell him that it wasn't a game as far as she was concerned. To tell him that she did have feelings for him. Real feelings. Deep feelings. To tell him ... it was love.

CHAPTER TWENTY-FOUR

Mark wanted to kill someone. At the very least, he wanted to smash something to bits. To pummel something with his fists until they bled and maybe then he would feel the pain in his hands instead of in his heart.

Shit, he thought. The one time I let my guard down and open up my heart, she rips it out. And not only does she rip it out, she stomps on it several times to make sure there's no life left in it. But if there's no life left in it, why the fuck does it hurt so much?

His head was spinning. How could he have been so stupid? He'd been so careful until now. He'd always managed to avoid falling in love, at least, the head over heels, would do anything, even die for, kind. All his relationships had either been very short and based purely on lust or had started off that way and then drifted into something longer and comfortable but in no way posing any real threat to his heart. Until Willa.

He turned and was a little surprised to see that she was not in the corridor. He wondered where she was. Was she still in his room? Should he go back and talk to her? See if she was okay. Of course, she was okay. What was the matter with him?

Just the thought of her was making his blood boil. He needed to calm down. To cool off. But there wasn't enough ice in the whole of Greece to do that. He did know where there was a large amount of ice at the moment though. It still may not be enough to stop him from combusting but it would at least get him away from the fire.

'Right. That's it. I definitely need to get out of here,' he said out loud. He dialled his father's number on his mobile and headed down the stairs.

Less than ten minutes later, it was all arranged. All he had to do now was avoid Willa at all costs. He needed to find Harry and Aristaios and then get drunk. But not too drunk. He didn't want to end up doing something else he would later regret.

He spotted them, looking rather dejected, both slouching in chairs on the terrace and marched over to them.

'The game's up then?' he said. 'Let's go down to see Loukas and tell him, shall we?'

'Fine,' Harry mumbled. 'Can you believe those fucking women?'

'I think it is very unwise to ever believe women,' Aristaios said.

Mark sneered and dragged his hand through his hair. 'Tell me about. It's a mistake I don't intend to make again. Are you coming?'

They both stood up and the three of them walked listlessly towards Demeter's.

***

'It seems women are better at playing games than men after all, Harry,' Loukas said when they explained what had happened.

'Yeah, okay. Don't rub it in. I'm beginning to wish I hadn't come on this sodding holiday.'

'Why? Surely you have enjoyed it so far? And what does this matter? It is just a little set- back. There are other women here besides Willa and Blossom. And it is only Wednesday. You have three nights and two more days.' Loukas patted Harry on the back.

Harry seemed to brighten at the prospect. 'That's true. Although it must be about nine-thirty now so tonight is almost over.'

'The night is young, Harry. And more importantly, Sonia and Susan had dinner here and have just gone downstairs to my disco, Persephone's. You could do a lot worse than go and join them.'

'That's not a bad idea. Mark, Aristaios, are you up for

197

that?'

Mark shook his head. 'Not me. Sorry. I'm leaving early in the morning.'

'Leaving?' the other three said simultaneously.

Mark nodded. 'Yeah, I just spoke with my dad. He's up in the Arctic doing a wildlife documentary and I ... I'm going to join him. I was ... lucky enough to be able to get a flight back to the UK tomorrow at eight-fifteen. I'll sort something out from there.'

'Oh, Mark. This is ... sad news,' Loukas said. 'I have enjoyed meeting you. I hope we shall remain friends.'

'The same for me,' Aristaios said. 'Is this because of what has happened tonight? Surely things will look better in the morning?'

Mark ran his hands through his hair and sighed. 'I ... I just think it's best if I leave. Dad could use another pair of hands anyway. Things could get ... more difficult if I stay and to be honest, I don't need the hassle. I've got assignments for most of the summer so ... it's just better if I leave now. I'll stay in touch. It was a pleasure to meet you all.'

'Perhaps you shall return here one day?' Loukas asked.

Mark shook his head emphatically. 'No. I don't think so. At least, not in the summer.'

'Not when Willa is here, you mean?' Loukas said.

Mark met his eyes. 'Definitely not when Willa is here.'

Loukas stood up and went to get the Metaxa bottle containing the wager money. He smashed the bottle open and shook the fragments of glass from the 3,000 euros.

'The bet was not won so your money is returned.'

Mark shook his head. 'I don't want mine back. Will you give it to a local animal charity if there is one please, Loukas?'

Loukas raised his eyebrows. 'Of course, Mark. If you so wish.'

Mark nodded. 'Thanks. And now I think I'd like to get a little bit drunk.'

CHAPTER TWENTY-FIVE

Willa glanced at her reflection in the long mirror on one of the walls of the hotel reception as she passed on her way to the restaurant. She didn't like what she saw and quickly looked away. She had hardly slept and had spent the night alternating between pacing her room, crying, drinking coffee, making things to eat only to discard them as she couldn't face food.

Several times during the seemingly endless night, she considered going to Mark's room, banging on the door and demanding to be let him so that she could tell him how she felt. Surely it couldn't have been all a game on his part? The way he'd held her. The way he'd kissed her. Surely he couldn't have faked that? His erection was definitely real. She'd felt that. Of course that didn't mean he cared about her; that just meant he wanted to have sex with her, but even so. There was something in the way he'd said her name. Something in his eyes. Something in his kisses.

She had been going mad but she knew she couldn't go to his room, no matter how compelling the urge was to do so. She, Blossom and Suki had been drinking on the terrace, going over the events of the evening when shortly after midnight she heard Mark and Harry staggering through the gardens. They weren't alone. Susan and Sonia were with them and they all had their arms around one another.

The shock had been almost unbearable. As the four drunken revellers stumbled into the hotel without so much as a glance in her direction, Willa realised that they probably hadn't finished partying. She found herself wondering which the women Mark had taken to bed. Finally, she spent most of the night imagining all the wonderful things he would be doing to whichever one it was. Wonderful things that she wished more than anything, he was doing to her instead.

She trudged over to the table where Suki was having breakfast.

'Mind if I join you?' she asked.

'Not at all, honey. Shit. You look rough. Are you okay? I suppose that's a silly question isn't it?'

Willa sighed and nodded. 'I don't think I got one wink of sleep last night. I kept imagining ... well, I think you can guess what I kept imagining. I even considered going to his room and demanding he throw out whichever woman he was with and have sex with me instead. How insane is that?'

Suki chuckled. 'Sorry, honey, I didn't mean to laugh. I know it's not at all funny but I could just picture his face ... and hers. Mind you, I think he would have done just that. In fact, I'm almost certain he would have.'

Willa sneered. 'Yeah. To teach me a lesson probably. To show me just how bloody fantastic he is. Oh God, part of me can't wait to see him today to see how he reacts and to find out whether he did spend the night with one of the girls but ... part of me is dreading finding out that he definitely did. But I don't even know why I'm wondering about it. I saw them all staggering through the gardens. We all did. They certainly looked as if they were having a bloody good time. Of course he spent the night with one of them.'

'And yet,' Suki said, 'if he gave you the slightest indication that he'd spend tonight with you, you'd be waiting at his door, wouldn't you?'

Willa nodded. 'And that's the worst part of it. I'd be happy to accept any crumbs he throws me. Shit. I'm like a starving pigeon.'

'No, honey. You're just a girl in love. It drives us all a little mad.'

'It definitely does me,' Willa said, pouring herself a cup of coffee, drinking it in several gulps and then pouring another.

'The thing to do is to try to stay calm, honey. I know that's easier said than done. But what will be , will be and you must accept that. I was quite surprised at Mark's behaviour yesterday, to be honest and when I saw him last night, squeezed between Sonia and Susan, well ... it totally threw me, I can tell you. I didn't have him down as the kind of man who will go to bed with any available woman. Harry, yes, although he's a dear but Mark ... no.'

'Haven't you read that article about him in *Only The Best Will Do*? He slept with that woman and then left the next day without so much as a please or thank you.'

'What the article you 'doctored', you mean, honey? The one that's been the cause of most of this trouble. Yes, I read it. I think every red-blooded woman on the internet will have read it before long. That's where I first saw it. Anyway, that was different. When you're in that sort of situation, emotions are hyped. I think all single men would have done the same. This is different. Mark hasn't shown any interest in either of those girls until last night.'

'He's been flirting with them both since he arrived!' Willa said.

'I don't think he has, honey. Not really. Only when he thought you were watching. The rest of the time, he's just been cool and friendly and he's avoided being alone with either of them – and believe me, both of them made it very clear what was on offer. As lovely as those girls are, they didn't waste any time making their intentions clear.'

Willa let her head drop to her chest. 'That just makes it worse. He obviously took one of them to his room last night. Oh God, how am I going to get through the next two and a half days?'

'You'll manage. Although, if you're still going on that date that isn't a date thing with him this evening, I'd try to get some rest if I were you. You want to look your best, regardless of the outcome.'

Willa's head shot up. 'God! I'd forgotten about that. I ... I wonder if he'll cancel. Oh God, I'd better see if I can sneak back to the apartment at some stage today and get some sleep.'

'Don't look now, honey but Harry has just walked in ... with Susan and Sonia.'

Willa's back stiffened and she sat up straight. 'No Mark?'

Suki shook her head. 'No sign of him so far. Morning, Harry!' she yelled. 'Hope you slept well and there are no ill feelings about yesterday. It was all just a bit of fun really. Speaking of which, where's Mark? I haven't seen him yet this morning.'

Willa cringed and waited anxiously, turning just a fraction so that she could see Harry and the women.

Harry sauntered over to the table and beamed at them both whilst Susan and Sonia waved enthusiastically at Suki and Willa and went off in search of food from the breakfast buffet.

'Good morning, ladies. Actually, I didn't sleep at all. Those two gorgeous girls kept me awake all night. And I do mean all night, if you get my drift. Are you okay, Willa? You look ... a little less than your usually gorgeous self this morning. Did someone keep you up all night too?'

'She's got a bit of bug or something, haven't you, honey? So, do I take it from that that you spent the night with *both* of the girls? You are a devil, Harry.'

Harry winked. 'Well what can I say? Guilty as charged.'

'And ... and Mark?' Willa sounded as if she did have a bug. Her voice came out as a squeak.

'Mark? Oh, I see. Was he with us, you mean? No. He wanted to get a couple of hours sleep so he went to bed. Alone sadly for him ... but not for me. Morning Aristaios.'

Aristaios came over to the table and smiled sheepishly at Willa and Suki. 'Good morning. I hope all is well with us today.'

'Morning Aristaios,' Suki said. 'Yep. Everything is fine apart from the fact that Willa has a bug or some sort. She's not really at all herself. Are you, honey?'

Willa shook her head. That part was true at least. She definitely didn't feel at all herself.

'I am sorry to hear that, Willa. I hope you feel better soon. If there is anything I can get you, please just ask.'

'Thank you, Aristaios. And, I'm sorry about yesterday ... and the game we played.'

'No, I am sorry. We are all sorry, aren't we, Harry? It was wrong of us and we apologise. I hope you can find it in your heart to forgive three very foolish and very drunken men for doing such an appalling thing. It will never happen again. You have my word.'

'And mine,' Harry said. 'Although it was fun, I have to say. Speaking of fun, excuse me, people. My tag team awaits.' He jogged over to Susan and Sonia, whispered something to them and all three headed towards the lifts.

'Dear God,' Suki said. 'Where does the man get his energy from?'

'Willa,' Aristaios said, 'Mark asked me to give you this.' He held out his hand with an envelope in it.

Willa glanced from it to his face and back to the envelope again.

'I ... I don't understand. Is ... is it a complaint form or something?'

'Or something, I should think,' Aristaios replied.

She was utterly confused. Was he trying to avoid her at all costs? Even to lodge a complaint form ... or something. For one moment, one brief, crazy moment, she wondered if he did feel the same as her and he couldn't face her to say it, so he'd written it down instead. Was it ... a love letter?

'Why ... why couldn't he give it to me himself?'

'Because he is not here. He has gone.'

'Gone? Gone where? Sailing, do you mean?'

Aristaios' brows knit together. 'No. He has left. This morning. He took a taxi to the airport around three-thirty a.m. He had booked an eight-fifteen flight to the UK.'

The words didn't register. Gone. Left. Flown back to the UK. How could this be? What was Aristaios talking about? Was this another game? She glanced at her wrist but she still didn't have her watch.

203

'I must buy a new watch,' she said, unable to think clearly.

'I hope ... well, if there is anything I can do ... once you have read this, anything you need, please do not be afraid to ask. In spite of what I have done this week, I do care about you, Willa, as a friend.'

Aristaios smiled, a little sadly, Willa thought and left her and Suki alone.

'Do you want me to leave while you read it, honey? I'll go and sit somewhere else, if you like.'

'What?' Willa raised her eyes to Suki's and saw her concern. 'No. I ... I may need moral support, if that's okay with you?'

Suki reached out and squeezed her hand.

Willa smiled sheepishly. She tore open the envelope and unfolded the handwritten note. It read:

By the time you read this I'll be in a plane somewhere over Europe. I'm going to the Arctic to work with my dad on a documentary he's making. It was a spur of the moment decision and one I may live to regret although I don't think so. What I do regret though is the way I behaved towards you and for that, I sincerely apologise, from the bottom of my heart.

Despite what you obviously think of me, I'm not the womanising little shit you seem to think I am and when I kissed you that first time on Sunday it was because I genuinely wanted to. You took my breath away the minute I saw you at Athens airport and, to be honest, I think I went a bit crazy. That's not an excuse. I shouldn't have done it and I definitely shouldn't have entered into that wager. Again, I apologise.

I know none of this means anything to you and you probably couldn't care less but I just want you to know that I did like you, Willa. I liked you a lot. Far too much in fact and that's why I've left. I don't usually run away and believe it or not, I have been in real life- threatening situations and managed to stand my ground – and no, I'm not talking about the ones with Candice Cornwell. I mean really dangerous situations where I wasn't sure I'd come out alive.

And that's sort of how I felt about the situation I was in with you. It probably was all a game to you but it wasn't all a game to me. I really wanted you and that's a feeling I didn't like. I love what I do and I don't want to change my life for anyone or anything. I know that wasn't really an issue as far as you were concerned but if I hadn't left this morning, the next two days would have been very difficult for me. I don't want to get my heart broken and you almost did that when I discovered your performance was an act.

I don't know whether you did like me at all. I really thought at one point that you wanted me as much as I wanted you but I was probably wrong. In any event, it's better this way. I need to get out now before it's too late. If you do feel anything for me, then I'm sorry it has to end this way. I suspect you don't though, in which case you, Blossom and Suki can all read this and have a good laugh. That's fine.

Don't worry about the review. I've got enough detail to write it and I'll do that soon. It'll be on my blog if you want to read it - you can Google the web address – but I'll also send a copy to your dad as originally agreed. I'm pretty sure you won't be on the next plane back to Eastbourne.

I hope you have a hugely successful summer and that your sailing holidays go from strength to strength. I'm sure they'll be a huge hit. I also wish you true happiness, Willa. You can probably tell from my ramblings, that I'm a little bit drunk. It's three a.m. and I'm leaving in half an hour. Ridiculously, part of me wants to stay. I'll drop this into reception with a note to ask Aristaios to give it to you. Take care of yourself, Willa. It has been a pleasure – and a curse, to meet you.

Love, Mark.

She couldn't understand it and even though she read it

again three times, she still wasn't quite sure what he was telling her. She looked up at Suki and handed the note to her.

'Would you see if you can make sense of this because I definitely can't? He ... he seems to be saying that he left because he ... likes me. A lot. But that doesn't make sense because then why would he go? And he also seems to be saying that he thinks I don't like him although at one point he thought I did. Then he says that it wouldn't work anyway because he's not prepared to change his way of life so we're both better off just forgetting it and going our merry little ways. Or something along those lines ... I think.'

Suki raised her eyebrows and read the note.

'Hi,' Blossom said, hurriedly approaching the table. 'I may be wrong but I could have sworn I just saw Harry in the lift with Susan and Sonia and they were doing a lot more than pressing the button to close the lift door, if you get my meaning. Oh! What's wrong?'

'Mark's gone and he's left me a note.'

'Gone. Gone where?'

'Back to the UK. This morning. He left by taxi at three a.m.'

'Fuck!' Blossom said. 'That was about the time you were pacing around the kitchen, wasn't it? Who gave you the note? Did he leave it for you in reception?'

'No, he left it for Aristaios to give to me. Suki's reading it now. I can't make head or tail of it.'

'Can I read it after you, Suki?'

Suki handed Blossom the note. 'I could be wrong, honey,' she said. 'But I think Mark Thornton has fallen in love and he doesn't know what to do about it.'

'In love? W ...with me, you mean?'

'No, honey. The Goddess Aphrodite. Of course, with you.'

'But he can't have. I ... I think he did like me and perhaps even quite a lot but he definitely doesn't love me. I mean. Last night. All the things he said. The way he looked at me.'

'I think he was in a state of shock and was probably hurt. From what you told us afterwards, it got a bit passionate. There is nothing that will make a man act more irrationally than realising he's in love with a woman and then thinking she doesn't give a damn about him. Especially if he thought he was going to get the chance to ... show her exactly how he felt, shall we say?'

Blossom glanced up from reading the note. 'Screw the living daylights out of her, you mean? Sorry, Suki but one person in a time warp is quite enough, thanks. What? Don't look at me like that. I haven't got time for all that hearts and flowers stuff. Get to the point, that's my motto.'

'And you so often do,' Willa said, managing a smile in spite of the very real pain she felt in her heart since hearing of Mark's departure.

'Not often enough for my liking but I'm working on it.' Blossom continued reading the note and then looked up. 'Wow! I agree with Suki. The man's up shit creek without a paddle and he doesn't know how to swim.'

'Ever the romantic I see, honey,' Suki said.

Blossom shrugged. 'So are you going to reply?'

'Reply? What do you mean reply? There's no address.'

'Are you completely mad? Hellooo. This is the age of computers and emails, blogs and Twitter and Facebook. There are a million and one ways you can get in touch with someone without having their address. God, you even managed to realise that when you were eighteen and you cyber-stalked that arsehole rep who shagged you and dumped you.'

'Yes! Thank you, Blossom for sharing that with the world.'

'Oops! Sorry. I keep forgetting it's a secret. Suki won't tell, will you Suki?'

'Suki shook her head. 'Of course I won't. But I must admit to being interested in hearing the story. Of course, honey, if you'd rather not tell me I completely understand. But if you tell me your most embarrassing secret, I'll tell you mine. In fact, I'll tell you mine anyway. When I discovered my husband was having an affair I put itching powder in all his underpants. It gave him dermatitis and these really nasty lesions formed on his privates. I told him he must be allergic to the new washing powder I was using but I told my female friends at the gym that he'd got some awful sores 'down below' and that I thought he must be sleeping around because it looked like he'd got a sexually transmitted disease from someone.'

'Oh my God, Suki! That's the sort of thing I'd do,' Blossom said, laughing. 'We should have done something like that with the men instead of seducing them.'

'That's awful though,' Willa added, suppressing a giggle and forgetting about Mark for a few minutes. 'It must have really hurt.'

'I bloody well hope so, honey. He hurt me. All's fair in love and war.'

'But didn't he go to the doctor's?' Blossom said.

'Yes. But he told the doctor what I'd said about the washing powder and because it was dermatitis, the doctor thought that was what had caused it, so he gave him some cream. It cleared up after a while because I bought him new underpants and threw the old ones out – just in case. I still like to think of how many weeks of sex he missed because of that. I do sometimes feel a little guilty – but not often.'

'Okay,' Willa said. 'I was on my first season as a holiday rep. It was in Spain – Marbella, to be precise. I was eighteen and there was a rep there from another company. He was twenty-two and drop-dead gorgeous. He offered to show me the ropes and being the idiot that I am, I fell for him and believed all the spiel he was feeding me. This was my first time and ... well I wanted to do anything to please him – as you do.'

'Don't we know it, honey? The things we do for men.'

'That's true. Well, one day he said he'd always wanted

208

to have sex outdoors in a particularly idyllic part of the gardens of the hotel where we were working. It was a fairly secluded spot so like a complete twit, I agreed. I had no idea that he'd been given a written warning already for having sex with another young rep from his own employers. Anyway, we were seen by several holiday guests, one of whom sent a complaint form to my dad. I'm still not sure whether he was more concerned about the fact that I was having sex with someone or that it had meant him receiving a holiday complaint form. The guy left the next day.'

'Tell her about the cyber-stalking,' Blossom said.

Willa sighed. 'It wasn't really that bad. I thought he'd been sacked because of me so I sent him an email saying I'd talk to my dad and tell him we were in love. I said I'd sort it all out and get him a job with us. He didn't reply so I sent another one, then another then ... Well, you get the picture. I sent about forty emails and texts, I think until I finally got one back. Only it wasn't from him. It was from his fiancée telling me to leave her fiancé alone and that she'd contacted my employers – basically, my dad. I had a bit of a 'drowning my sorrows' session and needless to say, Dad dragged me home to Eastbourne and I wasn't allowed to do another season for a couple of years. I haven't mixed business with pleasure since.'

'Until now,' Blossom said.

'Until now.' Willa felt the rush of pain anew.

Suki shook her head. 'Men. Some of them really know how to screw us, the little darlings. And I don't mean in a good way.'

'I kept telling her she should have had a few flings long ago – just to get it out of her system but she wouldn't,' Blossom added.

'Are you saying that he's the only man you've had sex with, honey?'

'No! Just the only one during a summer season. I've had boyfriends back in Eastbourne. Some lasted a few years, some not very long but I just can't handle the whole 'quick fling with no emotions involved' bit. I'm afraid I go into relationships hoping they'll last. Stupid I know.'

'It's not stupid, honey. As much as I'd like to pretend otherwise, I'm the same. And my ex-husband *is* the only man I've ever slept with.'

Willa didn't know who was more surprised. Her or Blossom.

CHAPTER TWENTY-SIX

'So. Do you want to talk about it yet? Or would you rather continue stomping around here like a polar bear with a sore head?' James Thornton asked.

Mark glanced across at his father. He hadn't told his dad why he'd had the sudden change of heart and decided to join him, and his father hadn't asked. He'd just said that something had come up and he would be joining him after all.

'Have I been that bad?'

James shrugged. 'Let's just say you're not your usual cheery, happy-go-lucky, self. Is it a woman?'

Mark smirked. 'What makes you think it's just one?'

'Because if there were several, you wouldn't be bothered. It's always the one that gets us every time.'

'The one?'

'Yes, son. The one.'

Mark dragged his hands through his hair and then held them out in front of the stove.

'I thought it was supposed to get warm here in the spring? I'm freezing.'

'Freezing? It was a balmy two degrees centigrade out there today and it's as warm as toast in here now. Here, drink this.' James handed Mark a mug of coffee and topped it up with a large dash of brandy.

'Cold toast maybe,' Mark said. 'Don't forget I was basking in temperatures of twenty-five degrees or more just three days ago.'

'And the attentions of a woman I'm assuming. If you're not ready to talk about it, that's fine but holding it in isn't helping you or anyone else. We're here for four more weeks, son and personally, I don't want to have to keep staring at that miserable expression on your face for another twenty-eight days.'

Mark sighed. 'I don't know where to start, Dad.'

'The beginning is as good a place as any. We've got all night and plenty more coffee and brandy. What's her name for a start?'

'It's Willa, Wilhelmina Daventry.'

'The daughter? Didn't you say it was Daventry Travel Sailing Solo Holidays or something?'

Mark nodded. 'Yeah. The singles sailing holidays were her idea.'

'I take it she's single then. Although that doesn't necessarily follow, of course.'

Mark smirked. 'No. But she is. At least ... I assume she is. D'you know, Dad, that hadn't even occurred to me. That she might have a boyfriend back in the UK, I mean.'

'Surely she would have told you?'

'I'm not sure she would have. I'm not sure of anything about her, to be honest. I'm not sure if she pretended to like me to get a good review. I'm not sure if she pretended not to like me to get me to want her all the more. Not that I could've wanted her much more than I did. I'm not sure that is humanly possible.' He sighed loudly.

'I'm not sure you're making much sense, son. Let's start again, shall we? You arrived at Athens airport and then ...?'

'I think I fell in love. Only I didn't realise I had. I just thought she was stunning and I'd been ...'

'Stunned,' James said facetiously.

'Knocked for six. Is ... is that how you felt about Mum when you first saw her?'

'Good God no! I hated the woman on sight.'

'Are you joking?'

'Nope. I'm serious. I absolutely hated her. And as you know, I don't hate many people. I think that should have been a warning to run, not walk away from her but we rarely listen to what our head tells us when it comes to matters of the heart.'

'So ... how did you go from hating her to loving her?'

'I really have no idea. We were on a camping trip with

212

some mutual friends. A big group of us, and all the woman did was moan. The ground was too hard. The sleeping bag scratched. There were insects in the tents. The food wasn't edible. And the funniest – she had nowhere to plug in her heated curlers.' He chuckled at the memory. 'Actually, now that I come to think of it, why did I fall in love with her? We were total opposites from the very beginning.'

'They say opposites attract.'

'They say a lot of things and most of them are rubbish. I think what did it for me was the fact that she seemed so vulnerable. Well that and the fact that she had a body to die for. Sorry, Mark. I don't suppose you want to hear that about your own mother but Jesus, that woman could cause a bush fire just by walking past a twig.'

'Mum told me the sex was pretty good between you.'

'She said that? Praise indeed. When were you and she discussing the ancient history of our sex life?'

'A few days ago. She was telling me that I grow more like you by the day. Then she said she'd read that article in *Only The Best Will Do* and no, before you ask, she wasn't reading a pseudo travel mag. The women at her spa read it out to her. Anyway, she said I was a devil – only in a semi-complimentary way. I facetiously asked if I was like you in that way too and she said that yes, as loathe as she was to admit it, you were very good in that department.'

James roared with laughter. 'God. I bet that was like pulling a tooth as far as she was concerned, to pay me a compliment. Assuming it was a compliment. You never can tell with your mother.'

'Do ... do you still care about her, Dad? Even after everything?'

James ran his hands through his hair and Mark realised that he'd got that habit from his father too.

'I care that she's okay and I want her to be happy but I don't love her. That faded a long, long time ago. It took me a while to get over it as you well know, but after a couple of years, the pain and the feelings of betrayal subsided. Then I thought about her less and less. We still spoke, mainly about you of course but we had little to do with one another. I haven't seen her since just before she remarried. So that's twenty years, I think you said she'd been married. She'll always be the mother of my child though. So anyway, tell me about Willa and why you ran away from her – or did she tell you to go?'

Mark told his father the whole story from first seeing her at the airport, right the way through to the night he decided to leave.

'Well,' James said when he'd finished, 'you certainly ballsed that up, didn't you, son? What were you thinking? Making a bet over a woman. I'm surprised she didn't castrate you – although in a way I guess she has. You're useless as far as any other woman is concerned now. Until you get over her at least.'

'Thanks for the support, Dad. I don't think I believed in love at first sight but I sure as hell do now. It's ridiculous though. I don't really know anything about her. How can I possibly be in love with her? Shit. I hope I get over this pretty damn quick.'

'We all get over love eventually, Mark. And you don't have to know someone to fall in love with them. But I don't know why you won't give it a chance. If you feel that strongly about her, why did you run away like a wounded animal?'

'Because that's exactly how I felt. I couldn't face her again. I didn't want to face her again. I didn't like what I was feeling. I needed time to think and if I'd seen her again, even for just a minute, I thought I might say something I'd regret and make an even bigger fool of myself than I had already.'

'Well, whatever you decide, you know I'll always back you up but part of me feels you got what you deserved. I mean, Jesus, son – a wager! Oh well. At least you didn't lose, I suppose. Although again, I guess you did and rather heavily by the looks of you. So are you going back?'

214

'Back? To Greece you mean?'

'No, to Uzbekistan. Of course to Greece.'

Mark shook his head. 'No way. What's the point?'

'Now that I'm sorry to say is your mother talking. The point my boy, is that you love her. And if you love her, isn't it worth spending some time to find out if she feels anything for you? From what you've told me, I'd say she does. She doesn't sound like the sort of woman who would sleep with you to get a five-star review, so you can dismiss that idea. But she does sound like the sort of woman who wants a long-term relationship and not just a holiday romance.'

'And that's the problem. Okay, let's just say she feels something for me and we start dating. She's based in Greece all summer and I'll be in about six different countries between now and October. Then she goes back to the UK for the rest of the year and again, I'm all over the place. How could we ever make that work? That's what tore you and Mum apart. She was left at home and she started looking for attention elsewhere. I couldn't bear that. It was bad enough as a kid. I couldn't bear to have my heart ripped out by the woman I loved.'

'Like your mother ripped mine out, you mean?' James shook his head. 'It wasn't the absences that tore us apart, Mark. Your mother never loved me as much as I loved her. It's true, and I think I always knew that. Plus, your mother didn't want that life. She wanted to be the party hostess, to have cocktail dresses and diamonds and a glamorous lifestyle. I never wanted any of that. You've got to stop comparing women with her. Willa works in the travel business, so you've got that in common. She's thirty-two you said, so she's obviously had relationships before. Do you know why they ended?'

Mark shook his head. 'We haven't talked about it other than when she said she'd had hundreds of men.'

'Yes. Well, that probably isn't true. Would it bother you if she had?'

215

'Of course not. The past wouldn't bother me. It's if she had hundreds in the future that I'd have a problem with.'

'But the past does bother you, Mark. It haunts you. You keep worrying that you'll fall in love with a woman, have a family and then she'll up and leave you like your mother left us. Not every woman is like your mother. In fact, I'd go as far as to say that very few women are like your mother so for fuck's sake, son, will you please let it go! Enough is enough. If I can get over it, then it's about time you did.'

Mark was surprised by his father's outburst. 'Okay, Dad! So much for support.'

'This is support. Don't let the best thing that has happened to you in your life be ruined by some stupid theory that no woman can adapt to our lifestyle. They can and do. Besides, if you love her enough, you won't want to travel so much. Have you never wondered why I was only too happy to get another assignment? Your mother and I just couldn't get on if we were together for more than a few weeks at a time. That didn't mean I didn't love her. I just couldn't live with her but the truth of the matter is I didn't really love her enough. Not enough to want to change my life for her and she certainly didn't love me enough to change hers.'

'But ... you were heartbroken when she left.'

'I was devastated, yes. I was left with a young boy to look after and although I would have stopped travelling for you, I needed the money. The divorce cost me and I was having a few financial problems before that. That's another reason your mother left. Anyway, I did still love her, so yes, I was heartbroken but do you know what? Part of me was glad I wouldn't have to go through all the rows. But the guilt. That was part of the reason it took me so long to come to terms with it. I felt so guilty for not trying harder, for your sake.'

'Wow, Dad. I had no idea.'

'Yes, well, that's clearly another thing you get from me. We never reveal our true feelings until it's much too late. I think you should go back to Greece and tell Willa how you feel. You've faced polar bears and killer whales. Snakes and poisonous spiders. Wolves and Grizzlies. You've even had an article written about you in *Only The Best Will Do*. Telling a woman you love her should be a walk in the park compared to that.'

'Do you know what, Dad? I'd rather face ten polar bears and everything else at the same time than do that.'

CHAPTER TWENTY-SEVEN

Willa was dreading telling her father that Mark had left so she was both surprised and relieved when her dad emailed her on Thursday lunchtime, just a few hours after Mark would have caught his flight. He told her he had received an email from Mr Thornton explaining that he had had to leave earlier than expected to help his father on a documentary but that it wouldn't affect his being able to do the review.

She was even more surprised when he called her two days later on the Saturday when Mark should have actually left.

'Wilhelmina, my darling,' he said. 'I'm calling to congratulate you. I am absolutely thrilled and this is only your first week.'

The fact that he was congratulating her was astonishing. It was something he'd never done before and as for him being thrilled, well, that was a word used only for high days and holidays.

'Thanks, Dad,' she said, lost for words.

'I've discussed it with Daniel and we both agree that we will leave the running of the Sailing Solo holidays to you from now on. I have complete faith in your abilities, Wilhelmina. We will, of course, be on hand if you feel you want to run something by us but you can make all the day-to-day decisions and I'll leave you to handle the negotiations with Mr Nikolades for next season. You're more than capable.'

She thought she must be dreaming. 'Wow! Thanks, Dad. I promise I won't let you down. Will ... will there definitely be a next season then?'

'I should say so, darling. We're already taking advanced bookings. Oh, and I'm increasing your advertising budget. Not that you'll need to advertise at this rate but it helps to spread the name of the company and our other holidays, so I think we should do it.'

Willa collapsed in her chair. She was amazed that she hadn't passed out.

'And I love your idea of using social media and a tongue-in-cheek video. What was the name of the young man you are working with on that? Harry something?'

Harry had offered to sort out the video for her by way of an apology, which had also left her speechless.

'Harry Bullen, Dad.' She couldn't believe this and she had to push her luck. 'He's about Daniel's age and he's very good-looking.'

There was just the slightest hesitation before he responded. 'There's nothing wrong with that, Wilhelmina. As long as he's good at what he does and you trust him, that's good enough for me.'

Okay, she thought. Now I'm worried. Has he lost his mind? She decided to phone Daniel as soon as she could and ask him if their father had hit his head or something.

'And the icing on the cake, darling, is that the phones have been ringing non-stop with people eager to book after reading Mr Thornton's review and recommendation and it's only been public since last night, or so his email says. I assume you've got a copy of it.'

Willa nearly fell off her chair. 'Er ... I haven't seen it yet, Dad. Perhaps he forgot to email it to me. Would you get someone to send me a copy, please? I ... I take it it's good then?'

'I'll send you a copy right now. He has an odd style but Daniel says that's how the young chap writes. He has nothing but praise for the holiday and for you and your team. You must have made him very happy, Wilhelmina. Well done. I couldn't be more pleased. We'll have a lavish celebration when you come home at the end of the season. Anywhere you want to go. Absolutely anywhere.'

'Thank you, Dad.'

Willa could feel the tears pricking at the corners of her

eyes. This was too much. It was all too much. She'd been dreaming of this moment ever since she was eighteen and yet, now that it was here, as wonderful as it was, she'd give it all up just to see Mark and one of his lopsided grins again.

'Well, I'll let you get on, Wilhelmina. Congratulations again my darling and if there's anything you want, just ask me.'

'Dad. There is one thing I'd love.'

Anything, darling. You name it.'

'Do you think you could start calling me, Willa? Everyone else does. I like Wilhelmina but it sounds so ... so formal.'

'Of course I can, dar ... Willa. Oh yes, I rather like the sound of that. Willa it is then. Bye for now ... Willa. I love you, sweetheart.'

That was it. It was official. Her father had clearly lost his mind.

***

Willa sat at her desk pondering the conversation she'd just had. She heard her email ping and her heart raced. That would be the copy of Mark's review. She needed a drink – and Blossom by her side, if she was going to read it and she had to be quick. The guests would be leaving in an hour to go to Athens airport and the next party of guests would be arriving.

She sat up and dialled Blossom's number.

'Get in here quick, please and grab Suki if you can. I've just got a copy of Mark's review of his holiday.'

Blossom and Suki appeared in under a minute.

'We were having a coffee on the terrace,' Blossom said. 'So come on then. What does it say?'

'I haven't read it. Dad's just sent it to me. Oh, and you won't believe the conversation I've just had with him. I don't believe it and I was a party to it.'

220

'Was he pleased or furious?' Blossom asked. 'Your dad, I mean.'

'Pleased. Thrilled, in fact.'

'Gosh, honey. Mark must have given you a very good review,' Suki said.

'Will one of you read it please? I don't think I can.'

'Give it here,' Blossom said, perching on the edge of Willa's desk. She took the laptop Willa passed her. 'Okay, this is it.'

Then she read out the review, which said:

I must be honest, I wasn't particularly looking forward to spending a week in Greece on a Sailing Solo Holiday courtesy of Daventry Travel. I'm not a fan of the singles holiday concept although I'd never actually been on one until now. I've sailed around the Greek islands so I felt I'd 'been there, done that' and I know the Peloponnese peninsula as well as I know the ingredients of pure Greek yoghurt.

Imagine my surprise when I discovered that, not only was I having fun, I was having one of the most memorable holiday experiences of my – up to now – entire life. So, how wrong was I with my preconceived idea of a singles sailing holiday? Completely and utterly, off the sailing chart, one hundred per cent, wrong. Let me tell you why.

Nestled between the golden sand beaches of the bay of Argolis and the hills of the Argolida district clad in heavenly scented pine trees, sits the picturesque fishing village of Kritiopoli. A village as traditionally Greek as the aged olive trees surrounding it, this is a place to take a leisurely stroll through the narrow streets framed by whitewashed houses. The air is heavy with perfume from a kaleidoscope of brightly coloured flowers hanging at every door and the grey, rain-soaked streets of the UK are soon but a distant memory. Sit awhile at a table overlooking the bay on a peaceful, late afternoon and enjoy a glass of ouzo whilst a gentle breeze from a cloudless sky cools your sun-kissed skin.

Less than two kilometres away, you'll find the haven of tranquillity that is the Argolis Bay Hotel. Built by Niko Nikolades for his artist wife, Sara, in the 1960s and now owned and run by his grandson, Aristaios Nikolades, who looks more like a film star than an hotelier, this stunning building perches above the bay in gardens filled with olives, figs and prickly pear trees. The vista from each of the forty spacious and airy bedrooms is simply breathtaking.

You are assured of a warm welcome at the Argolis Bay Hotel and a week spent here relaxing by the pool or swimming in the calm, clear waters of the bay will make your daily grind feel like ancient history.

Speaking of ancient history, if that's your thing, you'll be spoilt for choice as the drive down from Athens airport reveals one famous landmark after another. From Olympia, where the first games were held in 776 BC to Nafplio, which is surely one of the most beautiful and romantic cities in the whole of Greece; the theatre at Epidavros, which seats fourteen thousand people and is used to this day for the Epidavros Festival held in July and August. These are but a few of the treasures on offer. The area is steeped in them and even the most cynical of you will be transported back to a time when men knew the meaning of the word 'hero' and the gods fought their battles over this paradise on earth.

Let's not forget Corinth, where the myth and majesty of the ancient city meets modern day madness at the Corinth Canal. Begun by the Emperor Nero in AD 67 and completed by a French company in 1893, the Canal is a sight not to be missed either at ground level or from one of the bridges high above. You can even bungee jump from the specially constructed tower at a heart-stopping, gravity-pulling seventy-nine metres. It is classed as one of the top ten bungee jumps in the world and if you're so inclined, you are guaranteed the thrill of a lifetime. For those of you who prefer your feet on the ground, stand and wait for a ship to pass through. You'll be holding your breath as every sized vessel from a simple sailing dinghy to a gleaming cruise ship passes within a hair's breadth of the limestone walls.

After a day walking in the footsteps of the gods, or pretending you're immortal by throwing yourself off a bridge, you can be sure you will dine like the gods. Fresh fish caught that morning in the balmy waters of the Gulf of Argolis or the Aegean Sea, prepared by expert hands before being delivered to your table. Local wines that taste as they did in the days of Dionysus. Figs plucked from the tree, their skins still warm from the sun and oranges so rich and fresh you won't have tasted their like before. The place is a veritable cornucopia of ambrosial delights that will awaken your micro-wave-numbed palate.

I came for the sailing and I was not disappointed. Run by Loukas Diamantidis, another film star lookalike – there must be something in the water around here. He and his team make Jason and the Argonauts look like boys playing with toy boats. His patience with beginners and expert tuition, coupled with sound and knowledgeable advice given to those more experienced, leaves nothing to chance. Whether you are looking for a few hours bobbing about on the water or the thrill of racing under sail, you'll find it here. There's a large selection of boats but if windsurfing, kitesurfing or even bodysurfing are more to your liking, you'll be able to do those too. The winds here are perfect for sailing. This bay is sheltered from the Meltemi – the summer wind that often affect much of the Aegean, causing sailors to seek shelter and ferries to stay in harbour. You'll be tacking, gybing and trimming your sails whilst others are sitting about and tapping their toes.

Back on dry land, Wilhelmina (Willa) Daventry, who runs the holidays and her colleague Blossom Appleyard, who will give you the best Pilates workout you are likely to experience, deserve a special mention. Their warm smiles and 'can do' attitudes ensure that guests want for nothing and from the moment I arrived until the second I left, I felt that I was amongst friends. They pulled out all the stops to make my holiday an experience I can honestly say I will never forget. And I know that I'm not alone in saying that. They're pretty good to look at too, guy. In fact, I wouldn't be at all surprised if the Goddess Aphrodite has taken human form and called herself Willa, whilst Blossom, I think would give Athena a run for her money. Willa, in particular, has a professional, hands-on approach that raises the bar for all others to aspire to, as far as I'm concerned.

I could spend hours extolling the virtues and pleasures of a Daventry Travel's Sailing Solo Holiday – but I won't. Instead, I suggest or rather, recommend that you go to their website or pick up the phone and book without delay. Holidays like this are few and far between. Grab your bag and get on the next available flight, especially if you're aged between twenty and fifty, free and single. This is the playground of the gods, and as we all know, the gods knew a thing or two about how to have a good time.

Don't just take my word for it. Go see for yourself. I can promise that you'll be very glad you did. And tell Willa I said, Thanks.

The holiday demands a five-star review. I would give it more if I could.

'Wow! Blossom exclaimed, meeting Willa's eyes. 'What's wrong with you? You don't look very pleased.'

'What does he mean, "And tell Willa I said, Thanks"? I told you he was sarcastic. He just had to have a dig at me, didn't he? He couldn't just let it go.'

'Whoa. Hold your horses. I think it's a really good review and "Thanks" is great, especially when you bear in mind what he could have said. You should be really happy,' Blossom said.

'Happy! What? With all that drivel about Aphrodite? He said I look nothing like her and now he's saying I do. And I'll give him "hands-on approach". If I ever see him again, he'll really get to see my hands-on approach – as I'm strangling the life out of him!'

'I think he's paying you a compliment, honey,' Suki said, 'but he's also sending you a message. He's got it bad. I'm certain of that. He just doesn't know how to tell you.'

'Well, I think leaving in the middle of the night told me all I needed to know and those drunken ramblings confirmed it. He's happy with his life the way it is and he doesn't plan to change it, for me or anyone else. I just hope, for his sake and mine that I never hear that sarcastic voice or see that lopsided grin of his ever again!'

CHAPTER TWENTY-EIGHT

Willa now had a routine. Every morning as soon as she woke up, she repeated her regular mantra, 'I am over Mark Thornton'. So far it hadn't worked, and today was no exception she realised as she sat at her desk reading Mark's latest blog update. Oh well, she thought, it has only been one hundred and thirty-nine days. Not that she was counting.

She hoped that by the time she returned to the UK she might have achieved her goal but as that was in only seven days' time she felt she was probably doomed to failure. Perhaps it would be easier once she was back in Eastbourne. Everything here reminded her of him. Everywhere she looked, she thought she saw him. Every time she heard the name Mark, her heart skipped a beat. She still couldn't believe how many guests there had been over the summer with that name. It was as if the gods were conspiring against her.

Neither could she believe the summer was over. Today she and Blossom would take the last guests of the season back to Athens airport and then return to the apartment for one more week. They would have some time to relax and do some final paperwork before packing their things and heading home.

She reminded herself that she had achieved her goal. The Sailing Solo Holidays was now a very successful part of Daventry Travel's business and they were already more than half full with advanced bookings for next year. Her father had been true to his word and allowed her to renegotiate the deal with Aristaios. He'd been thrilled when she managed to get a better one than he had, mainly due to the fact that the Sailing Solo guests had proved far more lucrative for Aristaios and Loukas than they had first anticipated and they could afford some leeway.

Willa knew she should be happy but she wasn't. She was beginning to wonder if she ever would be again.

'Where is he today then?' Blossom asked, handing Willa a cup of coffee.

'Who?'

Blossom tutted. 'Don't be an idiot. I know you're reading his blog. It's the first thing you do every single day even if he hasn't posted an update.'

Willa sighed. 'He's still in Norway. It looks absolutely beautiful from the photos he's posted. I've never been to Norway, have you?'

'No. And if you're thinking of setting up sailing holidays there, count me out. It looks permanently cold. I know it isn't, before you start giving me a lecture on the Norwegian climate. I'm just saying it looks it.' She perched on the edge of Willa's desk and gave her a concerned look.

'What?' Willa said.

'Why do you do this to yourself? Why do you read his blog and his articles when it hurts you so much? And don't say it doesn't because I know it does. You haven't been the same since that bloody man came here and then did a runner like some pathetic little wimp.'

'He's not a wimp! You should see the things he does. And I don't just mean the wildlife documentaries and stuff. He was with his dad in the Arctic after he left here and all through June. Then he was climbing in Switzerland in July, skiing in New Zealand in August, tagging whales with some marine ecologists in Alaska in September and now he's writing about a cruise of the Norwegian Fjords.'

'The man certainly gets around, I'll give him that. No wonder he hasn't got time for a real relationship. He doesn't stand still for long enough. It's pointless thinking about him, Willa. I agree with what Suki says about that. That's what he meant in that note he left. It wasn't that he didn't want to have a relationship with you. It was that he *couldn't* have a relationship with you – or anyone for that matter – because he does so much travelling. It would never

227

work'

'I know. But that doesn't stop me wondering about it. I'm still not sure that was what he was saying in that note though. I'm not sure he wanted to have any sort of relationship with me.'

'Well, you'd know that better than us. You read that every day too.'

'I don't! Not every day. In fact, I haven't read it for almost a week. I know. It's pathetic. It's even worse than when I was eighteen.'

'Except you haven't sent Mark even one text or email. You haven't even posted a thank you on the comments on his blog for that review he gave you. I know. Don't tell me again. You got Daniel to send him a thank you email. I still think you should have at least acknowledged it. That's all I'm saying.'

'I couldn't, Blossom. If I'd started writing even one word to him, I would have ended up pouring my heart out and I couldn't do that.'

'Yeah, I know. Anyway. We're leaving for the airport in about half an hour. I'm really looking forward to seeing Suki again. She's texted me to say her flight's on time so she'll be there when we arrive.'

'I can't believe she wanted to come back after the week she had with us. Although she's not with Sailing Solo this week, of course, so I suppose that's a bit different. It will be good to see her, you're right. Emailing, texting and posting on Facebook isn't the same somehow. I'm dying to hear about this guy she's been emailing. Do you know anything about him?'

Blossom shook her head. 'No, she's being very secretive about it but she said she'd tell us when she gets here, so we'll know soon enough. Right. I've got a couple of things to do so I'll see you on the coach. And will you turn that bloody thing off. Let's see if we can get through the rest of the day without thinking about Mark Thornton, shall we?'

Mark's eyes scanned the arrivals hall even though he told himself he was being stupid. The last time he'd been here was exactly twenty-two weeks ago when Willa had been waiting for him. He could still see her standing there, holding a piece of paper with his name on and as he'd walked up to her he kept saying to himself, 'That *cannot* be Wilhelmina Daventry.' Well, she wouldn't be here this time, thank God.

He turned to his father. 'Did you say we're hiring a car or that your friend is meeting us? I'm so jetlagged I can barely remember which country I'm in, let alone what you told me on the phone last night.'

'My friend's meeting us. She should be around here somewhere.'

Mark dropped his bag on the floor. He stretched his long frame and ran his hands through his hair. 'I could sleep for a week,' he said. 'Have we got time to grab a coffee? I need something to help me stay awake. Good God! It can't be!'

Mark thought he must be more exhausted than he suspected. It seemed he was now imagining things. That couldn't possibly be Suki Thane standing just a few feet away and beaming at him.

'Is it you, Suki? It is, isn't it? Sorry, I'm shattered and not really with it. How the hell are you? What are you doing here?'

He walked towards her as he spoke and when he reached her he held out his hand but she threw her arms around him and kissed him on the cheek.

'Hello, Mark. How lovely to see you. You do look as if you could use a good night's sleep, I have to say. Still you've been so busy, haven't you? I follow your blog, you know.'

'Really? That's good of you. Oh, sorry. Suki, this is my dad, James. Dad, this is Suki Thane. She ... she was on that sailing holiday I told you about. The one I did the review for.'

Suki and James smiled at one another and Mark was surprised to see his father take both of Suki's hands in his and kiss her on both cheeks. That was something he only did to people he knew really well.

'Hello, Suki,' James said. 'It's lovely to finally meet you and I have to say, you look even better in the flesh.'

'It's lovely to meet you too, James. And the same goes for you.'

Mark tried to figure out what they were talking about. The words, 'finally meet' and 'better in the flesh' seemed to suggest that they weren't the complete strangers he'd assumed they were but he couldn't think for the life of him how they could possibly know one another. He noticed his dad was still holding Suki's hands. How very odd, he thought.

He didn't know why but he suddenly had the strangest feeling that something was going on. He realised he hadn't asked his father for details of the urgent assignment he'd called and asked Mark to join him on. All his dad had told him was that it was in Greece and it was a rush job. He said he needed Mark to make up the numbers and although Mark had only just got back from Norway four hours earlier, he'd unpacked his bag, repacked it with clean clothes and headed straight to Heathrow airport where his father was waiting.

'Why do I get the feeling I'm missing something?' Mark asked.

'Not something, son. Someone. And unless I'm very much mistaken, here she is.'

Mark heard Blossom's voice first. She was calling out 'Hello' to Suki. He had his back to her but he knew from the look Suki gave him that Willa wasn't far behind. He turned around just in time to see the look of horror turn to surprise and then ... to anger on the face of the woman he'd been unable to forget, in spite of his very best efforts.

'You! What are you doing here?' she said.

'Hello, Willa,' Mark said. 'I'm actually just asking myself the same question.'

He tried to look away from her to his father but his eyes seemed to be fixed like glue on her flushed face. Her skin had a deeper tan than when he'd seen her last but her cheeks still displayed the red bloom of anger. Her hazel eyes flashed and those lovely soft lips that he could still taste when he was alone in his bed, wore a definite scowl.

Willa's eyes darted from him to Suki to Blossom and then to James.

'Hello,' James said. 'You must be Willa. I've heard a lot about you. I'm James Thornton, Mark's father. I'm very pleased to meet you.'

He held out his hand to her and she took it although she looked as if she had no idea what she was doing, Mark thought.

'H ... hello,' she said. 'Um. Sorry. Yes, it's lovely to meet you too. Er ... do you know Suki?'

'Yes,' James said. 'Although this is the first time we've met face to face. We've been emailing and we've had several chats via Skype.'

Mark noticed that Willa glared at Blossom as if she were accusing her of something.

'Okay,' Mark said. 'Perhaps someone would like to explain to me what's going on here. And very slowly please, so that I can take it in. My brain doesn't appear to be functioning properly at the moment.'

'It's really very simple, son,' James said. 'I thought you needed a holiday so I've booked us both a week at the Argolis Bay Hotel. Well, it sounded so good from your review. Suki's staying there too and I believe all your guests have gone, Willa, so other than 'tidying up', you've got a week off too. Oh, sorry. You must be Blossom. Hello.'

Blossom burst out laughing. 'Hello, James. It's good to meet you,' she said. 'Well, well, Suki. It seems like you're the one playing games now.'

231

***

'I see we're taking the motorway,' Mark said when they were all in Willa's car heading towards Kritiopoli.

Due to more game playing on Suki and his father's part, he was sitting in the front with Willa who was driving. His dad, Suki and Blossom were squeezed in the back. Not that Suki or his dad seemed to mind one bit. Unless he was very much mistaken, there was a romance starting to bud. They both looked half in love with one another already.

Not that he was an expert on love, of course. He'd made a complete mess of his love life and now, just when he'd started to think that possibly, in several more months, he'd be able to stop wondering what Willa was doing or what she was wearing or who she was with, here he was right back at square one.

'What?' Willa said.

'I said I see we're taking the motorway.'

'Yes. It's the fastest route to Kritiopoli – unless you want me to drop you at Stavros' and you can make your own way down later.'

'No, no. That's fine with me. The sooner we get there the better. I can't wait to slide between the sheets.'

Willa's head shot round and her mouth fell open.

'What did you say?' Willa asked, clearly astonished.

Mark had to grab the wheel and yank it towards him to stop her veering off the road.

'And I'd quite like to get there in one piece. Are you having trouble with your hearing today? I said I can't wait to go to bed.'

'I heard what you said quite clearly, thank you. And there is nothing wrong with my hearing, I assure you.'

'Then why did you ask me what I said – twice?'

'Because ... because I can't believe that you've only been here for half an hour and you're already flirting with me again! I don't hear from you in five months and the first thing you do is proposition me! You really are a piece of work, Mark.'

Mark frowned, trying to understand how she thought he was propositioning her.

'Oh! You thought I meant I couldn't wait to slide between the sheets with you. Well, I'm sorry to disappoint you, Willa but that was the last thing on my mind. I've been travelling almost nonstop for months now and I'm absolutely knackered. I only got back from Norway last night and I was up at the crack of dawn to get the flight here. All I want to do is sleep – for a week.'

Willa sucked in a huge breath. 'I am not disappointed, believe me. I just assumed you were up to your old tricks again, that's all. A leopard doesn't change its spots. I wonder how many women you've kissed in the Arctic, Switzerland, New Zealand, Alaska and Norway. And you can do whatever you like this week. I'll make sure I stay out of your way, that's for sure. I really don't know why you even came here.'

'You've been following me,' Mark said, grinning. A flicker of hope sparked inside him. 'As to why I'm here, your guess is as good as mine. I thought I was coming here on an assignment. I had no intention of seeing you. In fact, I was really hoping I wouldn't. And for your information, I haven't kissed even one woman since I left here. Not one. And I've had offers, believe me.'

'I do believe you. I'm sure women everywhere just fall at your feet, don't they? I'm sure they're all just hoping for the magnificent Mark Thornton to take them in his arms and ravage them.'

'Ravage them? Don't tell me you're still reading Candice Cornwell articles?'

Willa looked him full in the face.

'Why? Has she written another one about you? Have ... have you seen her again?'

'No. I haven't seen her again. Why on earth would I want to see her again? God. I haven't even thought about her once since I left here, until just now. I don't even know why I did then. I must be more tired than I thought. It's just that ravage is the sort of word she'd use, that's all.'

'Sometimes Willa forgets what century she's in,' Blossom piped up from the back seat.

Both Mark and Willa's heads shot round as if they were surprised to find her there. Mark grabbed at the wheel again.

'Will you please keep your eyes on the road, Willa? Are you trying to kill us all?'

'I'd quite like to kill one of us,' she hissed.

'What was that?' Mark asked.

'Something wrong with your hearing?'

'No. There's nothing wrong with my hearing.' His brain seemed to be waking up and he remembered something she'd said. 'It's ... magnificent, like the rest of me, according to you. For God's sake, Willa. The road!'

'Okay,' James said. 'That's enough you two. As amusing as this is for the rest of us, I really don't think you should be having this discussion whilst Willa's driving. May I suggest that I take over and you sit in the back? I'm sure you're an excellent driver, Willa but your mind does seem to be elsewhere at the moment.'

Mark saw Willa's hands tighten on the wheel and he thought she was going to argue. Instead, she indicated and pulled over.

'Fine,' she said. 'I'll sit in the back and you can drive, James. No. You stay where you are, Mark.'

He had been planning to get out and exchange places with Suki and the look on Willa's face made him want to all the more; just out of devilment but his dad shook his head.

'Leave it for now, son,' he said. 'You've got all week to sort it out.'

The rest of the journey passed relatively peacefully. Willa sat scowling in the back diagonally opposite him, sitting as close to the door and as far away from him as she possibly could. Suki, Blossom and James chatted amicably and after five minutes or so, Mark fell asleep, feeling the happiest he'd felt for twenty-two weeks.

CHAPTER TWENTY-NINE

Willa didn't know what to think. When she'd seen Mark at the airport she thought she'd have a heart attack on the spot. Part of her wanted to throw her arms around him and shower him with kisses. Part of her wanted to punch him in the face. She'd been both elated at the sight of him and furious that he'd stayed away for so long.

When she discovered that his father and Suki had got him here under false pretences though, she'd been less than thrilled. It meant he'd had no intention of coming of his own free will and that meant he hadn't changed his mind and suddenly realised he wanted to see her again. She had to be very careful that her heart didn't get broken for the second time this summer.

She was even more disappointed when they got to the hotel and Mark did exactly what he had said he would. After he'd shared a beer and a bite to eat with his father, Aristaios and Loukas, he'd gone up to his room to bed and he hadn't been down since. That was at nine o'clock last night and it was already nine-thirty the following morning. He'd miss breakfast if he didn't come down soon and that would be a pity.

Not that she cared about whether he ate or not. She just wanted to see him. More importantly, she wanted him to see her. Despite tossing and turning most nights since he'd left all those weeks ago, last night she had slept very well and she'd had the most amazing dreams. Dreams she knew couldn't possibly come true of course but she'd woken up feeling happier than she had for a very long time and she was really looking forward to the day even though she wasn't sure why.

She'd made an extra effort with her hair and although she only wore mascara and lipstick as usual, she'd chosen the most flattering colour lipstick she could find. She'd even painted her fingernails and toenails to match. It was called Grecian Dream and it was a deep, dark, shimmering rose-brown.

The sundress she'd chosen matched perfectly and showed off her tan. It was white with a myriad of rose, brown and red flower buds with tiny butterflies strewn across the figure hugging bodice and skirt, as if they'd been scattered there by the hands of Demeter herself. She wore brown sandals with a slight heel, and no jewellery save the new watch she'd bought after being nagged by Blossom to do so.

She thought she looked quite pretty and she hoped that Mark thought so too. She wanted him to see her. She wanted to see his lopsided grin. She wanted to see that light flicker in his eyes again as she was sure it had when he'd looked at her at the airport, even if it was only for a moment. She wanted him to flirt with her but more importantly, she wanted to be able to get up and walk away as if she couldn't care less whether he was there or not. The fact that nothing could be further from the truth was irrelevant. She just wanted to be able to do it.

Where was everyone? She'd been sitting in the restaurant for almost an hour now and there was no sign of Blossom although that wasn't a surprise. She'd stayed up late with Aristaios, Suki and James talking on the terrace, long after Willa had gone to bed. She couldn't even remember her coming in last night and she'd left her to sleep this morning.

There was no sign of Aristaios either which was odd. She saw him at breakfast every day during the season. Perhaps now that there were fewer guests, he'd decided it wasn't so important to make an appearance.

She was surprised that Suki wasn't down yet. She'd been a fairly early riser during the week she was here in May and when they'd kept in touch over the summer she was always saying that she was out jogging or swimming or something by seven-thirty a.m. at the latest.

And what about James? Surely he wasn't the stay in bed type? Or perhaps he was. Perhaps he spent so much of his life under canvas or in similarly sparse environments that he liked a bit of luxury now and again and was making the most of a luxuriously comfy bed.

She heard Blossom's laugh and her head shot up.

'At last!' she said out loud.

Then her mouth fell open and stayed there. Blossom was holding hands with Aristaios. And more than that. She was wearing the same dress she was wearing yesterday when Willa had left her on the terrace last night. At least she had the decency to blush when she realised Willa had seen her. She didn't let go of Aristaios' hand though, Willa noticed.

'Have you ...? Are you two ...?' she began but was so surprised that she couldn't find the words.

'Yes to both,' Blossom said, a huge grin plastered across her beautiful face which somehow looked even lovelier this morning as she looked up into Aristaios' puppy-like eyes.

Wow, Willa thought. He's got it bad. The she saw that Blossom clearly felt the same.

'But how ...? When ...?'

'I have loved her for most of the summer,' Aristaios said, raising Blossom's hand to his lips and kissing it before planting a lingering kiss on her lips.

'Get a room you two,' Suki's voice said from behind them. 'You own a hotel, Aristaios. You have a choice of several.'

They turned and grinned at her.

'And we're going to try out all forty of them,' Aristaios said, winking.

'And then we'll move on to the gardens,' Blossom added, kissing Aristaios again.

'Please,' Willa said, finding her voice finally. 'Some of us are trying to have breakfast here.'

It was only then that she noticed that Suki and James were holding hands too.

'Oh my God!' she exclaimed, unable to help herself.

'Not you as well. What happened last night? Oops. Sorry. I shouldn't have said that.'

'That's quite all right,' James replied, wrapping his arms around Suki as he stood behind her. 'We're as surprised about us as you are. Well, maybe not quite as surprised. We have both known that something has been developing between us for several weeks now. We just didn't realise exactly what until last night.'

'You speak for yourself, honey,' Suki said, smiling lovingly up at him. 'I've known since the moment you replied to my first email and we had that Skype call.'

He kissed her on her nose. 'I think I have too,' he said. 'Well, at least I hoped.'

'Wow,' Willa said in a very downbeat way. 'How ... how long have you two been 'developing' this then?'

'Since a few days after I went back to the UK,' Suki said. 'I Googled his name, got his email address and wrote to him saying I had just spent a few days with his son. We've been 'chatting' on an almost daily basis ever since.

She made her way to the table where Willa was sitting, trailing James along behind her. He seemed reluctant to let her out of his arms.

'Not in front of the children, Dad.'

Everyone turned to look at Mark who was standing in the doorway. He was wearing baggy shorts and a T-shirt but the only thing Willa really noticed was that he was wearing his lopsided grin. She completely forgot about her plan to get up and walk out as soon as he came in and she stayed where she was, hoping that he too would come and join her as Aristaios, Blossom, Suki and James had.

'You'd better get used to it, son.' James turned to face him. 'I'm not going to let this one go – ever – and we're going to be doing a lot more of this, I can assure you.'

Mark ran his hands through his hair and smiled. 'Does that mean there's a possibility that I may have a wicked step-mother at some point in the future? Shall I call you *Mum* from now on, Suki?'

Suki blushed. 'Well. It is early days but ...' Her voice trailed off.

'I'd say that's a very definite possibility. In fact, I'd lay odds on it if I were a betting man – which I'm not. I leave that sort of thing to my numbskull son. That's why you two are trying to avoid looking at one another, isn't it? Because of some ridiculous bet that left you both not knowing whether you were coming or going. You're only here for a week, son. Don't waste any more time.'

'Thanks, Dad. Do you think you could keep your mind on your own love life please and stay out of mine?'

'I would, son but you've made such a mess of it so far. Personally, I think we should get it all out in the open and deal with the problem head on.'

Willa could feel her cheeks burning and now she wanted to run, not walk from the restaurant.

'I agree,' Suki said. 'The pair of you need your heads banging together.'

'Okay, *Mum*,' Mark said. 'Let's not get too into the wicked step-mother role, shall we? Don't start beating the children just yet.' He grinned at her and shook his head. 'I need food before I do anything else. I'm starving.'

'Well, that's romantic,' Blossom said.

'Don't you start,' Mark replied, still grinning. 'And you're hardly one to talk are you? Although I see you've at last come to your senses and realised you're crazy about Aristaios. Everyone could see how jealous you were when he went on that date with Willa, and all that 'but I don't like him in that way' stuff wasn't fooling anybody.'

Willa was astonished. She had no idea that Blossom felt anything for Aristaios but as her confused brain processed what Mark had said, she realised it was obvious – or it should have been. Maybe if she hadn't been so focused on her own feelings about Mark, she would have seen that Blossom was in love but trying to pretend she wasn't.

'I wasn't sure at first,' Blossom said. 'And when I was, I was absolutely terrified. Having a fling with someone is one thing but actually being head over heels in love, well – that's a different thing entirely.'

'And you were just as bad, Aristaios. I can't believe it took you so long,' Mark said.

'I did not want to rush things and risk losing the best thing that has happened to me in my life,' he said. 'And I did not know she felt anything for me. In fact, I thought she did not think of me at all. If I had known, things may have gone very much quicker, I think.'

'So that just leaves you two,' Suki said, glancing from Willa to Mark.

'Okay,' Willa said, jumping to her feet. 'That's quite enough, thank you. Just because the four of you are all hearts and flowers and loved up doesn't mean that Mark and I will be. In fact, I'm pretty sure we won't. Now, I've got things I should be doing. If you'll excuse me I'll leave you to it.' She walked around the table and started towards the door but stopped in her tracks. 'And I'd really rather you didn't make any more ridiculous plans to try and get the pair of us together. Don't you agree, Mark?'

Mark ran his hands through his hair and let out a long sigh. 'I agree entirely,' he said. 'You can all stop making plans to try to get Willa and me together because they won't work. Is that what you wanted me to say, Willa?' He smiled at her.

She was more than a little disappointed that he'd said it. A tiny part of her was hoping he'd say he didn't mind and that they just might work. At least now, she knew that nothing had changed.

'Yes,' she said. 'Thank you.' She turned and headed towards her office hoping she could get there and close the door before the tears she could feel welling up, started streaming down her, now deep scarlet, cheeks.

CHAPTER THIRTY

'I think we need to talk,' Mark said approximately ten minutes later as he burst into Willa's office.

'Don't bother to knock, will you?' she said, startled but glad that at least she wasn't crying. She'd realised she was far too angry to shed tears.

He grinned. 'Nope. You would probably have told me to go away, so there didn't seem much point.'

'You're right, I would have. It's lovely to see you Mark but I am really busy. Perhaps this could wait until later?'

'Nope' he said again. 'It can't. It's more than twenty weeks overdue already.'

'Overdue? What ... what's overdue?'

'Us.'

'Us? What do you mean, "us"? You ... you just said that you didn't want there to be an "us".'

'No, I didn't. I said that their plans won't work. Which is probably true. They wouldn't. And besides.' He reached her side of the desk in three large strides, took her hands in his and gently pulled her to her feet. 'I have a few plans of my own. I would've told you that in the restaurant but I was starving and I had to have something to eat first. I need the energy for what I plan to do.'

He wrapped his arms around her waist and eased her towards him, his lopsided grin spreading into a full smile and his blue eyes twinkling with delight. She put her hands against his chest to push him away but he was too strong for her.

'What plans? What do you think you're doing?' she said, wanting more than anything to be exactly where she was but not wanting him to know that.

'I'm holding you in my arms,' he said, staring longingly into her eyes.

She stared back for what seemed like an eternity.

'Is that it?' she said. 'Are you just going to stand there with your arms around me?'

'For now. Yes.'

'W ... why?'

'Because I like having my arms around you and it's been a very long time since I have. Do you mind?'

'I ... I told you, Mark. I don't like playing games.'

'I'm not playing games. I've never been more serious in my life.'

'I don't understand. You ran off and left me without a word.'

'I left a note.'

'Yes. One that seemed to say that you didn't want to see me again – ever. And that you weren't prepared to change your life for me or anyone else.'

'I don't think it said I didn't want to see you ever again. As for not being prepared to change my life, that part was true, I guess.'

'You guess? Mark, will you please let me go?'

He shook his head. 'No. Sorry.'

Willa tutted. 'This is ridiculous! If you want to talk, fine, we'll talk.'

'I don't want to talk.'

'You said you did.'

'I was wrong.'

'Then ... what do you want to do? Please be serious, Mark.'

'I am being serious. I told you. I'm being very serious. As to what I want to do – I want to kiss you. Several times in fact. Probably all day and all night.'

Willa sucked in her breath and tried to wriggle free. 'How many times do I have to tell you? I'm not interested in a one-night stand.'

'Nor am I. Please stop struggling, Willa. I'm not going to let you go.'

'So you think you can just come in here and force yourself on me. Is that your plan? I'll scream.'

243

Mark raised his eyebrows and his smile grew even wider.

'Other than keeping you in my arms, I have no intention of forcing myself on you. As for you screaming. I sort of hope you will – but from pleasure when we're in bed together. And we will be in bed together, Willa. You know that as well as I do. It's just a question of time.'

'Of all the arrogant ... we will not! I assure you. Now. Let. Me. Go.'

'No.'

'We can't just stand here like this.'

'I'm happy to stand here for as long as it takes.'

'As long as it takes ... for what?'

'For you to ask me to kiss you. I told you, if you remember that, although I wanted to kiss you again, I wouldn't, but that you only had to ask. I'm waiting for you to ask me to.'

'You're mad! We'll be standing here all day then because there is no way I'm going to ask you to kiss me.'

'Don't you want to kiss me? I want to kiss you, Willa. You have no idea how difficult this is, just waiting.'

'This is crazy, Mark. What's the point in starting all this up again? Nothing's changed.'

'Everything's changed. For me at least. Do you know how many airports I've been to over the last five months?'

'I have no idea. A ... are you saying you're tired of all the travelling?'

'No. Well, yes, a little I suppose. What I'm saying is that at every airport I've been to I've had to stop myself from getting on the next flight to Athens and coming down here.'

'Oh! But ... Suki and your dad had to trick you to get you here. You had no intention of coming of your own free will. You even admitted that.'

'They tricked me here, yes. But I would have come to you before much longer.'

'I'm only here for this week. You wouldn't have found me.'

'I would've flown to Eastbourne.'

'Planes don't fly to Eastbourne.'

Mark chuckled. 'I'd have got there, don't worry about that. When you're in love you can sprout wings or some such drivel.'

'In ... in love? Are you saying you're in love with me?'

'Isn't that obvious?'

'No.'

'Well I am ... and it should be. And if you'll ask me to kiss you, I can show you just how much in love with you I am.'

Willa felt her heart skip several beats.

'But ... I don't understand. Are you saying you want to have a relationship with me? A real relationship? Not just a holiday romance?'

'I definitely don't want a holiday romance, Willa and yes, I want a real relationship with you. A forever kind of relationship in fact. If you'd like that too, of course.'

'Um. Yes. Yes, I'd like that very much but ... are you sure?'

'Absolutely.'

'And ... and this isn't a game or ... or some kind of bet?'

'Neither. I love you, Willa. Madly. Passionately. Insanely.'

Oh! But ... but how will it work? I don't understand. I ... I mean what with you travelling all over the world and me out here every summer season.'

'I've thought about that. I could stay here during the summertime and write. Perhaps my next book will be about finding love on a singles sailing holiday in Greece. Then we could travel on my assignments during the winter. Providing your dad's happy about you having time off, that is. You might not want to go on all of my trips of course, so we'll have to choose which ones I do and which ones I don't.'

'You'd ... you'd give up some of your trips ... for me?'

'Yes.'

245

'But you don't have to do that, Mark. I'd love to go with you. And if there are a few I wouldn't want to go on – for example, I don't like the idea of jungles – too many creepy crawlies for my liking, well … I don't see why you should have to give them up. I'm happy to wait for you.'

'Would you be? Happy to wait for me, I mean?'

'I've waited five months for you, haven't I? And that was without knowing if I'd ever see you again. I could wait for months as long as I knew you'd be coming back to me. What makes you think I wouldn't?'

'It's because of my mother. I won't bore you with it now but I will explain it to you sometime. And I'll also explain why I left.'

'I think I know why you left. And I even think I understand ... now.'

'Good. So ...?'

Willa stared into his eyes. She'd never been this happy. 'Sorry. What?' she said.

'I'd really like to kiss you.'

'So what are you waiting for?' She tilted her head back a fraction.

Mark sighed. 'I'm waiting for you to ask me to. Remember?'

'Oh! Sorry. Mark, will you kiss me ... *please*?'

'About bloody time,' he said.

Mark was right when he said that he would show her just how much he loved her. By the time they eventually came up for air, Willa was in absolutely no doubt whatsoever.

He looked lovingly into her eyes. 'God. I've missed you so much, Willa. I've been an absolute idiot about all this.'

'So have I,' she said. 'Remember when I told you that you would never get me into your bed?'

'How could I forget?'

'Well, I was wrong. I don't think you're ever going to be able to get me out of it.' She looked up into his eyes and gave him her sexiest smile.

'Remind me to thank Suki and my dad tomorrow, will

you?'

'Tomorrow? What do you mean tomorrow? It's only about eleven a.m.' She couldn't drag her eyes away to look at her watch.

'Yes,' he said, grinning, 'but somewhere in the world it's night. I don't think I can wait for another twelve hours before I make love to you.'

'Then what are we standing here for? Oh! And I want to thank you personally for that fabulous review you gave us. Very, very personally. And several times, in fact.'

Mark beamed at her, threw back his head and howled like a wolf.

THE END

To be the first to hear about new releases and other news, you can subscribe to my newsletter via the 'Sign me up' box on my website.

To see more of my books or to contact me, pop over to my website, Facebook or Twitter.

***

Author contacts :

http://www.emilyharvale.com

http://www.twitter.com/emilyharvale

http://www.facebook.com/emilyharvale

http://www.facebook.com/emilyharvalewriter

http://www.emilyharvale.com/blog

http://www.pinterest.com/emilyharvale

http://www.amazon.co.uk/Emily-Harvale/e/B007BKQ1SW

***

COMING IN AUTUMN/WINTER 2013

TWO NEW BOOKS BY EMILY HARVALE

READ ON FOR DETAILS

CAROLE SINGER'S CHRISTMAS

Should she choose love past, present or possibly, future?

Carole Singer hates her name, especially around Christmastime when everyone seems to think it's okay to make a joke about it. She can't wait to marry her boyfriend Dominic and change her surname to 'Smith,' and she's sure he'll pop the question any day now.

When her gran has a nasty fall, Carole has to return to the Sussex village of Jutsdown, to care for her – and that's sixty miles from London ... and Dominic. It also means coming face to face with Sebastian, the man who broke her heart ten years earlier.

As Carole juggles her career as an illustrator, caring for her meddlesome gran, and missing Dominic, she struggles with her rekindled feelings for Sebastian. Getting roped in to help with the Christmas Musical at the local theatre and discovering her gran has invested in a garden centre owned by the moody but gorgeous, Nick, doesn't help. Carole's Christmas now looks as if it'll be anything but peaceful.

With the Christmas holidays looming and Dominic coming to stay, Carole is facing a dilemma. Should she choose her past boyfriend, Sebastian, her present boyfriend, Dominic or could there be any sort of a future with the dark and secretive Nick?

***

A SLIPPERY SLOPE

Love shouldn't be an uphill struggle

Verity Lawton expects a big surprise from her husband,

Tony for her upcoming fortieth birthday but telling her he's leaving, isn't what she had in mind. To make matters worse, their daughter, Lucy has landed a job as a chalet girl for the ski season so Verity will be facing her marriage breakdown alone, and that's not a pleasant prospect.

Twenty-one year old Lucy doesn't want to leave her heartbroken mum, so when her co-worker drops out, she persuades Verity to take her place. It'll mean they can have some 'together time' in a luxury chalet in the up market ski resort of Meribel, France and Verity will have time to consider her options. Her cooking may be more 'bleugh!' than cordon bleu but how difficult can it be to make crème brûlée? She's about to find out.

But being a chalet girl involves a lot more than sitting by a roaring fire watching snow fall as her employer, Josh Calder tells her – repeatedly. He owns several chalets in the French Alps and expects his staff to be exceptional, not set the kitchen on fire, ignore the rules, take in stray dogs and snap at him every time he opens his mouth. Verity Lawton has to go. He just has to find a way to tell her and why that is proving to be so difficult, he has no idea.

Verity's on a slippery slope and when her own mother arrives, she knows things can only get worse. Add to the mix several raucous holidaymakers, two sexy ski instructors, her repentant husband and a mountain rescue dog that clearly doesn't understand its job description and you've got a recipe for more than just upside down cake.

Will things work out for the best or is it all downhill from here?

***

250

Printed in Great Britain
by Amazon

68183775R00149